TESTIMONY OF THE SENSES

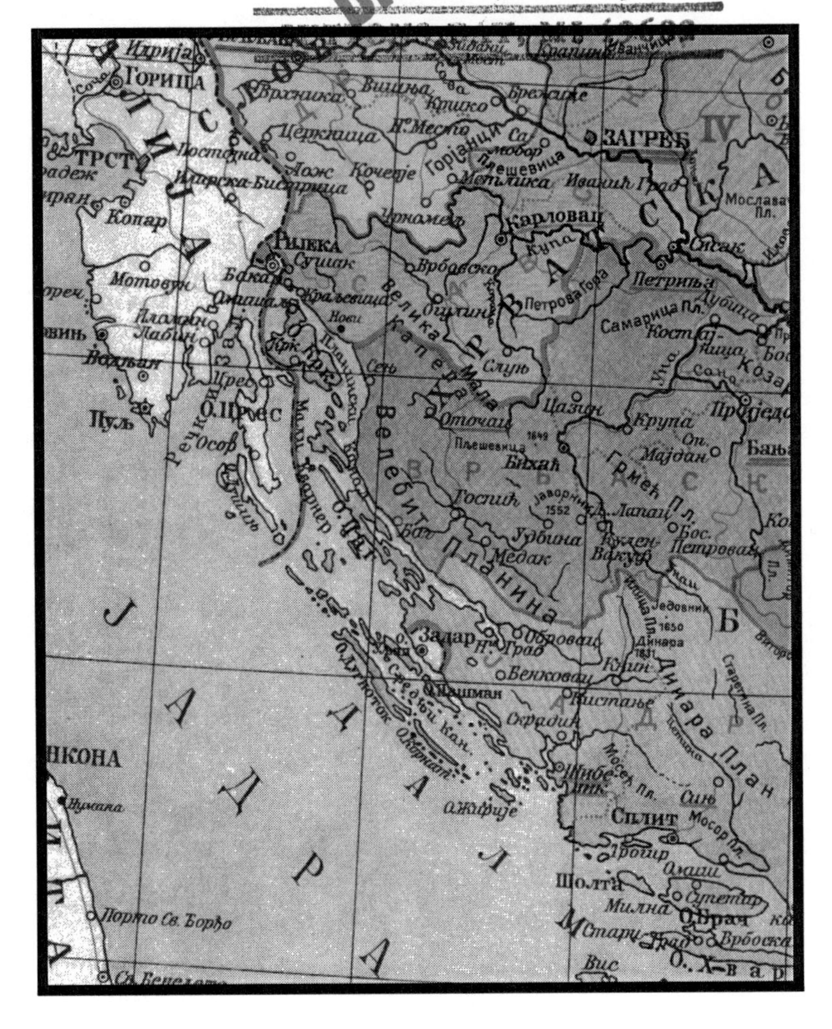
Горица
ТРСТ
Копар
Мотовун
Лабин
Пуљ
Осор
О. Црес
Сушак
Бакар
Краљевица
Нови
Велика Капела
Велебит
Планина
Плешевица
Оточац
Госпић
Медак
Удбина
Бихаћ
Цазин
Крупа
Слуњ
Петрова Гора
Карловац
Купа
Врбовско
Чрномељ
Метлика
ЗАГРЕБ
Сисак
Петриња
Самарица Пл.
Грмеч Пл.
Задар
Бенковац
Кистање
Скрадин
Шибеник
Динара План
Сплит
Сињ
Мосор Пл.
Трогир
Шолта
Милна
О. Брач
Врбоска
Вис
АНКОНА
Порто Св. Ђорђо

CORY OLDWEILER

TESTIMONY OF THE SENSES

This is a work of fiction. Names, characters, places, and incidents are products of the author's imagination or used fictitiously. Resemblance to actual persons, locations, or events is coincidental.

Quotations from Ovid's *Metamorphoses* are from Loeb Classical Library edition, first published 1916.

First Cy Daedalus Books Edition: May 2015
www.cydaedalusbooks.com

Library of Congress Control Number: 2015904224
ISBN: 978-0-692-40843-8

Book design by Cory Oldweiler.

Cover stairway photograph © Michal Dziedziak/Thinkstock.
Back cover photograph © Sofia Kozlova/Thinkstock.

Printed in the United States of America.

For Rich O'Malley

il miglior peregrin

Lo, mine eye hath seen all *this*, mine ear hath heard and understood it.

—*Job*, 13:1

I would not speak about 'absolute' truths, even for believers ... Truth is a relationship. As such, each one of us receives the truth and expresses it from within, that is to say, according to one's own circumstances, culture, and situation in life, etc. This does not mean that truth is variable and subjective, quite the contrary. But it does signify that it comes to us always and only as a way and a life.

—Pope Francis, letter to Dr. Eugenio Scalfari,
4 September 2013

An unseasonable *bora* blows mercilessly down from the Trieste Gap, imprisoning me here in Split. I want to rail and thrash against the elements, scream until I'm mute. Blow, Boreas, blow! Petulant god of the north winds! You shall not keep me caged!

But I must quash such urges. I am impotent against the gusts. The storm is not my true jailer anyway, merely a manifestation of the charges against me. If I am to be absolved, I cannot be defiant or proud. I must be penitent. Express myself exactingly. Choose the best word, play the optimal note. State things simply.

I feel trapped. (Good.) I feel trapped and turn to my maps. (Continue.) Constant companions, my maps, they are as grapnels tossed over the sides of my drifting body and mind. I need their anchoring because I never seem to stop long enough to unpack. *Nam omnia mecum porto mea.* (Whoa. Not Latin. Lucidity.) Everything I am, I carry with me, and after these past thirty years, that load feels heavy indeed. My maps don't relieve this burden, but they ease it a bit, distract me, slow me down as I determine where I currently stand or sit. They make me believe that at least one thing is knowable with certainty: Here I am. Alone, unknown, an outsider, but here. And I can fare no further until I unburden my soul, put this ordeal in the past, at last.

So, spread before me on this café table, contouring its smooth marble top, is 1960s Yugoslavia, a country that no longer exists, but mutable boundaries contrived by men do not concern me. This is a relief map, its pertinent characteristics constant for centuries. I trace my finger along the coast, but because the *noms de pays* are written in Cyrillic, initially I cannot find myself. Panic familiarly sets in and then I realize my mistake, searching for Split starting with S instead of C. Adriatic beginning with J should have clued me in quicker.

Here I am. Halfway from the top, lying in a fold of the map. It looks as if I should be better sheltered back in this little bay, Marjan Hill looming to the west, the thin island bulwarks of *Brač* and *Hvar* offshore to the south. But my walk down to the sea this morning was so blustery that I abandoned it, searched for the calm of this café. Any café actually, to enjoy a white coffee, or *bijela kava* as the Croats say. Given the insidious doubts as to my innocence, the kava's color may also signify my surrender. I'm tired from the chase. (But it's over isn't it? Don't answer that.) While my coffee still steams somewhere under my map, beneath Bulgaria I believe, I shall evaluate my options one final time.

Ideally I would go west, sailing after Phoebus over the left edge of my map into Italy, where after docking I would take two trains, changing in Bologna, step down on the second platform, cross the street to the bus depot with its twelve angled parking spots, and when my bus number pulls into its assigned slot, climb aboard and ride twenty minutes to a comforting stop. But I can't go that way today. Boats are forbidden on the Adriatic, docked due to tempestuous seas.

To the north, where these gales are being generated, the passages that cling to the sheer karst faces of the Velebit Mountains (bloodred on my map but chalky white in my mind) are closed because of the high winds, halting bus travel in that direction. A flyer resting alongside the piles of tourist brochures by the café's front door touts a new high-speed train which makes the trip to Zagreb in less than six hours, but today's newspaper informed me that the *Hrvatske željeznice* employees are striking, unconcerned about fulfilling the promises of café leaflets. The way is blockaded.

Continuing clockwise, the east offers no easy escape. The bright yellow valleys (this map is so vivid) cradle a roundabout route to Sarajevo, where I could spend days in some *ćevabdžinica* or *kafana* swapping war stories, but they would not be mine. Another man's apologia for murder will not exonerate me. All roads out of Bosnia lead toward Belgrade, but I find the Serbs too frustrating to let them succor me. Forever fixating on the past in the hope that it will lead to a future unlike the present is a familiar fallacy, one that has enslaved me most of my life, but that does not mean I encourage it in others. Romania's blotchy Carpathian peaks are unknown to me, but they are more a barrier than a gateway, demarcating eventual visa requirements that I do not meet and bribery demands that I cannot pay. The east is not the way for me.

So south it must be, if I were to leave immediately. Take the highway around Dubrovnik, just admire in passing that gem of a city in its lapidary setting alee of the Lapad Peninsula, and drive on, further, to Tirana, navigate the Sar Mountains and their southern massifs (at which point I clamber off the bottom of this map and without digging out another, continue on mnemonically) to Skopje, up the steep western slopes of the Osogovos to Sophia, squeeze out and down into the upper Thracian plain, cross to Istanbul née Constantinople, bridge to Asia, then Ankara, and disappear. *Abracadabra*. Wraithlike I'd blow anonymously in an abecedarian line through eastern Anatolia, Armenia, Azerbaijan, beyond Baku, clear Caspian Sea, dive down, and drown.

But no, I won't go. I'm too tired for that final route. Today is my forty-seventh birthday and I am unduly aged by grief. Jerzi Wojtek, an old friend who was, before his lies came to light, like a father to me for much of my forsaken, fatherless youth, claimed to treasure a birthday spent alone. He mused on the preceding year, he said, remembering it and surely reinterpreting it as well, seeking to understand both how he had arrived at that age and how he could continue on. Despite his betrayal, he shaped me as much as anyone, and so I will take my initial cue from him. I will fold up my map, attend to my long-dormant coffee and appeal for mercy. I will allow Boreas to arrest me, and in solitude, I will mount a defense. I will present those factors that fostered the man I am, ponder my faults and crimes, strive to enlighten, shy away from blame, and await the judgment that I know is mine. I hold no hope for acquittal, but I shall stay and try.

Setting off is tough since no coherent map of my past exists. I must be both explorer and cartographer. As I begin the descent through the dimly lit underworld of my mind, I hear no sounds. Eyes shut tightly, I write the journey as I create it. I catch glimpses of photographic reminiscences, tenuously attached by dendritic clips on the neurons where my thoughts drip dry. The initial recollections are blurred, unfocused. Some experiences were exposed to the light too long, others were never fully developed and lie in opaque coils in the glia at my feet. Along some axons are scorch marks, the consequences of overactive synapses that got too close and burned. Clear images do exist but they are probably contrived, mosaics of lies, collages of pictures I did not shoot or compose, snapshots stolen from other peoples' lives. Negatives recording my psyche are smudged. Dangling films of processed emotions are permanently damaged by incorrect handling and clumsy examination. It is almost impassable at points, Gordian nerves in each ganglion I encounter. I trudge on, roughly achronologically, searching for my nativity.

Eventually my eyes grow tired from straining to see truths in this chimerical cavern, so I shut them against the murk, leave sight behind. (In my mind I mean, as I've already blacked out this café.) Instead I listen with patient ears. To silence. Purity. Nothingness. I rest for a beat or two. Hold my breath. Still naught. This is a waste of wait …

There. Almost imperceptibly, something stirs. One note. On a single string. A *pianissimo* memory. I take a tentative step. There is another. I move slightly again. One more, but discordant. I creep forward, backward in time toward the start, the tempo *più mosso*. A phrase now. A theme. An entire idea. Colors begin to show, synesthetically, and the notes blend *legato* with the images. No longer missing my eyes, I confidently chase the melody. I round a corner and scores of notes stream out, measure after measure, bar after bar, a lifetime of sound and light blaring past my blind, staring mind.

And just as suddenly it is gone. Hushed. I am deafened. There is nothing. Not a breeze. Not a whisper. I open my eyes onto a sable void. No flicker. No trace of dimension. This is the beginning. And I am alone.

1. Satz.

Langsam. (Adagio.)

My earliest memory, imagined or intrinsic to my dormant temporal lobes, is the murmur of lapping liquid. Maybe I sensed my personal Cocytus, unfrozen in my innocence, securely cradling the fetal me. Or maybe the annihilating depths of the fast-flowing Lethe as I strived to remain at rest, preferring continued death to the reincarnation that would result once my parched lips sipped from that font of forgetfulness. Or the wake from the ferryman's craft carving a path past me through the thick, cool languidness of Styx, of Acheron. Or molten Phlegethon splashing against some rocky outcropping, my uterine Marjan Hill, where I was dumped to sleep off my destructive creation.

I am a symbolist, small s, *non maudit* but still accursed, and I believe all five infernal waters cushioned me as I awoke to consciousness. It was an extended process. I know not how long I lay listening to them, but I know exactly when they stopped their serenade: forty-nine years to the day before my birth, when Gustav Mahler's *Symphony No. 7 in E minor* premiered in Prague. And just as the origin of the universe endures at some unfathomable depth in space, so does the Seventh's premiere resound at the periphery of my mind, where even now I can sense the sighing strings, bassoons, and clarinets, their rhythms inspired by oars, Mahler said, oars dipping into the *Wörthersee* in southern Austria, oars propelling him home to his wife, Alma, who awaited him in Krumpendorf, a seven-hour drive from where I sit here in Split. I hear the tenor horn call, hesitantly in the key of B, minor and major indeterminately, and slowly oboes and flutes join in, and eventually horns, tuba, timpani, the aural efflorescence of my orchestrated essence.

Initial reviews of the Seventh were sympathetic, but it never acquired the following of Mahler's other works. Today many still regard it as almost a bastard child. The Mahler scholar

Henry-Louis de la Grange writes in volume three of his exhaustive biography that the symphony has been criticized for its "total self-deception" and "mood of self-indulgence." Mahler himself was "torn by doubts" about the work, likely because it seemed imitative of earlier compositions and not completely cohesive. One critic even referred to the final movement as "a sort of 'monster.'" (Well, we shall see, as that movement alone has yet to be rendered through me.)

There is no time to cover all the clues to raveling the symphony within me (and that tome can't be entered into evidence since I no longer lug its three-plus pounds around), but quickly I must mention that the fractured nature of the Seventh may be due in part to the fact that it was composed in distinct phases, the odd-numbered movements written nearly a year after completion of the even-numbered ones, which were sparked by the same creative fires that annealed Mahler's Sixth Symphony. That work, a nightmarish masterpiece of tormented beauty, ends with a blazing *fortissimo* blast of the entire orchestra from the dying otic embers. That information is particularly relevant to my testimony because, after almost a half century of prenatal listening, I had become the Seventh. My existence would be predicated on my internalization of it, and I too would require an explosive catalyst for my birth.

On the forty-ninth anniversary of the symphony's premiere, that agent finally arrived, in the form of the United States' first underground nuclear detonation, carried out beneath the Rainier Mesa, northwest of Las Vegas, Nevada. The 1.7-kiloton bomb resembled the Seventh diagrammatically: the hemispheres of its outer beryllium shell matched the symphony's first and fifth movements; its inner plutonium sphere, the twinned second and fourth *Nachtmusiken*; and in the center, hollow yet replete with deuterium and tritium atoms, the volatile *Scherzo*, waiting to explode.

The energy released by the morning's blast instantaneously vaporized the surrounding earth forming an ovoid cavity, its walls coated with molten rock, its floor puddled with lava-like matter. With a larger detonation, the cavity can be so big that the ground above the blast site collapses under its own weight forming a crater, a terrestrial scar. That did not happen after the Rainier test. Some dust rose on top of the mesa, but the cavity itself remained absurdly pristine. Once the temperature dropped, the molten rock solidified, sealing any cracks, leaving an airtight void. Scientists found no evidence of the detonation in the two-thousand-foot tunnel that spiraled into the blast chamber. All energy, all radiation, all memory of violence had been successfully contained.

I have never escaped the currents of those initial waters, never silenced the eternal night of the Seventh, never awoken from the fires of the Rainier blast, in whose tenebrific womb, at 10 a.m., Thursday, September 19, 1957, I, Emilio Tramonti, was born.

• • •

My corporeal childhood commenced in Corona, Queens. Mamma rented the second floor of a gable-front house owned by the elderly couple downstairs. A shallow wooden porch ran the width of the facade but only one step off the ground and sloping toward the sidewalk, making it appear as if the building was going to topple forward onto 44th Avenue. Along the south side of the one-way street, as far as the eye could see in either direction, a concrete wall tried to hide the Long Island Rail Road shuttling commuters between Penn Station and Port Washington. From my bedroom window, top left when facing the house, I could see over the barrier, giving me an unobstructed view into the ten-car trains rumbling by night and day.

For the first six and a half years of my life, Mamma and I were never physically far apart. Most mornings began before dawn when she would gently shake awake *Caro Emilio, mio carino* and moments later carry him (me), still benighted, somewhere between swaddled and smothered in nightshirt and sweatpants, feet stuck hastily into socks and boots, down the stairs and out onto the still slumbering streets. Once outside she would set me down and, in a somnolent haze huddled beneath the folds of her heavy woolen cloak, one arm wrapped tightly around her leg, I would blindly make the four-block walk to *Due G's*, the bakery named for my paternal grandparents Giuliano and Giorgina Esposito, where Mamma worked. We would enter the side door on the driveway next to the mortuary, squeezing single file past the hearse if it was parked there and not out ferrying caskets, and climb the carpeted stairs to Nonna and Nonno's apartment where I would collapse onto the couch in the den, hoping to return to the dream I had abandoned fifteen minutes before while still in my own bed. Mamma, after covering me with the old blanket draped on the back of the couch, would go down the kitchen stairs to the *pasticceria* which opened at 6 a.m. She took over the ovens from Nonna, who had been baking bread since three, and made biscotti, cakes, cookies, cannoli, tiramisu, tarts.

Nonna's day was not done however. She merely changed jobs, unlocked the front door and, still wearing her apron and hairnet, served customers at the counter. One of those served was her husband, who sat and smoked, spinning an entire morning's worth of *canzoni* and anecdota out of a single cappuccino that he stirred incessantly with a small spoon, pausing only when he took the infrequent sip. As a consequence of Giuliano's sedentariness, most people called the place Gina's. He was not offended. Their love was impregnable, a fact not always evident to the casual observer. They had been married just two months when they boarded a ship to America in 1919. Their first child, a daughter conceived in the middle of the Atlantic Ocean, died as an infant. I never knew her name or what caused her death and am not sure they did either, but I do know that such loss, combined with their youth and the disorientation that dominated the early months and years of their immigration, could have blown them apart. Instead it drew them closer together.

Corona underwent intense changes during their first years in America. A rural village before World War One, by the 1920s it was an urban destination. Both the arrival in 1917 of the elevated train (the No. 7, overarching every aspect of my life) and the easing, and eventual elimination, of wartime building and materials restrictions contributed to the boom. When the *pasticceria* was completed, my grandparents lived in the back. In 1925 they added a second story. The next year, my father was born.

I never heard Nonno talk about his son, but hanging above the couch where I slept was a photograph of him, the only photograph of my father that I saw until I turned seventeen. He stood, starkly defined in black and white, like the early, overdeveloped daguerreotype *L'Atelier de l'artiste*, in his Sunday suit, age three, in front of *Due G's*, holding a baguette in his hands on which two pigeons perched, eating their support out from under themselves. Because of the high contrast, his eyes are lost in the shadow of a wing. Unknowing, naïve, I imagined him watching over me as I slept. When I could not fall back asleep some mornings, I used to lie there and wonder whether the pigeons succeeded in devouring their foundation. I wished the photographer had taken successive shots to document their progress. It was irrelevant I eventually realized, because pigeons, if they find themselves falling, can fly. Mamma could not.

I grew up believing that my father died five months before I was born, hit and killed by a driver who decided not to stop at the white neon WALK beckoning my father to cross. I did not blame my father for his death, but neither could I forgive him for it. A pouting child may yearn for a parent's death, but it is beyond his mind to confront such a loss. Throughout my adolescence I struggled with my fate, but each time I threatened progress, something would set me back and the resulting anger would shut down my reasoning. I equated acceptance with acquiescence, forgetting with forfeiting. By the time I started high school, I had buried all the sorrow and its resultant rage deep beneath the radioactive bed of my mind. When I found out the truth on my seventeenth birthday, all that energy began to leak into my lair and I wished he really had died.

I did have moments of childish contentment growing up, exemplified by the occasional walks Mamma and I would take to listen to the light trumpet peals of Louis Armstrong, who lived just eight blocks from us. In my mental atlas, I can still trace the route we took on those summer days, strolling north on 108th Street, wading through the heat that hovered several feet above the softening asphalt, holding Mamma's hand which remained comforting, cool and dry, still accustomed to the temperature and humidity of southern Italy where she was born and lived until coming to New York with my father after World War Two. We sought the sounds of Satchmo's horn. Approaching the intersection with 37th Avenue, his playing was as faint as the distant clangor of the 7 train whose wooden tracks we subambulated four blocks back. We turned left and the notes crescendoed slowly, still dampened by the intervening trees and houses until we turned onto 107th Street and could see Louis blowing down from his redbrick balcony, his notes as bright and intense as the sun. I slipped free from Mamma's grasp (in reality, she let me go, again and again) and ran the half block to join the crowd of children who stood staring up at him with a reverence adults reserved for deities. Some days, Louis would come down and sit on his stairs and the kids would all gather around and a lucky one or two would get to hold his trumpet, the same one he just had played some crazy, jazzy tune upon.

I was happy those days but self-conscious. Unlike the other children whom Mamma and I passed on the sidewalks before I broke away, only one of my hands was held by a parent, the other uncomfortably hung at my side uncertain what to do: swing in time as I walked or seek the safety of a pocket. I wanted the alien joy on the other young faces to infect me, but, alas, I was immune. And though I smiled outwardly at Louis's playing, it didn't send me. (My ears must already have been aware of the martial phrases dominating my mental orchestral accompaniment, the Seventh playing in the background, though I did not yet know it.) So I let the others enjoy the spectacle and lingered at the back of the crowd, wondering at this man who, having no children of his own, nevertheless loved children so much that he would spend part of his day whenever he was not on the road bringing music into their lives.

The spring of 1964 I was about to finish kindergarten. Most children my age were finishing the first grade, but Mamma had held off enrolling me for a year, for what reason I cannot say with complete certainty. Whether it was because I was older or because Mamma had kept me so close, I did not adjust well to school and made no friends. I satisfactorily completed the work required, not terribly difficult in kindergarten it is true, but never felt part of a group, even when we were forced to work together. After school I would hurry across the street to the park where Mamma would meet me and hold my hand walking back to the bakery. Most nights we would have dinner there and then go home. I was in bed by seven while the cantabile play of the neighborhood children unwittingly mocked me through my bedroom window, always open a crack, even in winter, to prevent my asphyxiation by our stove's leaky valve.

Yes, my life was rather simple and unremarkable until that spring, that spring when a god came down and, not even bothering to disguise himself as a swan or a bull, took Mamma from me, leaving me parentless and alone. She didn't die, but she may as well have.

It was late April, I strangely don't remember the day, and Mamma was not waiting for me in the park after school. Nonno was. He stood smoking and staring at the ground. I panicked.

Dov'è la mamma? He spoke English, but inaccurately at times and I needed to be certain that nothing was wrong.

All'esposizione, per vedere la Pietà. Nonno was kind but not exactly talkative. He softly started to sing and began walking off. Halfway to the *pasticceria* he finally explained that Signora Labetti, a woman I knew of solely from watching her worry prayerfully over her rosary at *Due G's*, had shown up that morning with three passes to the opening of the Vatican Pavilion at the World's Fair. She had convinced Nonna to close up shop for the day, something which Nonno could not remember ever happening spontaneously. *Dio l'ha convertita*, he said with a laugh. Nonno did not believe in much of anything.

For the rest of the afternoon I felt happy for Mamma. I had known that Michelangelo's masterpiece would be at the Fair, it was impossible to be in New York and not know, let alone live in an Italian neighborhood one block from where the statue was to be displayed. It was the first—and last—time that the *Pietà* was shown outside the Vatican. Tickets were readily available, even the local banks were giving them away, but Mamma had shown no interest in them. She said that she had grown up less than two hundred miles from the *Pietà* and had never seen it, so maybe it was not meant for her to see. Unfortunately for me, she was wrong.

At the Vatican Pavilion that day, Mamma met Robert Hupka, known at the time solely in secular circles for his zealous idolatry of Arturo Toscanini. Hupka's monomania manifested itself in the taking of hundreds of photographs of the maestro conducting, many without his knowledge during orchestra rehearsals.

Sometime after Toscanini's death, God found Hupka or Hupka came to God. (Never having been sought after nor caught seeking salvation, I know not how the game is played.) Hupka was put in charge of music for the Vatican Pavilion at the World's Fair and wanted a photograph for the cover of a souvenir record album. Once started, he could not stop, and Michelangelo's *Pietà* took Toscanini's spot on the podium. Hupka got complete access to the sculpture, behind the seven sheets of floor-to-ceiling bullet-proof glass, and took some five thousand photographs of it. As far as I know, Mamma was there for almost every frame, in what capacity I never was told. She simply could have been attracted to the opportunity for a job outside the bakery, whether that job was helping with lighting or developing or just carrying equipment. Or she could have been attempting to replace my father, the first photographer in her life—an entry on his résumé that I wouldn't learn of for several years. Regardless of her original intent, she began to worship, whether sculptor or photographer or the Divine Will that she believed shaped one or the other or both of them was not and is not relevant. Her fixation became Hupka's, became all-consuming, and suffered not her little child to come between them.

By my bedtime, Mamma was not back from the Fair so I lay down beneath the sightless eyes of my father in his frame. I fell asleep listening to Nonna as she cleaned up after dinner. Nonno had gone out for a walk. Mamma woke me in the morning.

Emilio, come. We must go home and get you ready for school.

This type of greeting, matter-of-fact and far-from-maternal, was what I got from Mamma for the rest of our life together. Something changed in her that day at the Fair and while I should not say that she stopped loving me, it often felt that way. Most nights during the ensuing eighteen months, I would awaken on the couch to Mamma telling me to follow her home. Those walks had nothing in common with the ones we used to take together.

Now Mamma, instead of tending to me, attended to her rosary, muttering her *Ave Maria*s and *Padre Nostro*s as she fingered its beads. Now both my hands were free to dangle at my sides.

Crucifixes appeared nailed to every available surface in our home, including above my bed, providing me with another absent father's pointless gaze overseeing my sleep. Maybe Mamma believed that by finding a heavenly father for herself, she somehow provided me with a terrestrial one, albeit one who could never take me to see the Mets play in their new stadium, which opened two days before the Vatican Pavilion and was half the distance from my house.

Instead of returning to P.S. 16 for first grade I was sent to St. Leo's Parochial School, around the corner from *Due G's*. It did not go well. The students in my class knew each other from the previous year, I was older than all of them, and out of spite, I flatly refused to acknowledge God's existence. I would not participate in prayers, sitting silently and devoting my thoughts to my temporal troubles instead of focusing on the ethereal mysteries of eternity. Never once did I refer to the nuns with the titles they desired, although disrespecting Sister Sofia did make me feel guilty given that she was so young and beautiful. I had no siblings, heavenly or otherwise, I said to her when she asked why I referred to her as Ms. Sofia. She pretended not to hear my whispered explanation that my father had not stuck around long enough to provide me with any. While I performed adequately academically, I stifled my potential, not wishing to reveal anything that might make me attractive to the school. I feigned illness whenever there was a field trip of an ecclesiastical nature, which meant that I missed the best chance I had to confront Mamma's *idée fixe*. Yes, the day St. Leo's visited the Vatican Pavilion, Emilio was absent with a virus. (I could have been Laszlo Toth!) After one year, I was back in public school, mercifully asked to trouble the Sisters no more.

Mamma's obsession gradually alienated Nonna—and consequently Nonno. She cut back on her hours at the *pasticceria* to work with Hupka, increasing the already heavy burden carried by her nominal mother-in-law. As soon as Mamma finished the morning's baking, she was finished. No apologizes or questions. She left without even a good-bye many days, save a pious laying of her hand on my cheek if I was there and not already in school. Cleaning up the kitchen was left to Nonna, as was raising me. Mamma rarely finished with Hupka before midnight and so I spent afternoons and evenings above the bakery watching TV or reading or sitting staring at the photograph above the couch until it was time to lie down and try to sleep, even though I knew that I would be woken up in a few hours to walk home. On weekends and during the summer, I practically lived at *Due G's*, rarely getting set free, unless it was to run down Corona Avenue to Spaghetti Park and tell Nonno it was time to stop playing bocce and come eat.

Perhaps Nonna would have liked to fill the role of surrogate mother to me but the *pasticceria* did not permit her the time. I never really got to know her despite eating with her almost every night until I was a teenager. There was always a barrier around her that I could not break through, and it was not due to language as it was with her husband. Maybe she simply believed that I was the reason she lost her son, feelings for which I could not fault her as they were similar to those that fed my hatred for Mamma's God.

When the Fair ended, things did not go back to the way they were pre-*Pietà*. Mamma never resurrected her relationship with her earthly family. Whether her true allegiances lay with God or His golden calf, once the marble manifestation of her idolatry was back in Italy, her faith became fanatical. She claimed to see visions and hear voices. She took to body mortification, including extreme fasting that at least once resulted in her collapsing in the bakery and having to be hospitalized for malnutrition. She wore a hair shirt, which I suppose should have made me feel that at least she was paying penance for her actions, except that eavesdropping on her constant muttering it became clear that I was seen as one of the sins for which she believed she must atone. Eventually she joined a group that worshipped at a park bench installed on the site near where the *Pietà* had sat. More hewn stone altars for Mamma.

I do not know where she is today.

She actually did take me to the World's Fair once, but it was not to watch her and Hupka work. It was early October and the giant exposition ended in less than two weeks. I desperately wanted to go see the wonders of GE, Illinois, Belgium, the Ford Motor Company, and all the others, so when Mamma told me on Friday night that I would not be going to school on Monday, I irrationally hoped that maybe I would finally get to float through the Small, Small World or ride the Carousel of Progress or see Florida's water-skiers, all subjects of the what-I-did-on-my-summer-vacation stories being continually related by my restored classmates at P.S. 16, who appeared to have no recollection that I had attended their school two years prior. But none of that concerned Mamma. Frivolity was for the faithless. She was taking me to see the pope.

We arrived at the Fair around noon that day and walked past the observation towers, straight to the north side of the New York State Pavilion, where we sat, as placid as Lake Ontario on a still autumn night, behind the temporary barrier the police had erected. And then we waited more than ten hours for the arrival of Pope Paul VI. Even though when we took up our positions, he was addressing the United Nations General Assembly and still had to meet with President Johnson and then bless the crowd at Yankee Stadium (such a scary borough the Bronx, Mamma had said), we sat and waited.

Being at the Fair, so close to the colors, the sounds, I asked if I could walk around the grounds and see what I had been missing.

I did not take you out of school to play, Emilio, was her response. She explained that since I had chosen through my actions to abandon any chance at a religious education, this opportunity was perhaps the last I would have for salvation. She hoped that the pope would see the sin on my face and save me. I told her I did not feel such an intercession was likely to occur.

I asked for food. Mamma replied only that our Lord survived forty days in the wilderness "*e morì in croce*." (Why she switched to Italian I have no idea, but I remember it distinctly because she crossed herself as she said *croce* and, since she was seated cross-legged on the curb, her elbow awkwardly banged into her right knee on the way down, which made me grin.) Because of these sacrifices, I apparently could live one day without dinner was the principle I took from her parable.

As if to hammer her point home, she added, This is to feed your soul, my son.

They were the last words she spoke to me that day. She looked away, bowed her head, and began to pray.

By the time the sun set, the crowd must have numbered in the tens of thousands. And the pope was late. It was after ten o'clock, well past the time Mamma insisted I be under the blanket above *Due G's*, even though Nonno always had the television on late watching *The Tonight Show*, but all the lights made it seem more like midday. The crowd was eager and abuzz. Finally police cars and motorcycles began driving past us and I quickly got to my feet, not out of excitement as much as to avoid being stepped on. It was so crowded, and the push from the rows and rows of people behind us was so insistent that I found myself pinned up against the barricade. The combination of my height (under four feet) and the policemen stationed along the route (every five feet) limited my field of view to an area not much larger than the side of a small automobile. The pope would need remarkably quick powers of perception to spot me and put Mamma's plan to work. But she did not seem to remember her avowed purpose for this outing as she had not even looked down to see if I was still standing next to her, which I wasn't, having been shoved to the left as I stood up by a balding gentleman who now was holding fast to the barricade. Suddenly there was a noise that sounded like cannons firing, which I found out later it was, and the volume level of the crowd increased to *forte*.

Apparently the pope drove past me soon after the dynamics changed, but I never saw him. Unlike Napoleon's whiff of grapeshot, the pope's salvo did not calm the crowd. Voices screamed, flashbulbs went off by the score, both across the street and *staccato* from my right. The bald man appeared to be a professional photographer. (Maybe it was he! Hupka, not my father.) I became disoriented both aurally and visually. Then all at once, the wall of people that had been holding me securely against the barricade was gone and I fell backward. Brushed and kicked several times, I got up onto my hands and knees and crawled under the barricade and onto the now empty road. The crowd was chasing the motorcade in the direction of the Vatican Pavilion, where I guessed the pope was headed. I looked up over my shoulder to confirm what I already knew. Mamma was not there. No one was.

I sat in the street for a while, wondering if I should wait for her to return for me. My right hand throbbed from being stepped on in the stampede. I was angry and wanted to teach Mamma a lesson so I decided I was on my own. It was a nice night. I picked myself up and followed the bridge over Robert Moses's Grand Central Parkway and continued past General Motors and around a fountain and out the Henry Hudson gate. I was on 55th Avenue and I knew I shouldn't be that far south so late (in my mind I could hear Nonna and Mamma scolding me), but there were so many people on the streets because of the Fair and the pope that I didn't feel scared. It was the first of many a long walk that I have taken alone.

I walked over to Corona Avenue and turned right past Mauro's, past the Lemon Ice King and Corona Pizza and boys in leather jackets smoking cigarettes around girls in Spaghetti Park, past the Park Side, up to *Due G's* where the dull white glare of Nonno's TV flickered in the curtainless window above the store door, up 104th Street (née Alburtis Avenue) past the butcher's where Nonna sent me for meat some days after school, left onto 47th Avenue lined with single-family homes not yet entirely asleep, right on Nicolls Avenue where a group of older kids on the opposite side of the street stopped in the middle of the sidewalk and stared silently over at me making me wonder if I should run. They eventually kept walking, leaving me with nothing but shaky legs and my first adrenaline-induced stomachache. I reached the corner of National and 44th, where just two years ago they had torn down the Corona stop for the Long Island Rail Road. I wished that the stop were still there and I could get on a train and go east to the shore where a boat would be waiting to take me across the Atlantic to somewhere Mamma would never be able to find me once she bothered to realize I was gone, once she began to feel bad about neglecting me. I stared into the empty sky above the overpass. Nothing but darkness. No sound of anything approaching. I turned right and walked the two long blocks to my house, where I sat on the front porch waiting for Mamma.

I fell asleep and dreamed I was back in the fairgrounds, back in the middle of the intersection after the pope had driven past, but all the lights were turned off and the people were gone. I was crawling around looking for something in the glow of a rapidly waning moon and noticed the surface below me was not asphalt but something smoother, like black ice, but without the cold. Then gradually I became aware that my knees and toes were sinking when I crawled. I pushed at the ground with my fingers. It was no longer firm, but felt tacky, as if it was still cooling. I knew my innocence, my childhood, was slipping out of me into this thick gel and it would become lost to me forever once the surface hardened again. I also knew that if I didn't stand, keep moving, I too could become lost, stuck, trapped. I looked up for guidance, but the moon had waned to new and it was pitch dark. I closed my eyes. In the distance I heard the sound of brass instruments marching martially over thickets of strings and winds, and I slowly crawled toward the sound. I didn't realize it at the time, but the first stage of my life was ending. The key change of E from minor to major heralded the approaching ravine, but it was too late. I tumbled over the edge and rolled to the bottom.

I awoke to find myself still in the dark on the porch, but I would not remain alone for long.

2. Satz.
NACHTMUSIK.

Allegro moderato.

Distant church towers toll the hours, calling me back from the depths of my recollections and, disoriented, I hear a child stridently urging his mother to look, to listen. (The boy speaks English, which still attracts my ear despite the expatriate years, and initially lacks individuality, melds with mine pleading with Mamma on the porch.) I raise my eyes and peer out the leaded-glass window to my left, seek the source of the resounding bells. (Did I count nine?) Met with the tessellated Split sky, low, slate-colored, latent with rain, I quickly look away, turn toward the mother and child. (*Per pietà.*) She holds today's *International Herald Tribune*, securely clamped to a wooden frame, by its carved handle and gazes into its pages as if she were about to inquire who is the fairest of them all. (Not you, madam, *non eri tu.*) The boy begs. She ignores. He persists. The empty interaction continues. Finally, without averting her eyes from her lusterless newsprint looking glass, she dismisses him for good with a disgusted *shhhh*. Annoyed on his behalf, I put down my pen, smoke a cigarette, and warily consider the approaching storm. (Don't judge yet. Return to the task, recount the facts. Fall back to the bottom of the starless ravine where the call of the first French horn awaits its distant, muted reply.)

• • •

When I first heard Jerzi straining to distinguish himself from the squeal of the espresso machine steaming milk for some customer's cappuccino, it was the Sunday after the pope's visit. Drawn to him for a reason I have never been able to pinpoint, I acted out in an attempt to attract his attention to my little table by the counter. Pretending to finish the book in front of me I dramatically closed its cover and, with a satisfied sigh, smiled while turning my eyes to the ceiling the way the nuns at St. Leo's did after sharing a psalm. Not getting any response, I greeted a woman approaching the temporarily untended counter with a "*Giorno signora*," tossed lazily over my shoulder. "*La mia Nonna*," I explained, "she owns *la pasticceria, ritornerà subito*, right back, she's in the *cucina*." The woman had been coming to Gina's since before I was born and eyed me reproachfully. Nonna returned as I finished my facile elucidation and just shrugged to her friend who mouthed the word *pazzo*. Their wordless rebukes chastened me and I stayed quiet the rest of the morning. In fact for several weeks after that I did nothing. I watched and I listened.

He arrived early each morning, before I headed to school, and was gone by ten. On weekends I was there to see him go. During those hours he drank a coffee, enhanced differently depending on the day, and thoroughly read two newspapers, one in English and one in a language whose l's appeared to have been shot through with arrows, perhaps by the suspicious number of z's hiding unsuspectingly next to common c's and d's and r's and s's. Periodically Jerzi would tap the toe of one worn, leather shoe against a hard-shelled suitcase beneath his table, as if reassuring himself that it still sat at his feet. Some people addressed him in English, others in the language of the archer z's, which I later learned was his native Polish. He responded to both tongues with polite words, but in a voice which often visibly frightened the unsuspecting because of its extraordinarily gruff timbre. That rough edge was smoothed however by his soothingly precise and assiduously considered diction. Such introspection, as I originally assumed it to be, could lead to lags in conversation, but no one appeared to mind. I came to prefer his disconnected cadence to the free-flowing blather of those smug in unfounded convictions. (In retrospect, Jerzi's deliberation was probably a *sine qua non* to keep track of the myriad lies he told and to whom they had been repeated.)

Then one December day I was decided. I piled my books and pushed them to the center of my table and slid off the side of my chair. I walked to where he sat.

"My name is Milo, what's yours?" even though I knew. (Since the night at the Fair, I had begun referring to myself with the diminutive of Emilio, retaining the Italian i with its long-e sound, but taking a first tentative step toward today's liberated Miles.)

"My name is Jerzi, Milo. I am pleased to meet you."

"Please to meet you" and I limply put out my small hand to be held by his proffered one, simply letting it sit loosely in his grip as if it were disinterested. He did not squeeze too hard.

"What's in that suitcase that you always have?" I asked him as I pulled out the chair across from him, climbed onto it, sat on my feet.

"A *skrzypce*." I smiled widely. (I loved the sound of Slavic languages that I heard occasionally in the neighborhood, fricative-heavy consonantal jungles, affricates shoved into each thought.) "That means a violin, Milo. Have you ever seen one?"

"No, I haven't," I told him without shame because there was nothing accusatory or threatening in his voice, unlike those of the teachers at school who judged you for your lack of knowledge before you had even showed that you didn't possess any.

"If you would care to, I will let you see this one. It is very special to me and very old."

Jerzi never used contractions. Maybe it was an immigrant tic, but it made me feel as if he enjoyed the conversation and did not wish it to be hurried along by compressing his clauses.

"Actually, I did see a man play one in church once," I confessed, leaning forward. "But never up close like this," I added, standing on my knees in the center of the seat while he reached under the table for his case.

"Well, that is what I do. I play the violin. But never in churches."

(Amen to those final four words. He who abjures churches has my blessing.)

"Do you play alone?"

"Sometimes. Mainly to practice, for when I work I play with other musicians in an orchestra."

And with that lie—the first that Jerzi told me—the mnemonic tape spooling from reel to synaptic reel snaps. I don't care to splice it. The memory still stings, not because it was a consequential lie, but because it, along with so many of the other falsehoods, was a tenet upon which I based my belief in Jerzi. When they were disproved, that edifice crumbled.

The eight-year-old me sitting in *Due G's* did not possess the same sensibilities as the misanthrope that sits here in Split. I desperately wanted someone I could trust, someone who would parent me, and Mamma was with her God and Nonna was working and Nonno was with other old men playing bocce and my father was dead. Or so they all said. I had sat at my table in an empty coffee shop all day, all summer long, not permitted to go outside because my ostensible guardians didn't want me stabbed like Kitty Genovese or ensnared by the Dukes or Club 54 or any of the other neighborhood gangs with their loud, easy laughter and greased hair and girls. These concerns were baseless, but such empty edicts, handed down solely so as to seem to govern, were typical of the disinterested, albeit well-intentioned way in which I was raised. I was safe, not because I was actually being protected, but because I was isolated, no one to believe in but myself.

So Jerzi became my friend that day, at least from my perspective, which is the only vantage point considered by youth. I aped his character in a childish fashion initially, but over time I came to share so many of his traits, it was almost as if he had passed them down to me genetically. I'm certain that if he had spoken to me about the Gemini program orbiting Earth (mission VII, I swear it's true, was above us that first afternoon), I would have wanted to go to the moon. But he was not an astronaut, he was a dishonest (ex-)musician and he spoke about the camaraderie born of an orchestra and the even closer symbiosis of a string quartet. Music had been around me all along, with Louis's trumpet and *le canzoni cantate da Nonno* (and in the firmament of my nuclear womb), but Jerzi taught me to listen, showed me how to hear. I never learned to play an instrument, never even had the opportunity to once Jerzi was gone, but the reverence for music that began with him persists in me to this day.

• • •

Intermezzo No. 1: Earlier I wrote that I had never "been sought after nor caught seeking salvation," but I'd like to revise my characterization. Indeed it is my first lie in this narrative. My life has been nothing but, emphasis added, an unsuccessful succession of attempts to find something or someone to trust in, hang on to, learn from, believe in, follow, love, save me. Maybe that someone should have been Mamma, but her God, being the vengeful one (cf. Hebrews 10:30), condemned me to this fate, neither cradled nor cried over, when I turned from her as she in turn turned her attention to the marble Madonna mourning its marble son (namely Him, not me). Jerzi was the first person I turned to for deliverance. And there would be others. But they all played out. And that is why my maps are so comforting, not just physically but psychically. With no one to tell me where I am or where I should go, I must locate myself, find a temporary way. And now I really have reached a dead end. The route I've been following, this *côté de Tramonti*, the plan, the dream, charted and recharted in my head for thirty years, has landed me here. *Hic ego sum*. But my hands feel unclean, incarnadine. (Object. Stop jumping ahead. Stay sequential and calm. I request a recess.)

• • •

Stepping outside briefly helped to settle me down. A few undisciplined raindrops fell on my face, but the deluge remained restrained above. (It is not yet time.) The further I go along this path, the more this day progresses, the more frequently I anticipate requiring these respites. I will probably stop writing about them as it has already grown tedious. There are no rules. I am going through this for my benefit. It is my attempt at self-preservation. I will stop and start as I decide, until the imperium is taken from me.

Persevering. For the first few months, my interaction with Jerzi was limited to quick hellos during the school week and longer conversations on Saturdays and Sundays. I looked forward to those weekend talks enormously. I started to read more in my free time and to daydream less because I wanted to have new things to talk about with him. I didn't bring up my childhood often and he didn't ask about it. He showed interest in the topics I did raise, the simple stories I related, and he brought me books, books about music, books about different types of instruments, brief biographies of musicians with onionskin-protected pencil sketches of the "Great Composers." He talked about growing up in Poland and being a child prodigy and moving to America and in 1943 joining the New York Philharmonic Orchestra whose incoming music director, Artur Rodzinski, was a fellow Pole who, incidentally, was born here in Split while his father served in the Hapsburg military. He talked about playing at Carnegie Hall and teaching at Queens College. All these anecdotes touched on Jerzi's life, but they were only highlights, showpieces from his complex and dark story. I heard additional passages as our relationship moved outside the *pasticceria*, but by the time I heard the whole score run through on an autumn afternoon when I was sixteen, it was too late to apply what I knew, too late to try and help. Less than a year later, Jerzi would be out of my life.

As far as I know, he accurately related to me his life prior to 1959, but that year, the year that Leonard Bernstein asked him to leave the Philharmonic, Jerzi changed. He never told me why he was asked to leave, he actually never even told me he had left, and I know very little about what happened during the ensuing six years, until we met. But I'm getting ahead again. *A tempo.*

One morning before school, I decided to introduce Jerzi to Mamma, who was still baking. I did not participate in their conversation, which Mamma informed me was for adults. Afterward, she took me aside and told me that if I wanted to go to Jerzi's after school that afternoon it was okay with her, as long as I was home by dinner, a proscription that even at that age I found bizarre since our last supper together had been almost two years earlier. Mamma then returned to the kitchen and Jerzi said that if I waited at Linden Park after school he would meet me and we could walk to his home where I could hear some of the music that we had been discussing. I eagerly agreed, and as I hurried out the door so as not to be late, I was as excited as I remembered the children huddled around Louis had been when I watched them from the back of the crowd.

Jerzi lived in my neighborhood at that time, just a few blocks from P.S. 16 on a dead-end bit of 100th Street that couldn't be reached from 39th Avenue but only by walking up 99th and corkscrewing in via 38th and down. (Yes, the paths to my wombs are always involuted.) He rented a basement apartment from a couple who also taught at Queens College (although he did not). The house was close to the 7 train (too close when the noise from the tracks rumbled over a *pianissimo* passage playing on his phonograph), which he said he took to Flushing where he changed to a bus for the last leg of his commute to work (although, again, he didn't). We climbed the three stairs of the porch and went in the front door. It was locked I recall because Jerzi had trouble finding his key, which gave me time to get nervous and wonder if this was a good idea, me being there with him.

Thinking back, I wonder at Mamma's apparent transference of faith from her Christian God to the unknown Jew Jerzi. Why exactly did she let me go to the basement apartment of a forty-one-year-old man who was a stranger to her? I was eight. What was she thinking? Despite her increasing indifference when it came to her role as parent, I don't believe that she was casting me aside. Jerzi never told me what he and Mamma had discussed, if she had asked questions or received assurances. Maybe her God told her that it was okay, that he was okay. Or maybe she simply knew she couldn't watch over me anymore.

The basement stairs were reached through a pocket door halfway down a short entry hall. The hallway walls were bare and white. A heavy runner ran along the narrow, darkly polished floor. At the far end of the hall was a closed door with a curtained window where Jerzi said his teacher friends lived. In all the years that I visited him, I never saw them, although once I heard one of their voices. Jerzi's stairway had a small landing where it turned to the left on the way down.

His apartment was different in every sense from what I was used to at home, wherever I considered that to be at the time, either Mamma's or above *Due G's*. First of all, it was simpler: one big space separated from a galley kitchen by a pass-through window beneath which a wooden table sat. In the rear were two doors, one to the bedroom (which I never caught even a glimpse of) and the other to a toilet. I had grown up with carpeting, wall to wall, but Jerzi's floors were linoleum, more worn than the wood in the upstairs hallway. One well-trafficked Turkish rug sprawled in the middle of the main room. The kitchen, redolent of recent cooking, recalled more of the rich aromas of Nonna's than the cool void of Mamma's empty cabinets and refrigerator. Very little natural light came through the two thin windows up near the ceiling. The most striking difference though was wooden shelf upon wooden shelf piled upon wooden shelf holding books and albums and sheet music, climbing from floor to ceiling and back again across the walls. There were more books about Brahms (five) than Mamma had Bibles (just four).

Keeping watch over the room from nooks in the bookcases were framed drawings of composers—Mozart, Brahms, Wagner, Beethoven—similar in style to those in the books Jerzi lent me. There was also a spot on the wall above the table where a fifth portrait once hung. I later learned it had been Chopin's spot, its existence memorialized or betrayed, depending on your point of view, by an umbra of slightly lighter blue that still clung to the wallpaper. (Frederic had been purged like the Decembrists from the halls of the Hermitage, Jerzi once drunkenly slurred.) When he noticed me staring at the portraits, he told me they had belonged to his father. He said that when he fled Europe, he brought the prints, rolled carefully in a cardboard tube. Coincidently or not, identical posters could be purchased for a dollar or two at Patelson's Music Store behind Carnegie Hall.

For most of the afternoon, Jerzi lovingly placed side after vinyl side upon his phonograph and then returned silently to his perch on a wobbly wooden chair at the table. I sat on the rug and flipped absentmindedly through a large book of photos of something which made no impression on me, absorbed as I was by the chords, the notes, the sounds overtaking the small room and infusing everything with … with what? I don't know exactly what overcame me that day. (Maybe a messenger from Euterpe stole in and activated a dormant musical gene in me? Not that again.) Whatever it was, I realized that I was feeling something intensely, more intensely than I had felt before. And one of the first things Jerzi explained to me that afternoon was that music is all about feeling, how you feel when you listen to it, and how those feelings change, how sometimes those feelings are not even describable.

"Sometimes we have feelings so deep and so special," Jerzi said, "that we have no words for them. And that's where music is so marvelous, because music names them for us, only in notes instead of words."

That explanation, that sentiment, connected with me and I repeated it like a mantra, under my breath, as I sat on the floor until it was more than memorized, it was a part of me. Many nights during my youth, I mused upon what Jerzi had said: "Music names them for us, only in notes instead of words." Fourteen syllables, an uncomplicated statement, but one that informed my whole life. (Even now I wish I had access to notes instead of solely my rote array of words, it could only help my cause.)

• • •

Intermezzo No. 2: Many years later I was killing time before an evening appointment by watching an episode of Leonard Bernstein's Concerts for Young People in the performing arts library at Lincoln Center. The first episode, entitled "What Does Music Mean," was filmed at Carnegie Hall with the New York Philharmonic and broadcast in January 1958, just two weeks after Bernstein took over as music director and almost exactly a year before Jerzi was fired. My anger toward my old friend had dissipated significantly by that time and as the video began I wondered whether I would spy him in the orchestra.

It was a good program—*William Tell* overture, *Don Quixote*, Beethoven Six, Mussorgsky *Pictures*, and then Tchaikovsky, the Fifth, I think. Bernstein was warm and funny and, as usual, related magically to the children, most of whom were shown sitting with mothers or nannies or aunts. Very few fathers were in attendance. The first half hour elicited strong déjà vu, but I was familiar with all the works being presented so I dismissed the sensations. I looked at my watch, knowing I needed to go soon, but then got lost in the Tchaikovsky, which was definitely the Fifth because Bernstein was contrasting the emotion conveyed by the first-movement E-minor incarnation of the main theme versus its fourth-movement E-major manifestation (and I was comparing Lenny's tempi with a performance led by Beecham that Jerzi had played for me, a reading that began agonizingly melancholic, almost too much so, *tanto troppo*). Then something Bernstein said yanked me out of my reverie only to throw me back in time again. "Only in notes instead of words," I heard. I stopped the tape. Wound it back. "Music names them for us, only in notes instead of words." I watched the whole scene again. Suddenly my déjà vu was explained.

Everything Jerzi had said that first afternoon came back to me and it was almost word for word what Bernstein was saying on this tape. Over the next several weeks, my last ones in America, I watched all of the Young People's Concerts that the library had available. "What Makes Music Symphonic?" "What is Orchestration?" "What is Melody?" "What is Sonata Form?" In these episodes and others, language that Bernstein used was familiar to me from thoughts Jerzi had claimed as his own.

I was stunned. Six years since I had seen Jerzi in person and I was still discovering ways he had lied to me. He had claimed that everything we talked about came from the lectures he had delivered while teaching at Queens College. He had made me feel smart, like I was more than a child. But that gift belonged to Bernstein, as so many before me knew, not to Jerzi. My anger toward the liar was rekindled. Yes, maybe I should have focused on how I felt instead of how it was accomplished. *Exitus acta probat.* (Ovid, you originally wrote that. But it is not yet your time.) Even though I had read that one should never write down one's mantra, I copied down Bernstein's words on a piece of paper and stuck the scrap in my pocket. (It still travels in the bag with my maps.)

Irate, ready to leave, I pushed my chair back, looked up at the image frozen on the screen, and there on the left side, at the third desk, sat Jerzi. The cameraman was filming from several rows back in the audience and had framed Bernstein on the right, facing the audience from his podium. The picture was a little gritty, but it was undoubtedly my old friend. He wasn't looking at his conductor like all the other musicians but was staring into the audience at a young woman with dark hair. I could only see the back of her head, but I didn't need to see any more. I knew who she was by the expression on Jerzi's face. I had seen it once before, standing on a windy Brooklyn street corner, staring up at a closed and curtained window.

• • •

But back into Jerzi's basement that first day. We began by listening to Beethoven's *Kreutzer Sonata*. I am sure the choice was not an arbitrary one. The violinist was Arthur Grumiaux, Jerzi's violinist god. He wanted me to hear him first, he said, because while Heifetz, Szigeti, Kreisler, Menuhin, Milstein were all immortals, "Grumiaux simply speaks to me more than they do." Jerzi believed the Belgian infused his strings with passion on the fingerboard and released those feelings with his bow. His sound was warmer than other violinists, he said, especially noticeable on the e-string, which never sounded shrill or insubstantial. Although he could dash off the most virtuosic passages, he did so standing almost stock-still and without appearing flashy. Jerzi felt safe, comforted, listening to Grumiaux play. He often talked about the technique, but the terminology was largely meaningless to me and I am unable to recall specifically what he said.

Generally what I took away from these observations was the fact that never would I hear the way in which Jerzi heard, in which a musician heard. I know that music, like love and friendship, is experienced differently by different people, even different musicians, but I wish that once I could have heard Grumiaux play through Jerzi's ears.

The two men never met as far as I know, and in hindsight I'm surprised Jerzi didn't concoct a story about their meeting as I could never have learned the truth. Maybe some things actually were sacred to him and it would have been tantamount to blasphemy to lie about someone he respected so much.

Grumiaux' playing enthralled me, but if Jerzi's aim had been solely to dazzle, he would have put on the Mendelssohn E-minor concerto, for which Grumiaux was rightly renowned and by which I was rightly amazed when we did listen to it several weeks later. No, Jerzi chose the *Kreutzer* not only for the violinist, but also for the pianist, Clara Haskil. Jerzi explained that Clara and Arthur were close friends who dearly loved performing together, who understood and respected each other. Key to their unique collaboration was the fact that Clara also played the violin and Arthur was an excellent pianist, so they could switch instruments to hear the piece from the other's perspective. This closeness was evident, even to me, listening to the recording. It sounded as if the piano and the violin were speaking to each other, teasing each other, chasing each other around the keyboard, the fingerboard. Sadly, Jerzi said, the two would never again play together. In 1960 Clara fell down a stairway in the Brussels train station. She died from the injuries. She played her last concert with Arthur and was to have played with him again the day after her death.

Jerzi stared at the floor between his feet after telling me this, and it was a full minute before I realized that he was sobbing. As soon as I noticed though, he stopped, wiped his tears away with his thumb, one swipe under each eye, stood up and placed the side with the third variation on the phonograph again. "I would like us to listen to this part one more time," he said and we sat quietly and listened. I did not understand Jerzi's actions until much later, until the day we stood and listened to Marie, the girl with the dark hair from the Bernstein video.

Next came a recording of Bizet's *Symphony in C* by the Philharmonic-Symphony Orchestra of New York, conducted by Rodzinski, my host playing amid the thicket of violins. Knowing nothing about music, I asked Jerzi to point out his parts, thinking I would be able to hear each violinist individually. He smiled and said most of the time, the goal for an orchestra was for the strings to be indistinguishable from one another, to lose their individuality like the voices in a chorus, all the first violins playing together, the second violins playing together, the violas, and so on. I nodded but still did not expect what I heard. The total unity that Rodzinski commanded from the strings, whether they were playing *staccato* or *pizzicato* tripping atop the oboe solo, *spiccato* or *legato* furiously charging out for the finale, it was a revelation to me.

Jerzi could not remember how many players the first violins comprised for those three days in early 1945 when the symphony was recorded, but even had it been only a few, the fact that they could ache as one *con molto espressivo* during the second movement made me almost cry. (And it is that same moment, *ô ma* crafty Bizet, that you cribbed to have Don Jose sing to in "*Car tu n'avais eu qu'à paraître*" in *La fleur que tu m'avais jetée*.) The three other movements were just plain fun and I remember being filled with joy, even wanting to dance. (False friend that Mnemosyne is, I almost believe I imagined Balanchine's choreography in my mind's eye that afternoon, ten years before I saw it on stage.)

Besides trying to illustrate the truth of Bernstein's (stolen and unacknowledged) words, I believe Jerzi had an ulterior motive for choosing the Bizet symphony, as he had when selecting the Haskil and Grumiaux collaboration. Bizet wrote the piece in 1855 when he was a seventeen-year-old student of Charles Gounod in Paris. It was never performed during Bizet's lifetime and he never mentioned it in any of his writings. The score was not discovered until eighty years later, when it finally received its world premiere. Since then scholars have noticed remarkable similarities to Gounod's *Symphony No. 1 in D major*, which was popular when Bizet wrote *Symphony in C*. It is generally held that Bizet's is better, but the shape of the work and many of its ideas came (stolen and unacknowledged) from his teacher. I think that maybe Jerzi was subconsciously trying to justify his theft of Bernstein's ideas with the hope that his version, like Bizet's, might end up more enduring.

Finally Jerzi himself played for me. And here my probing fingers find preserved in the darkness of my mind, stuck in a sulcus, a crystal clear film of that half hour, beginning as Jerzi opens his violin case on the table.

"I must warm up, Milo, but while I do so, you would perhaps like to listen to some opera music?"

I knew nothing about the opera, although I thought I may have heard it on the radio at Nonna's. Jerzi had never mentioned it to me before then, but as I got to know him better, I came to believe that it was his true love, more than any symphony or concerto, more even than music for the violin. I was soaring from what I had heard so far that day and eagerly answered, "Sure."

"These two ensembles that I will play were recorded on the same day in February 1908. The first is '*Bella figlia dell'amore*' from the opera *Rigoletto* by Giuseppe Verdi. It is a quartet, meaning it has four voices. The second is '*Chi mi frena*' from *Lucia di Lammermoor* by Gaetano Donizetti. It has six voices, a sextet. Both feature the tenor Enrico Caruso, who had one of the most magnificent voices of all time. He begins the quartet by himself and the sextet singing with the baritone, the low voice. Once you have heard him sing, you will never forget it. It is like a canyon, deep and wide and open to the heavens. The soprano, the highest voice, who sings on both tracks is Marcella Sembrich, who went to the same conservatory as my great-grandmother in Lemberg, which at that time was part of the Austrian empire. They were dear friends. Great-grandmother sang too, but not as well as Madame Sembrich. It broke her heart when her seventeen-year-old friend moved to Vienna to continue her studies and eventually came to America to sing at the Metropolitan Opera. Great-grandmother was happy for her success, but never content with her own life. Not until my mother was born. But those are old stories," he said. "Let us listen to the music."

Caruso transfixed me from the start. The steady clarity with which the voice unspooled and its easy power and expression. Sembrich's soprano soared brightly above, sometimes strong, sometimes light, sometimes sounding artificial it was so unlike anything I was accustomed to hearing. I had trouble keeping the many voices separate, but never lost aural contact with Caruso. At the beginning of the sextet, his voice seemed the epitome of heroic. I barely listened to the orchestra accompanying the singers, partly because of the recording quality, but more so due to how enamored I was with the potential of the human voice. Sembrich was more ethereal in the sextet than in the quartet and the harmonies available with two additional voices were luxurious. I did not understand many of the feelings educed by the music, but I liked that I was moved.

So focused was I on the sound coming from the dark green Symphonic's lone speaker that at first I didn't notice Jerzi playing along. There is no reason it would have made an impact on me at that time, but years later, thinking about the night our friendship ended, I remembered how frequently he played melodies from the operatic repertory.

The Caruso selections finished, Jerzi stood up with his violin in his left hand and turned off the record player. He was not tall, but as he picked up his bow I worried that it was going to hit the low ceiling. That was when I noticed that above where he stood, just to the left of the table, two ceiling tiles had been removed, providing a small space with an additional eight inches of clearance. His back straight, feet slightly splayed, Jerzi looked down on me. He appeared older from that angle. His unruly hair, still black unlike the gray stubble on his slack chin and cheeks, fell across his forehead and accented his eyes, burying them even deeper in their sockets. He brushed the strands away with the back of his bow hand.

"This violin belonged to my father, Milo. At the end of his life, he was concertmaster in Lwów, for the orchestra of the opera company. The concertmaster is the leader of the violins and the assistant to the conductor. This violin was made for my father as a wedding present. It was made by one of the best luthiers in the Austro-Hungarian empire. A luthier makes stringed instruments, like violins and violas and guitars. This violin, it has a very beautiful, very dark sound, Milo. The darkness comes from here, the soundboard, which was crafted from an ancient spruce tree that grew high in the Carpathian mountains south of Lwów. The roots of that tree burrowed deep into the earth. My mother gave me this violin when she said good-bye to me."

Jerzi closed his eyes and took a deep breath. Outside a car horn honked and a siren drove into the distance. Then all was quiet. He drew his bow down across the strings and a low minor chord cut the silence. He played slowly. Trills and thirty-second notes took their time. His body seemed shut down, sacrificed to the solemn (I confess I even thought holy) creation of such grave sounds. He moved his left arm only above the elbow, the rest of his body reacting passively, as if entranced. It swayed but didn't initiate motion. His right arm appeared to be dragged along by the bow, to which it was seemingly tenuously attached by thumb and pinky. It was the first movement of Bach's A-minor Sonata.

One violin in a small space is capable of stealing all the air, transmuting oxygen into emotion. I did not want to breathe for fear of inhaling such sorrow.

When he finished, Jerzi lifted his bow off the strings and dropped his arm to his side. His eyes opened and he looked at me. I didn't know what to say, but my face was bright with amazement. He smiled back and drew his bow over the strings again. The first chord sounded like it was the same piece of music, but then more notes started to come, runs, scales, up and down, finishing higher each time, rising higher, the fingers of his left hand coming closer and closer to the bridge where his bow drew on the strings and then sliding back to the scroll. He stopped, winked at me, and then notes started to fly through the air faster than I imagined possible. They rained down on me. For a while the middle of the bow just rocked back and forth over the strings but the notes kept coming. Rapid, choppy, shreddy, tripping, metallic, bright, squealing, sawing, back and forth. It was Paganini's *Caprice No. 5 in A minor*. Same key as the Bach, such a different effect. I clapped wildly when he finished. I begged him to play it again.

"It is late, Milo. Your mother is expecting you home. There will be lots of time to listen." No light shone through the narrow windows behind the tops of the bookcases, but I didn't want to leave, to return to my reality.

Walking me to back to the bakery, neither of us spoke. For my part, I did not wish to still the lingering musical memory. Jerzi often intuited this desire and would remain silent until I said something, as if he too had struggled with holding onto a fast-fading phrase as it tried to flee. That night, as I lay on the couch waiting for Mamma to come for me, I resented my father for the first time. Tossing and turning under a thin cotton blanket, I wondered what he could have taught me if he had lived, whether Mamma would have been happier with him at her side, why her God had killed him. I sat up and lifted his photograph off the hook where it hung. Without looking, I slid the frame under the couch and quickly fell asleep.

• • •

It is difficult to delineate the events that occurred between that afternoon in Jerzi's basement and the night eight years later when I slipped into the shadows, leaving behind everyone I knew. The scenes seem to blend together *portamento*. There were jarring moments. My Mahlerian ears heard when the clarinet sang out clearly like a klezmer-band member, when a horn called from afar through the stage door left ajar, when the cowbells jangled, clanged, wrangled. These are pertinent sensations, but ones not tied uniquely to specific instances. Life at P.S. 16 never got any easier. Some mornings I couldn't imagine returning to the taunting and teasing. I would beg Mamma to let me stay home and after she said no, I would beg Nonna, who rarely countermanded Mamma by acceding to my pleas. To a small group of kids, mostly older, I wasn't Italian enough, I lacked *maschilismo*. They beat me up, not every day, and not so badly that anyone in a position to stop it would notice, but it had a cumulative effect over the years. Hit in the kidneys, smacked on the back of the neck—sometimes so hard I dropped to my knees, tripped, pushed, spit on. I lowered my eyes. My head hung down, chin near my chest, shoulders tensed up anticipating the next whack. My ankle stayed sprained and I began to limp (weight on my right leg for a quarter note, left leg for an eighth). I was alone, quiet, different, changed slowly by each punch or gibe or kick until I became a loner, quite diffident.

I saw life mainly through my ears during those years and learned a lot by listening. I decided to get good grades because I was afraid that anything less would land me back at St. Leo's, which would be worse. At least I was free from religion at P.S. 16, although still living my own blasphemous Passion, my isolation my cross to bear, no friends or family along my path except Jerzi (my Simon the Cyrene), but he claimed to have classes, rehearsals, concerts. (Not true, not true, not true, you thrice have lied to me! Perhaps he was Peter). I found salvation in my mind, my isolation, and I redeemed my world. *Quia per solitudem mentem Meum redimi mundum.*

• • •

On my tenth birthday, Jerzi took me to the Metropolitan Opera House to see Gounod's *Roméo et Juliette*. Franco Corelli and Mirella Freni sang the lead roles and Francesco Molinari-Pradelli conducted. Standing-room tickets had gone on sale Saturday morning, my birthday fell on the following Tuesday, and Jerzi said he waited all night Friday to buy the tickets (true), joining the line after he finished playing a concert with the Philharmonic (false). It was the first night of a new production and I wore the black suit that I had gotten for Nonno's funeral twelve months earlier. Four out of the next six years, the Met had a performance on my birthday and Jerzi and I went to them all. Let's test my memory: in 1968, a *Rigoletto* when MacNeil canceled before taking the stage; a 1970 triple-header on the Saturday I became a teenager, comprising a matinee *Ernani*, of which I would soon learn the significance to Jerzi's life, to Jerzi's existence, and an evening *Cavalleria Rusticana / Pagliacci*; opening night in 1972, Bernstein conducting *Carmen*, the drunken Jerzi in his tuxedo alternately crying and mumbling throughout, booing after Horne's *Habañera*; and in 1973, my introduction to Strauss through the electrifying *Salome*, the thirty-six-year-old Bumbry singing the sybaritic teen under Levine. Some facts have not fled my mind. And some will not, no matter how I try to forget them, e.g., in 1974, the Met was in Cleveland doing *Don Giovanni* on my birthday, the day my murdered father rose from the grave like the Commendatore. And Jerzi, Jerzi who I had worshipped and followed like a lowly Leporello, was consigned by me to Hell. (Midas coiled his tail eight times and I turned my back as Antaeus dragged him down and deposited him with the rest of the betrayers. *Che inferno! Che terror!* That day looms ahead in this cavern where I sojourn, I see the telltale prints, I passed them on my descent, fluttering near the shadowy outline of the *Scherzo*, that manic third phase where I start to see for myself instead of listening meekly to those who would use me.)

While I have had more memorable nights at the opera since then, nights where the music or singing moved me uniquely, nights when I at last felt as if I understood a particular work, nights my favorite singers sang for all they were worth, I have never been more overwhelmed than I was that first night.

It started with the subway trip to the city. The teachers were on strike, so Jerzi and I went into Manhattan in the early afternoon. New York was in the midst of a late-September heat wave, the temperature must have been in the eighties, and so we dressed casually and carried our suits, which Jerzi had a way of folding—jacket inside out, waist of the slacks up by the shoulders, sheet of waxed paper inserted between them—that somehow prevented wrinkles. We took the 7 train to Queensboro Plaza and transferred to the RR for the trip into Manhattan. Getting out on 57th Street, I saw Carnegie Hall for the first time. Even though the Philharmonic had moved to its new home in Lincoln Center five years earlier, Jerzi said he still knew some of the guys who worked there. (This assertion proved to be true, but I don't believe that Jerzi had played with the orchestra its last several seasons at Carnegie.) We hung around the stage doors on 56th until a guy came out who Jerzi recognized. He greeted him warmly and the two had a brief whispered conversation. I was introduced as a good friend and then we were taken inside. (I observed Jerzi using this *modus operandi*—waiting by a service door for a familiar face—many times to great effect and frequently used the technique in my later life.) There was a rehearsal going on at the time, so we didn't have free run of the place, but we got to look into the main auditorium from the balcony and use empty dressing rooms on the third floor to change clothes, the same dressing rooms used by visiting musicians, conductors, dancers. It was quite thrilling.

One of Jerzi's main purposes for the evening was to help me forget what had happened during dinner on my previous birthday. He had been busy that year because of rehearsal (lie), so I had eaten with Nonno, Nonna, and Mamma at the Park Side in Corona. The *primi* had just been delivered when Nonno suffered a massive, fatal heart attack, shaking under the table while Mamma prayed aloud and Nonna wailed and I sat there alone in shock. Accordingly, Jerzi and I did not eat a fancy meal before the opera. After leaving Carnegie Hall, we cut through Central Park, careful to avoid the fallen fan-shaped gingko leaves that suffuse the autumn air with the smell of sewage, and got a slice of pizza on Broadway.

Approaching Lincoln Center from the east, I was unable to hide my glee. I felt like skipping, or indeed, like singing. The travertine plaza shimmered white before me, the fountain glowed brightly, and the three soaring glass facades looking down on us made me feel like I was in a different city on another world. Ladies walked by in gowns and dresses, men in tuxedos. Illuminating the Met against deep-red walls and shining through its five-story windows, giant Swarovski chandeliers sparkled like interstellar prisms.

Inside, after having my ticket torn and being told to enjoy my evening, carefully climbing the curving, gently sloped staircase to the first landing, I tried not to fall while continuing to look up, up at the lights, up at the crowds looking down over the balconies, up into the din of hundreds of voices and the sounds of crystal on crystal and china beneath silver as well-heeled patrons toasted each other and dined. I was envious and in awe. Continuing up, carried along with the crowds spiraling up the stairways, up into the relative quiet of the auditorium and lastly up the final straight stair to the very top, as far from the stage as you could get, where we stopped and Jerzi confidently assured me the sound was the best in the house.

Smaller versions of the chandeliers in the lobby began to rise slowly toward the ceiling, dimming as they ascended. It was hard for me to see over the railing so Jerzi suggested I go and sit at the top of the stairs. Some nights, this one included, I got away with sitting there for the entire performance; other times an overzealous usher chased me back to my feet. Darkness silenced the audience to whispers. One glaring square awaited the conductor and illuminated the orchestra members in their pit far below. I blinked and glanced up at the golden painted ceiling above me. Molinari-Pradelli entered to applause, bowed, turned around, and raised his baton. With the first note, the rest of the night became a blur of Freni's childlike frame, she looked no older than me; Corelli's sheer volume, he had no hidden microphone!?; Freni waltzing through *Je veux vivre!,* ending with a soaring final C; the passionate orchestration eliciting those unclassifiable emotions again, especially from the aching strings; the familiar sadness of the story, Jerzi had taken me to see Zeffirelli's film version in preparation; Corelli's lingering and lingering *piano* ending to *A leve-toi soleil!*; the ovation shocking me, the man next to me began it *sforzando,* shouting BRAVO! BRAVO! and I jumped to my feet only to say YAY! YAY!; Freni reaching longingly over the balcony down to Corelli's outstretched hand; the spectacle; the applause; the final duet; the death; the love. During the curtain calls, I was conflicted: sorrowful at the night being over and joyous at what had awakened within me. I walked downstairs in a trance, and once out again in the still hot September night, in a trance I remained, a silly boyish grin plastered to my face. Jerzi conducted me home in a thick fog that did not dissipate for several days.

• • •

I grew more awkward, as growing boys do. I gawked awkwardly as the girls grew too. Some afternoons when school let out, I lingered on 104th Street (Mamma did not come for me anymore) so I could watch the prettier girls from St. Leo's walk past in their school skirts. I thought about them while lying in the dark beneath my father, back on the wall, resurrected after a full six days (twice as long as Jesus was gone) when Nonno found his lost son buried below the couch, an interment he blamed on Mamma. I thought about them in my bedroom, staring up at the undesired crucifix Mamma installed above the headboard, Christ metamorphosed into one of the girls, only the small cloth on her loins, breasts bare, her arms spread out to rescue me. I wanted her to unnail her limbs and climb down, lie on top of me.

I was too shy to approach even girls at my own school, although I would allow them to copy off me during exams, hoping these interactions might be a prelude toward a friendship outside class. One day I encountered a girl in the hallway who had just stared over my slumped shoulder for forty minutes during a math test. I asked if she thought she did okay. She turned to me, looked me in the eye, and knocked my books to the ground. She pushed me into the lockers and screamed in my face, "I didn't cheat off your test, *culo*!" Everyone laughed at me. She and her friends walked away. I stopped helping after that day, retreated further into my mind. (I am distressingly aware sitting here of all the memories where the subject is I instead of we.)

• • •

During the summer or on weekends, I occasionally would walk to Jerzi's after meeting up with him at the *pasticceria*. He would teach me about a composer or specific type of music or specific work, aided at all times (*sine confitentis Deo omnipotenti et alii*) by Bernstein and his Concerts for Young People. (It seems rather puerile to be so condemnatory about this particular transgression of Jerzi's. There were enough sins of commission committed that I don't need to punish him for his omission ones. But I do.) I often directed the conversation by asking about whatever topic was on my mind. Even if my question wasn't music related, Jerzi frequently answered me by playing a record on his Symphonic. That is just how his mind worked.

I would ask what it was like to be in love and he had me listen to *Tristan und Isolde* from "*O sink hernieder, Nacht der Liebe*" through Brangäne's warning, 1952 Covent Garden under Furtwängler. I talked about trying to forgive Mamma for her neglect and he put on Elizabeth Rethberg as the Contessa singing "*Più docile io sono e dico di sì.*" After Nonno died Jerzi suggested we listen to Verdi's *Requiem*, conducted by Toscanini. (I heard Hupka's shutter accompanying him metronomically). In March 1964, when I was in the last weeks of being loved by Mamma, Jerzi had watched Georg Solti conduct that same piece at the Met during a memorial for President Kennedy, who had been assassinated four months earlier. I did not mind religion in music, and each time the ferocious *Dies irae* came around I trembled more than ever I did in a church. When Robert Kennedy was assassinated, Jerzi put on the *Adagietto* of Mahler's Fifth Symphony for me (true), the day after he played it at St. Patrick's with the Philharmonic (false).

Sometimes Jerzi picked up his violin while we talked. Here is what I felt when walking away from my mother for the last time, he would play. Here was my excitement at seeing America for the first time. Here is what my father looked like. These leitmotifs of his life would be expanded upon lexically on that Brooklyn sidewalk I keep anticipating.

We also took aural excursions on those afternoons. Years before I would see it, I drifted along the Vltava in Bedřich Smetana's *Má Vlast*. I climbed high in the Alps with Richard Strauss through his *Alpensinfonie*. I marveled at Franz Liszt's *Totentanz*. (Now I know the terror Dante must have felt upon reaching the second circle and seeing the lustful, including Paolo, whose Francesca was buffeted by "*la bufera infernal, che mai non resta*," lost to him forever, she is lost to me forever. Enough!) I closed my eyes and saw the swans overhead in Sibelius's Second Symphony, and every time Beecham whipped the BBC Symphony Orchestra down its final stretch runs, first cellos and violas, then basses and flutes and bassoons, then second violins and oboes and clarinets, then the furious runs for the winds high above, the violins beginning their twined tremolo ascents, thirteen measures climbing to high-A, never stopping, expanding *allargando*, rest, rest, thirteen more up to D now, it always seemed to me as if it could not keep going, then the entire orchestra is on D and holding and holding, under *fermata*, me weeping, Beecham holding, holding, holding, holding, holding, and finally with the orchestra's breath fading, at last, a little longer, then, and, release.

Heading home, misery would return. It was still light outside with the summer sun setting late, but in my mind, to which I had already retreated by the top of Jerzi's basement stairs, all was dark.

• • •

In 1969 Jerzi moved to Lefrak City, a Brobdingnagian brick complex comprising twenty-story buildings and housing twenty-five-thousand families. There are only two characteristics I can determine that differentiate Lefrak from the giant blocks of workers' flats called *panelák* on the outskirts of erstwhile Soviet cities: 1) Lefrak buildings were oriented in groups of four forming X's as opposed to *panelák* which were lined up like dominoes, ready to topple the moment the first one fell, just like the Soviet bloc countries, and 2) communists built in concrete while Americans opted for brick.

When it opened, Lefrak was solidly middle-class and Jerzi was not the only immigrant from eastern Europe who called it home. Within a few years, however, lawsuits changed the economic makeup of the complex and by the mid-1970s when crime increased, as it did all across New York City, white flight began. When I last saw Jerzi, a brief encounter before I left the country, he said he planned to move. He'd been mugged. His apartment had been burgled. He didn't feel safe anymore. I didn't believe anything he said at that point. He might still live there today.

Jerzi's move first made me begin to question what I knew about him. He had told me that he was moving to Lefrak because he wanted more space (possibly), more light (certainly), and a chance to meet people (likely). Those reasons may have explained his forced relocation, but they were not the *causus abitio*. I learned the truth on the day I went to help him pack. I walked over from *Due G's* by myself after lunch and when I got to his outside door, I heard Jerzi's voice in the hallway inside. It is another of the indelible recordings in my Cimmerian mind.

"Yes, Martin, well, I informed you that I would need a bit more time."

"And how much time have we given you? Four months? Six? I don't even remember to be honest with you. Look, you're a dear friend, we wouldn't have let it go on this long if you weren't. I know it's been hard for you the past few years. I still miss having you on campus. But it just doesn't seem like you're trying to fix the problem. I wish that we could just afford to let you stay, but we need the income. Sara's brother has a job. You don't. I wish you could find one. I'd love for you to stay. Believe me. I'd rather you than him."

"I know. I should keep packing so I will be ready to go tomorrow. You said at noon, correct?"

"Yeah. Noon is fine."

At that point I turned and quickly walked quietly back to the sidewalk. I didn't know if someone was leaving the house or not, but didn't want to be caught having eavesdropped.

I heard no voices behind the door upon my second arrival. I found Jerzi in the basement amid his disarray, containers of cardboard, plastic, wood. There must have been a hundred boxes piled on the Turkish rug. Beethoven's *Triple Concerto* was playing on the record player, which I interpreted (correctly) as a sign that Jerzi was unsettled. His mood dictated the accompaniment he desired and so he rarely listened to the radio. When he needed to think, Jerzi chose—perhaps paradoxically—chamber music, which he said was easier to tune out since he knew it intimately. When he was cleaning or cooking, the prominent instrument was the piano, occasionally concertos but mainly solo works by Mozart, Beethoven, Rachmaninoff, Bach, Brahms, Debussy, anyone really, except poor Chopin, one of the best, but nevertheless his composer *non grata*. (Our minds are not always our own.) When he wanted to escape, orchestral music or opera. The selection of piano, cello, violin, and orchestra meant the inside of his head resembled the inside of his apartment.

We said hello. He was glad to see me it was clear, but whether for my actual assistance or merely companionship I could not tell. I found it almost frightening that Jerzi had lied to me about something so fundamental as where he worked, so I didn't bring up his conversation with Martin. I didn't even know how. (And

I don't know whether I do now, thirty-five years later. How do you ask someone if they have been lying to you since the day you met?)

I suggested that I could pack his clothes so that he wouldn't have to worry about me breaking any of his records. Jerzi trusted me, he said. (By which he meant "with the music," not "with the truth.") I was instructed to place his albums—one by one—into either the wooden crates or the reinforced cardboard boxes. It was actually an enjoyable task, having to individually handle each disc. I had heard many of them during the three years that we had been friends, but whole sections were unknown to me. All of Jerzi's albums were meticulously alphabetized by composer, then subdivided into categories—symphonies, concertos, chamber works, etc. I could not reach high enough on the shelves to begin at the letter A, so I started with G. I asked if we could listen to the Grieg A-minor concerto but he wouldn't let go, and chose Szymanowski's *Mythes*, which I find eerie under any conditions.

Hidden among the scores of Haydn symphonies, I spied an outlier—Gustav Mahler's *Symphony No. 7 in E minor*, New York Philharmonic, Leonard Bernstein conducting. Assuming he played on the recording, and surprised at finding it out of place, I held up the album to ask Jerzi's opinion of the work.

He snatched it out of my hand so quickly that an actual LP flew out of its sleeve and rolled under the table.

That is not for you, he said, and proceeded to crawl on the floor and retrieve the record. He picked it up and slid it back into the sleeve without pausing to see whether it had been scratched. I started to apologize but he waved me off, said it was nothing, it was nothing. Jerzi went into his room and when he came back a few minutes later, he smelled like Nonno did when I hugged him goodnight after he had drunk his grappa. He made several more trips to the bedroom that day. It was the first time I noticed Jerzi's drinking.

I should say as an aside that I never learned what about the Seventh, about that particular recording, made Jerzi so animated. I assume it related to his dismissal, but that is just a guess. (Sometimes when I'm particularly introspective, I believe that his more-musical ears heard my—as-yet-unrealized—connection with Mahler's music, and he was trying to protect me, to defuse me before I blew.)

It was early evening when we finished packing the main room. The shelves were empty and the boxes were full. I went to the bathroom, and when I came out, Jerzi was leaning against the table playing Wieniawski's *Légende* on his violin.

I said I would like to help him move, but he said he was starting early in the morning and I would still be working. Since Nonno died, I had been helping at the *pasticceria* on weekends.

I thought about telling Jerzi that I knew he wasn't starting until noon, but decided against it. His flash of temper over the Mahler record had given me pause and I didn't want to see him angry again. I stepped onto the stairs.

He looked up and said he would come by *Due G's* on Monday or Tuesday afternoon, once he got done teaching, and walk me over to see his new place. Then he looked back down at the scroll of his violin.

He was hunched over. His left elbow rested on the table. He was drunk. I felt sad for him. And I realized that the darkness he had said lived within his violin also inhabited him.

• • •

I began to accompany Jerzi into the city on nights when the Philharmonic performed. My intentions were twofold: first, to try and see what exactly he did since he apparently wasn't playing, and second, to go to the Met and stoke my burgeoning love affair with the opera. As far as I knew, Mamma did not bother to verify my whereabouts anymore (I was thirteen, fourteen, fifteen, during the years about which I am speaking), but I didn't like going into the city alone, so I only went to the opera when I could ride the subway there and back with Jerzi.

I continued to play along with his charade, but I was a bit more perspicacious, or at least more prying. We attended our respective performances, mine legitimate, his disingenuous, and then, since the opera usually finished later, I would inquire of the Lincoln Center parking attendants about where I was to meet Jerzi, who always went out for drinks with coworkers (i.e., friends) from the orchestra after their concerts. In retrospect, the valets probably knew what Jerzi was really up to (which I would not for several more years), because they stalled me, talked to me about the show, let me backstage early if I really wanted to meet one of the singers in their dressing room. (Maybe they genuinely liked me, but more plausibly they felt sorry for me because I was being lied to and they knew it.) After keeping me occupied for a half hour or so, they would tell me which nearby haunt held my guardian and I would go to meet him.

Not only did the valets know Jerzi, but it seemed that many of the patrons did too. In fact, anytime we arrived at Lincoln Center, which we always did by taking the same route we had on my tenth birthday, never staying on the 7 train long enough to transfer to the 1 because Times Square was too dangerous Jerzi said, people on the plaza recognized him. A fashionably dressed man would incline his head slightly in greeting or a woman would lower her eyes. Children, especially around the holidays, would tug on their parents' sleeves and point at him like he was Parpignol.

I assumed that the life of an orchestral musician was akin to that of a rock star, that I was basically approaching Shea Stadium in 1965 with one of The Beatles. I felt proud to be walking with him. Jerzi felt comfortable acting fatherly toward me at that time, and he regularly placed his hand on my shoulder or tousled my hair. I now believe that he used these walks through the plaza to garner sympathy, to make people think he had a son to support.

A few times we attended a Philharmonic rehearsal together, if school was on vacation or the teachers were on strike, which happened frequently in the early 1970s, but Jerzi always had an excuse for why he wasn't playing that day. And if he had been playing, he wouldn't have gotten tickets, because he obviously could not have attended, he stated. Many of his lies were tautological like this, making them difficult for a child to penetrate. What did not make sense to me (then or now) was the necessity of the deception.

All the ushers in Philharmonic Hall knew him and we always had seats held at the back of the first balcony. How he got us into those practice sessions I never learned, but we didn't present actual tickets like the others in attendance.

One night Jerzi, drunk in a cab on the way home, let on that he often played cards with some orchestra members—and often won—so maybe the access was periodically part of the pot.

That evening in the taxi wasn't the only time I saw Jerzi drunk during those years. Since moving to Lefrak, he didn't bother to hide his drinking anymore. At the new apartment, a bottle or two always sat on the kitchen table. I thought it was his way of winding down after a night of complex counting schemes in a contemporary work or bowing bored through another repertory piece. It was part of the camaraderie of being in the band.

But I honestly had no idea how adults behaved. (I did not really know anything about people in general.) I did not know what Mamma did for money, let alone relaxation, since she had cut down her hours at *Due G's* during the Fair. Nonna worked constantly, barely slept. Was that her entire existence? I had talked to a couple of teachers outside class, but it was always about what we discussed in class. Did teachers only teach?

I didn't truly know anyone except Jerzi. And I didn't know him at all, I only thought I did. A few years ago, I read an interview with Susan Sontag in which she said something to the effect that as a child, she knew more books than people. The same could have been said of me and Tchaikovsky symphonies, and there are only six of those, far fewer than the number of books in the world.

• • •

The Saturday before Thanksgiving in 1973, Jerzi showed up at the *pasticceria* early, while groups of aging Italian men wearing worn suits still argued around empty espressos and women stopped in to buy fresh bread. He no longer came by every day and I was happy to see him, but he looked tired and unkempt. I was in front of the counter cleaning off a table and shook his hand. He felt tired too.

"Is everything okay, Jerzi?"

"Today is a difficult day for me, Milo. I was wondering if you could come with me when you get finished with work. I am going to listen to some music. Chopin, I imagine." His eyes implored me. "It would be of great help to me if you would come."

"I'd love to," and I truly was excited by the invitation, both because I adored Chopin's music and because I could not envision what would make Jerzi actually listen to it. "Where?"

"In Greenpoint, a neighborhood in Brooklyn. I will wait until you are ready." With that he turned his back on me, slid his violin case beneath the table and, pulling a newspaper from his jacket pocket, sat down. I was unaware of a concert hall in Brooklyn that was not the Brooklyn Academy of Music, but I didn't ask anything else.

He began looking up at me anxiously around noon, so I asked what time the concert started. He answered cryptically, saying he was not entirely sure, but it was something he must not miss. He implored me to hurry.

The busy part of the day was past and I asked Nonna if I could leave since Jerzi seemed upset. She acquiesced. When I walked around the counter and said I was ready, Jerzi practically pushed me out the front door.

I had to jog to keep up with him on the way to the train. We got off at Queensboro Plaza but left the station, hurried one gritty block to Queens Plaza and, leaving the borough behind, got on the GG to Brooklyn. The Greenpoint Avenue stop emptied onto Java Street and we walked west to the corner of Franklin. After turning north, Jerzi stopped, which I appreciated because I had fallen behind by several steps.

"This building, Milo, is where I lived after first arriving in America."

A stolid brick arch outlined a short dark passage to the door. I tried to imagine Jerzi living there when he was just a few years older than me. I looked to him, waiting for him to elaborate, but he only stood silently for a moment and then turned and continued north. There were no other people on the street. The late autumn sun approached the top of Manhattan's skyline and dusk crept out of the east. After a few blocks I began to wonder again what kind of a concert hall we were seeking, and I was about to ask when Jerzi stopped at the intersection of Eagle Street, looked around, and quickly strode across kitty-corner. He stopped beneath the fire escape of a brick building with crumbling tuck-pointing and looked up. I crossed to him.

I had a cramp in my stomach from struggling to match his pace. Part of me wondered if Jerzi had brought me out here to abandon me.

"What's going on, Jerzi?"

"Please, Milo, she has begun already."

Above us a piano could be heard through an opened window.

I glanced at Jerzi to see if he was serious. This could not be the concert. He stood enraptured, eyes closed, staring up, his violin case in his left hand. I listened. It was Chopin's A-flat major etude, the oneiric, famous one, from Op. 25. I assumed that, for some reason, we were listening to a radio station or somebody's phonograph.

Taking the opportunity to rest, I leaned against the building and closed my eyes as Jerzi had. The next forty minutes may have been a dream, so magical did the playing seem. A *liederabend* composed itself in my mind, lyrical images flowing in and out of my consciousness, interrupted occasionally by Jerzi's narration explaining something about his life, or the music, or the scene unfolding in my head, or all three, I really don't know, so unified did they seem at the time. The echo of all I heard remains strong here in the fertile dark of my memory. I will try and replay it the way I lived it.

> *[No. 1 in Ab] Water sprites splash lightly about in the spray of a lazy waterfall, their lilting voices carrying the aroma of ambrosia over me and I am unsteady, wavering between two worlds. For another minute the naiads play on, droplets glissando down their diaphanous backs and bellies. Aeolus, slightly opening his billowing bag, dispatches a solitary aimless breeze which gently steals their final whispered words, and tired out at last, they crawl onto the grass and fall into a dewy slumber.*

Jerzi breaks the silence but speaks slowly, as if he does not want to ruin the spell: My mother was an only child. Her closest companion growing up was her grandmother, my great-grandmother, who was friends with the soprano Marcella Sembrich, as I told you. As a girl, mother was always singing, making up songs as she played with her doll or went on walks with her grandmother.

She had a beautiful voice, a winsome voice that never lost its innocence even as she grew older. Her grandmother was determined that mother should have the opportunity to develop that voice, so when mother turned thirteen, her grandmother went to the conservatory in Lwów and secured a position for her. No one in the family knew how she had accomplished this. If mother found out, she never shared the secret with me. When she started conservatory, she also began singing in the opera chorus. The small amount of money she earned she sent home to her grandmother. (Tinkling *presto* notes stop his voice. Fingers slip across keys.)

> *[No. 2 in Fm] Hermes races down and skates across the concave inner surface of my mind, quicksilver slick. One of the sleeping naiads, draped now all in cornflowers, is cradled safely in his arms. As they skate round and around the fogging hemisphere of my consciousness, the nymph awakes. Seeing where she is and being content in his grasp, she stretches back and wraps her arms around his neck. The outside world occluded, the purple-blue petals began to droop and the god, seeing that her day is done, glides carefully to the edge and lays her gently in the mist as a bell tolls four fading tones.*

Jerzi continued: Unlike mother, my father was never encouraged to pursue music as a child. He grew up in a small village, very poor, and he was an infant when his father died. His childhood was dominated by work. When he was eight, a group of Gypsies, Romany, passed through the village. My father heard them playing their mystic tunes and was mesmerized by the sound of the violin. He snuck into the Gypsies's camp and stole the instrument. It was too big for him, but he did not care. Whenever he had a free moment, he played. When he was twelve, his mother died. Father left the village. He went to Lwów. Four years later he got a job with the orchestra, which needed new musicians to replace those who had gone to fight in the war and never returned. Three years later my mother started with the chorus. Father was nineteen, mother fifteen. They fell in love very quickly.

> *[No. 3 in F] Such a young couple, walking hand in hand along the banks of the stream outside the city. The sun shines proudly, only an occasional cloud blocking its cheery mien. The couple stop beneath a fruit tree and he pulls her tightly to his chest and kisses her. This is not a game she sees. These emotions are not make-believe. He wants to be with her. Her heart races, but it is okay. She feels these things, too. She kisses him back playfully, she is just a child after all, nips him on the tip of his nose, pulls away, and laughing goes skipping into the grass, does a cartwheel. He chases her, they seem to bound nimbly up the hill. She outpaces him and he grows scared, fearing for a moment that she will lose him, that he has acted rashly. But she stops, bends down. She has picked a wildflower and turning back, walks toward him, the flower held so the petals tickle the underside of her chin. When they reach each other, she stares assuredly into his eyes, decided. I love, she says, you.*

Just months after my parents met, mother received a letter from home. Her grandmother was dead. One week later, she was expelled from the conservatory and kicked out of the chorus. No one at the school gave her an explanation. The timing could merely have been coincidence, since incidents of anti-Semitism were on the rise near the end of the war. My father tried to speak to the conservatory staff on her behalf, but she was not yet his wife and the conversation accomplished nothing. Mother went back to her village and wept. My father was desolate.

[No. 4 in Am] Though it has been so long, she wonders if he thinks of her. She thinks of him. She misses him. She stares into the night and hopes that somewhere, in the dark, the one she loves is coming to her. All is lost, the war is done, but everything is wrong. Everything is wrong. Suddenly the door blows open, and her love is standing there, he cries her name, he runs to her, he says that he can't live without her. But no. It isn't real, it all was just a shadow play. The door slams closed and wakes her up, she lights the lamp, puts it on the sill, and starts her vigil once again. She says her prayers, she prays for him, she pulls the shawl tight round her shoulders. One more night alone. Another night alone. She sleeps and dreams of love.

After the war, Artur Rodzinski came to Lwów with his wife. He had grown up there but studied in Vienna. Artur was initially in charge of the chorus at the Lwów opera house. He and my father had known each other as children but were not close. On Artur's first day, my father precociously asked him to secure mother's return to the chorus. The two men went out to dinner, talked, and Artur said he would try to help. And he did. Mother returned, both to the chorus and, eventually, to the conservatory. The four of them—my parents and Artur and his wife, Halina—became friends. In 1920 Artur conducted Verdi's *Ernani* in Lwów. My father and mother both were part of the production. It was Artur's conducting debut.

[No. 5 in Em] Confused by the man at the door, she blushes. He speaks with a confidence that is foreign to her. He appears more polished than before, but he's still impulsive or he would not have come. She is tired of being alone. They leave and travel at night, over passes and into valleys and then out again. In the diffuse morning light

falling through the hotel's muslin curtains, his caresses feel warm on her bare skin. She crawls onto him, into his arms, and he crawls into her. She gives herself to him completely, surrendering not only her passion but also her dreams. If he wants to, he can take them all, fulfill them or dash them. He doesn't know what to do. He is passive. Afterward she looks up at him, her cheek resting on his chest. He too should be loved. It is dizzying. The two travel again. When they arrive in the city, maybe she skips a little. Her future is now hers to make. She is free, thanks to him. She thinks back discordantly on what she left behind, those she left behind, but it is done. She is resigned. She puts her hands on her stomach and spins in place. Smiles. Sinks back onto the bed.

My parents were married in 1921 and within a year I was born. It was a sometimes challenging period for Poland, but she was independent for the first time since the eighteenth century and difficulties were to be expected. The arts, however, flourished, in both the country and within my family. I began playing the violin at the age of four and it was apparent immediately that I was gifted. I gave my first concert in Lwów at age nine and performed in Warsaw shortly after that. My father was promoted to concertmaster. Mother continued in the chorus, a voice in the crowd, she did not need the limelight of the soloist. The concert halls were full and our futures seemed bright.

[No. 6 in G#m] The breeze makes it hard to get the clothes down off the line. Staring across the city she wonders where he is. She is content and the child is a blessing but everything is always moving forward, the years racing along inexorably. Her hands never seem to stop. In these infrequent moments of solitude, her thoughts range to places

they have no business going. A choice was made, her life coupled to another, and they now are as one. Don't look back, she tells herself. It cannot be undone. And yet. Look at those two birds, one chasing the other down the winds, soaring and diving, twittering, stumbling through the air. Are they any happier than I? Why? She wonders. A last sigh and she turns and goes in, kisses her son goodnight, and goes to lay down in her cold empty bed.

It all fell apart in 1939. First the Germans invaded and then two weeks later, the Soviets annexed the eastern part of the country, including Lwów. It appeared as if that would be it, the Soviets would be our new masters. It was not easy. They changed the currency and immediately we were broke. Everyone was broke. We managed to survive. To supplement his income, my father began teaching at the newly reorganized, and now state-run, conservatory where I was studying. Then in 1941, the Germans attacked the Soviets. When they reached Lwów in June, they killed hundreds of professors, including my father. Mother was devastated. Getting me out of the country became her sole priority. She contacted Artur, who was then with the Cleveland Symphony Orchestra. He arranged for me to perform several concerts in America. I was twenty years old and very scared. Leaving mother was the hardest thing I have ever done. I never returned to Europe, and I never saw her again.

[No. 7 in C#m] So this is solitude. This is alone. It is more silent than she could have known. More hollow. She thinks her mind should make more noise given all the sorrow she carries around inside it. She can't understand why the stars should still twinkle so carelessly. Or why the moon should shine so brightly. She wants everything to fall into shadow, become black. Ugly. Lightless. She wants the world to be

clad in sables and crepe. She doesn't want to sit under this olive tree and see that it has so many new buds, so many signs of life. She doesn't want that basket of thorns and sticks to be an empty nest. She wants them to matter. She wants to forget, not be reminded of her mistake every time she hears him cry, every morning the first thing and every night the last. She wants her world back, but doesn't even remember what that was. She needs a new one. Quiet. Someone's approaching.

I sought asylum and it was granted. With Artur's help I enrolled at the Juilliard School where I finished my studies. I was living with a Polish couple who were big supporters of the arts and they let me stay with them as a favor to the school. I felt very lost and alone. Most of my time I spent at school, which was then up by Columbia University. It was a long trip home by subway, so often I would sleep in the practice room if I got tired, or at a friend's place where there was a spare bed. This latter situation was important to me too, because when I was not practicing the violin, I needed to be practicing my English. There were always people around to talk with, people from all over the world, many of them refugees like me. We tried to focus on music and our lives in New York and not talk only of the war. It was easier to try and forget that most people our age were fighting and dying. One night, very late, I decided not to take the subway home. Walking the halls during a break, I heard someone playing Franz Liszt's transcription of Isolde's *Liebestod*. It was painfully yearning and I stood outside the door and listened. When the music stopped, I knocked.

[No. 8 in Db] Everything has happened so fast. It's a merry-go-round. He sees unfamiliar faces. Always new. Every night if he wants to. Anything he wants to. He's found

success. Some nights, when the moon is shining through his window exactly right, he remembers the look she had on her face as she fell asleep but he never has enough time to focus on that because there is always another something. This is excitement. This is living. This is what he has to do. And he grabs his coat and runs out the door into the light.

Marie was from Warsaw, but she had immigrated with her parents before the war. We became inseparable, at first solely as friends. We made music together. She helped me with the language. We talked about our world, our city. When we graduated, we continued to see each other every day. One day we realized that we were in love. It was strange that we never noticed it before, but I think we enjoyed talking to each other and exploring and listening to each other play so much that we never, we never saw it. Once we acted on our new feelings, they were overwhelming. I was swept away. And in the midst of that bliss, I got a phone call from Artur asking me to join the Philharmonic, which he had recently taken over. My life could not have been better.

[No. 9 in Gb] He doesn't know how to capture these feelings before they are gone. They are too fleeting. Almost ephemeral. The rush has lost its luster. If he pinned them down, they would grow faded, get dusty. But he knows that the chase can't go on endlessly. Can it? Enjoy it while it lasts. Be lively. One got away. He tells himself he let it. Let her. Letter? She left right? If another one flies away, find a newer, brighter, younger, rarer. Some people never experience such heights, the sighting, sighing, let alone the capture. Confused. Left alone the capture? Left. A lone. Catch her.

When the war ended, I began in earnest to try to get in touch with mother. The last time I had heard from her was in a letter that I received six months after arriving in America. Honestly, it was difficult to put myself in her place given how wonderful my life had become. I thought about her, but not often enough. Now I hoped it would be possible for her to join us, Marie and me, in America. I sometimes discussed it with Artur after rehearsals. It helped to talk with someone who had known her, even if it was in another lifetime. Marie and I moved in together and this continued joy was a welcome distraction while I waited for word from my mother. We talked about marriage, but it was not urgent for either of us. It was enough to have found someone, to be together. There was no hurry. The war was over. We had our entire lives ahead of us. Then I found out that my mother was dead. She had been killed in the *Bełżec* extermination camp just north of Lwów. I doubt she lived more than a year after I last saw her.

[No. 10 in Bm] His carriage rattles through the starless night. He feels a stake of urgency being driven through his mind. Faster. Reach her. The black steeds' nostrils blow steam like coal trains. He can't arrive. Too late. She awakens slowly to the yellow light of the sun in her simple room. She is rested after her sleep. It is a blessing. She is getting used to being by herself, her child moved out, settled on his own. She walks through the empty rooms. Regretful? No. She misses things. Him. And him too. But that, she guesses, is just what people do. Move on. Forget? She has a lot to be thankful for. Devotion. She thinks about going for a walk but reconsiders. She is foolish. She needs a hobby. Something new to put her energy into. Belief. What should she do? What will he do? On the front stoop, he falters, his hand on the door knocker. What will she think when she sees how dark his heart has become? When she reads the desperation on his face? What motivates him? Loneliness or

love. Does he know the difference? How does he make her understand? Rage. He turns. Runs away. Again.

Marie and I stayed together for a few weeks, but something in me had changed. I was not naïve. I had known that terrible things were happening outside of my world, but I had ignored them, largely because there was nothing I could do. As difficult as leaving home had been, once I arrived here, the adjustment was just as challenging. It had been necessary to forget a little in order to survive. I could not live in New York with my mind in Lwów. But the barriers protecting me from the memories of my past cracked with the news of mother's death. I had been able to escape because of my talent. If my mother had been more talented, maybe she would be alive too. If it had not been for me, she would have focused more on her career, or she would have fled after my father was killed instead of worrying about my safety. I did not deserve to live just because those around me had sacrificed themselves for me, just because I was gifted. Guilt consumed me. And Marie could not live with it, so I left.

[No. 11 in Am] This is the death he undoubtedly deserves. By himself. In a cemetery. In the cold. The first gust comes cloaked as a breeze. And then Harpies bear down on him. Tearing, screaming, endless, deafening, repeating. He revels in the pain, its intricacy, its dexterity, its ferocity. He feels something genuine for the first time in years. When the initial assault is completed they rise as one. Dried leaves blow across his body and crack against his spilled blood. He wishes they would finish him. Then the clouds break and suddenly he has hope. Maybe. They fly out of his sight. I have been granted a reprieve, he believes. Somebody has saved me. Perhaps she prayed for me. Then they wheel and down they fall again, howling. Digging their claws into

him, they snatch up his body and when they reach the height of the bell tower, they let go. The winter wind is all that separates him from the tombstones below.

A metal trash can toppled over and its lid hit the ground with a cymbal clash. My eyes popped open. A sharp chill was blowing garbage down the sidewalk at our feet. I looked to Jerzi to finish his story but he remained silent. I closed my eyes again, eager to recapture the spell while it lasted.

[No. 12 in Cm] My lord, why has this happened to me? She kneels. Is penitent. My entire body feels pain, he laments. Then they are gone. Focus shifts inward. Clouds burst and rain begins, washing everything, everyone, washing away sin. The naiad stirs. She traipses across the lawn, taps shoulders, wakes her sisters. Donner swings his hammer. The water nymphs shed their gowns and dive into the pool. They look up at the sky and open their mouths, catching drops on their tongues, absorbing them, laughing, as the tears of the world come pouring down around them. This is beauty. Love. Eternity.

I shivered awake. Jerzi still did not speak. His eyes were open now, and in the gloom I could see tears streaked his cheeks. He looked both desperate and resigned, hopeful and bereft, as if his reason vied with his heart right there on his face. It was the look I would recognize nearly seven years later looking at him frozen in the past, on film, staring at Marie in the audience.

Then he started, breathed in deeply and looked as if he would speak. I quickly glanced up at the window. At the side of the sill, four fingers rested. Someone was hidden behind the wall, peeking out next to the window. Then the palm raised slowly as if the hand would wave, but it was withdrawn. An expressionless face, a woman's framed by dark curls, was visible for an instant in the emptiness of the apartment and then the window slammed shut. Red curtains drawn swiftly behind the glass.

• • •

Thursday, September 19, 1974.

My seventeenth birthday. Mamma not home. No opera for the evening. Jerzi working. No idea what I would do. Went to see Nonna. Up the familiar back stairs for the final time. She was out, at the grocery, as evinced by the contents of the paper bag that she would soon drop, breaking a jam jar and rolling onions and oranges toward my feet. I felt them hit, did not see, because for once I was not looking at the floor. I was staring into her disbelieving eyes. In my hand I held the piece of mail that I had picked up off the kitchen table after I arrived. In the upper right-hand corner Nonna had written a phone number in pencil. The letter was from the International Center for Photography, which had an address on Fifth Avenue.

"Dear Carlo" it began. I skimmed the surface. It congratulated "Dear Carlo" for having his work chosen for the Center's opening exhibition on documentary photography. "Dear Carlo" was invited, cordially I believe it said, to the ceremonies. Other things of no import. I read the letter again. Sat down in a chair.

The letter thanked "Dear Carlo" for submitting his photo for an exhibition that was two months in the future. I went into the unlighted den and stared into the shadows, searching once more for the eyes of "Dear Carlo" in the photo that hung above the couch. I smashed the glass with my fist and knocked "Dear Carlo" off his hook. I went back to the kitchen. I dialed the number that Nonna had written. Nineteen rings and no answer. I hung up.

When Nonna walked in she saw me and the letter in my

hand and said Oh no Emilio, oh no. Then the bag dropped. She said oh no again and I realized I needed to get out of that house before I hurt her. I shoved the letter in my pocket and started for the stairs. Nonna tried to put her hands on me, perhaps out of affection, or in an attempt at explanation, but I pushed her to the side. She screamed as her shoulder hit the wall.

At the bottom of the stairs I opened the door too quickly and smashed it into the hearse, which had returned since my arrival. I slammed the door three or four times into the side of the car until it was dented. I started to run. After a few blocks my side started to hurt and my limp left ankle ached. My feet slowed to a walk. My heart continued to race. My vision became blurry and white.

Mamma was gone when I got to the house. I assumed she knew, too. I hated. I tore all the crucifixes from the walls and threw them in a pile on the living room floor where she would see them as soon as she entered. I grabbed her Bible from beside her bed and ripped out its pages, ten, twenty, thirty at a time, and threw the loosed leaves on the pile of crosses. I went to her dresser and tore through the drawers, looking for anything that mattered. When it was empty I turned to the closet.

I opened the door. It was off track and the metal mechanism at the top ground to a halt. I started whaling on the door with both fists, punching, hitting, kicking with my feet, my left ankle seemingly breaking. I became aware I was screaming. The door fell inward and I picked it up and wrestled it out of the opening and threw it on Mamma's bed, which was already covered with the contents of her dresser. I pulled the clothes off the hangers. I was destruction. I grabbed at a box on the overhead closet shelf. When I held it in my hands and turned to toss it on the bed, another box stacked atop it was revealed. This second box hovered momentarily in midair, cartoonlike, poised to fall. Then it knocked me out.

I woke up alone on the closet floor. My head hurt and I pushed against my forehead to try to ease the pain and when I stopped, my right palm was covered in blood. I picked up the box that had hit me and opened it. Inside was a black rectangular cube with a carrying strap. I lifted it out. It hung heavily in my hands. On the side opposite the strap were several knobs and levers and a small attachment imprinted with the words Kalart Synchronized Range Finder. Another smaller viewfinder sat on top. I turned it around, feeling its weight, looking for some way to open it.

I knew what it was, although I don't know how. Maybe I had seen one on the street, or maybe Mamma had mentioned it to me at one time when she was telling me about my father, but I was sure. It was a camera. An old Speed Graphic, and it had been his. I set it down and reached into the bottom of the box. There were two red books tied together with a leather thong. I retrieved them and then grabbed the camera with my bloody hand.

In my room I put everything on my bed and took out my suitcase. Into it I threw some clothes, the two books, and whatever else I could fit and still get the lid closed and zipped. The front screen door banged shut. I heard Mamma see her faith on the floor. I picked up my father's camera again and toted the suitcase.

Walking out, I stared my mother in the eye for what seemed like the first time in memory. She had stopped by the *pasticceria*. She knew. She stuttered out some words.

He never wanted children, Emilio. I told him that I was pregnant and he said I should abort it. Abort you. I said no and he moved out the next morning. God. Emilio.

Those were the last words Mamma ever said to me. God and Emilio.

She might have gone on talking but a tinnitus filled my ears and they stopped hearing anything but a white noise akin to the blast that came from the speakers when I accidentally rubbed the needle of Jerzi's phonograph against my finger.

Jerzi.

I left. I walked to the 7 tracks, the bulky camera banging occasionally against my leg, blood dripping down into my eye, my suitcase urged along by friction with my side. I transferred trains. I felt fear. When I reached Lincoln Center the performance had already let out. A few stragglers lingered on the plaza. I went around back, under the overpass to Juilliard. I knew the musicians sometimes entered and exited there. I asked some type of security guard, the first man I saw, if Jerzi had left yet. He stared at the blood, which had slowed its flowing.

Jerzi? Wojtek? The hustler? He dropped by earlier to collect some money. Check the subway. He's probably still playing.

I gazed at him in incomprehension.

Right here. The Broadway Local. Around the corner. Where he always plays.

I couldn't hear more. I walked toward the end of the block to the stop where Jerzi had never let us get on or off. Too dangerous. We took a safer route. I entered on the downtown side and heard his violin before I was through the turnstile. I knew its tone. I turned left and there stood Jerzi. Eyes closed. Drawing his bow. At his feet, as ever, sat his hard case, now opened and upturned.

I screamed something and he opened his eyes, stopped playing. Everyone stared. He started to speak but the approaching train drowned out his words. I heard him no more.

I walked forward, my hand no longer empty or idle by my side. My father's camera was held tightly in my grip and it gathered momentum as it swung at the end of my arm. When Jerzi was within reach, I drew back the camera and smashed him in the face. He dropped his violin and fell backward.

I kept advancing and kicked the instrument behind me onto the subway tracks just as the train arrived. Strings snapped. Iron wheels tore the anguished wood apart, at last letting all the sadness out.

Jerzi stared at me above him through fingers that held his bleeding nose. I turned and calmly walked to his case, kicked it closed, and picked it up.

Then, without a glance back, I boarded the train as its doors closed, rode away from all the people that I had yet known. (And the violins *pizzicato* play the last notes as the darkness engulfs me again.)

3. Satz.
SCHERZO.

Schattenhaft.

Fließend, aber nicht zu schnell.

> My first thought when they told us Italy had surrendered was that it was a joke. Here we are sitting offshore ready to invade and they surrender? But it was true, and it was really General Eisenhower telling us it was true. A lot of us new guys got really excited but the ones who'd been around a while, who'd already seen combat, said we shouldn't pay any attention to the surrender. Forget it ever happened. Boy, they were right. Our Ducks hit the shore and the Germans were ready and they fought hard as ever and they're still fighting. And the Italians, well, they're still here too, but everything changed for them when Badoglio surrendered, and they seem kind of confused about what to do now. Some are helping us however they can, some are still fighting for Mussolini up north and killing their own countrymen and neighbors and family members, and some are trying to just forget the whole thing and return to normal. Whatever that is when you already lost everything but your life. It's awful. You can't imagine it before seeing it. There's so much death. I'm afraid and don't know exactly why I'm here, but all I can do is pray I survive and that we beat back these Nazis and that I get home soon.

My father wrote those words inside the front cover of volume one of a two-volume set of Ovid's *Metamorphoses*, 1921 Loeb Classics edition, with Latin and English texts facing off on opposing pages, the books that I found—the books that found me—in Mamma's closet. He did not date that entry, but Eisenhower announced the Italian surrender on the evening of September 8, 1943, so it was likely written sometime in mid-September, possibly even on the nineteenth, the date on which fourteen years later Mamma would lie alone in labor, giving birth to me.

A picture of Carlo, shirt off on the deck of a ship, is taped to the flyleaf opposite his neatly printed prologue. Around his neck hang his dog tags and a small 35mm camera, the manufacturer of which I have never been able to identify because a generic leather case masks any distinguishing characteristics. In his right hand he holds his Speed Graphic above the bellows, the same Speed Graphic that I used to send Jerzi sprawling. He's nobody's ideal of a military man, hollow-chested with a long neck and scrawny arms. He smokes a cigarette. The shallow brim of an Army-issue field cap casts a shadow over his eyes, preventing me once again from seeing them clearly. His pose does not project confidence, but neither does it betray timidity. He simply stands there, as if he had nothing else to do but be photographed.

At the time, Carlo was a seventeen-year-old stills photographer with the United States' 163rd Signal Photographic Corps, one of the many units that took part in Operation Avalanche, the Allies' first major ground attack against Hitler's hegemony in continental Europe. Sicily had fallen earlier in the year without much resistance, but the straits of Messina, where the mythical sentries Scylla and Charybdis stand, preclude that island from being considered continental in the strictest sense. It is doubtful Carlo was part of the first wave, which hit the beaches south of Salerno just hours after Eisenhower's announcement, but he probably came ashore during the next day or two.

When it comes to Carlo, I'm often just guessing, or trying to interpret rather, the scores of anecdotes, quotes, and seemingly random observations about the war that he wrote throughout his two volumes of Ovid. There are also academic notations—*lemmata* (glosses), *scholia* (marginalia), metaphrases (literal translations)—that likely originated during an antebellum Latin education and offer additional insight into his thinking.

Most of the notes are inscribed on the backs of photos, mainly black-and-white four-by-fives taken with his Speed Graphic, although several smaller prints made with another camera or taken by another photographer are included as well. The pictures are filed throughout the compact hardcovers, whose pages are not much larger than the photos themselves, usually at specific spots that Carlo felt were relevant to what he wanted to say, either in his shot or in his words or in the combination of the two. The volumes are robust and, despite the added thickness, only bulge slightly, as if they have adapted to the task of telling Carlo's tale.

There is also a neatly pressed dead lizard midway through Book V, where various words are covered with what, to my untrained eye, appears to be blood, which Carlo used *sic passim* to highlight certain passages. He generally wrote in ink his first four months in Italy, after which his notes are made in pencil. I speculate that as a seemingly dedicated student, at least in Latin, Carlo came to Italy with some sort of pen-and-pencil set, perhaps one he received as a gift from Nonna. Once the ink ran dry, he picked up the pencil. Perhaps an eventual lack of lead precipitated the switch to blood.

From these two books, which sit in front of me on the table in Split, I learned almost everything I know about the man who is my biological father.

After enlisting (he never writes why), Carlo attended some sort of basic training (nor where) and then went to the Signal Corps Photographic Center in Queens. When he shipped out, he headed for northern Africa, Oran most likely, and arrived after Rommel's defeat. He kept four photographs from that time in *Metamorphoses*. All are simply landscape photography, static desert scenes, and all are blank on the back.

He didn't go to Sicily, making Operation Avalanche his first exposure to live combat, his first vision of war. And although he became an excellent photographer, Carlo never appears to have been comfortable in the Signal Corps. Initially it may have been a struggle with his role: enlisted but not fighting, shooting but not killing, observing but not having any appreciable effect. Eventually though, it was not the weapon that he wielded, but rather the war itself, with which he disagreed, and I do not believe he would have felt any better had a gun replaced the camera in his hand. While no amount of preparation could have readied him for the proficient manner in which death targeted those closest to him, Carlo writes from the beginning as one who was totally unprepared for what he witnessed, the omnipresence of violence, its brutality, its constancy.

Unable to cope with his situation, Carlo turned to gods. But instead of seeking shelter in the theology of his childhood—a Catholicism that crumbled the more of the war he witnessed—or constructing his own pantheon, Carlo turned to his imagination, and to Ovid. That duo would fail too, and when it did, it dragged Carlo's sanity down with it. His writings in *Metamorphoses* record this fall, from belief to disillusion, from guileless observer to enraged killer, from that initial *exordium*—"all I can do is pray I survive"—to a closing *cri de coeur*, circa June 1944, written as a dialogue with the lizard cadaver he kept. The war didn't kill or physically cripple Carlo, but on the inside, where the camera could not see, it shattered him. And I don't know whether he ever completely healed.

Why do I now introduce this chronicle of my father's life, always in my bag next to my maps? Because Carlo is key to everything I am trying to unravel today. Because by ignoring him as long as I have, I am putting off the inevitable. That subway trip on the downtown local commenced the third stage of my development. I was still undeveloped and naïve, but I longed to be free, free from Mamma and her omnipotent scriptures, free from Jerzi and his faux-parental posturing, free from Nonna and her apparent disinterest. I could no longer lie larval in Corona if I was going to grow. And even though I didn't go to war, even though I only fled to Manhattan, it was far enough for my purposes. I lost track of myself so often (physically at first, then increasingly mentally) that I bought my first map just to have something concrete on which to show me my place.

I jumped on the Broadway train as a child, as Milo, but in the ensuing six years, I fought to slough him off, to abandon him. In the end, the decisions we made destroyed him. I had no choice, he became a casualty, his loss necessary for my survival. When I crawled out of his cocoon, I exploded into new life, an imago in the poisoned atmosphere of my subterranean cavern, an army of one, Miles, the man I am today, a soldier willing to take whatever steps necessary to win my personal war. I was reborn! And I was radioactive!

• • •

Carlo's first *Metamorphoses* photo after his pre-invasion portrait on the ship is filed at the end of Ovid's description of the four ages of man: Golden, Silver, Bronze and "hard iron," when "all evil burst forth." On the *verso* Carlo smeared blood across *nefas*, the Latin word for evil. In the margin he wrote "Evil comes from *ne* (not) + *fas* (divine law, dictates of religion)." The photo's shallow depth of field focuses on a young girl in the left foreground. No older than twelve or thirteen, she has soft features and thin plaits resting against a boyish chest. She wears a grungy white dress embroidered near the hem with a floral design. At one time it must have been lively, the outfit she wore to church or on holidays or simply to feel pretty. Now it clings limply to her slight frame. Her expression is blank, devoid of both sadness and joy, youth and resignation, laughter and sorrow. The ground is strewn with puddles and she stands barefoot in one of them, the water muddying her ankles. She stares straight ahead, past the plane of the photograph, away from the mob that rages behind her. The vigilantes, both men and women, surround a woman lying lifeless on the ground, nothing but a lump. One of the attackers, her face turned from the camera, grasps a clump of the lump's hair. Several men are frozen in the act of kicking the body. One looks straight into the camera lens from the blurred background of the shot and weighs a large rock in his left hand. The back of the photo reads:

> October 11. Napoli. Outskirts. The civil war comes (*prodit bellum*). Both sides (*utroque*) fight. This Italian woman was accused of going with the head of SS when they controlled the city. I see her daughter, at left, as Astraea, the goddess of Justice, innocent and pure. Astraea was the last immortal to abandon an earth dripping (*madentis* from *madeo*—to be wet, moist, dripping) with blood (*caedis*—slaughter/victims/blood/gore). How does this girl live her life after seeing this violence, after seeing her mother murdered? She will become Virgo with her scales, Libra, close at hand in the night sky. Who will care for her? Who will carry her to the heavens? [file at I 142–149]

Below that paragraph are two notes jotted at a later date in pencil. The first addition asks: "Did Mussolini and Petacci deserve this type of death more because their crimes were greater? Says who?" The second provides an answer, but to which question, who should judge the crimes or who will carry the girl to heaven, I do not know. It reads only "Me."

• • •

The first night that I did not return to Queens, my first night as a seventeen-year-old, was the most anxious of my life. Because my nerves were so jangled, my synapses firing so erratically, my heart beating so emphatically, I wasn't worried about finding a place to sleep. If I had laid down, I would only have gaped, glazed and bug-eyed, into space. My primary concern, melodramatic as it may seem now, was staying alive until the morning. The possibility of dying seemed almost tangible in the alien novelty of the city night. I was jumpy. I was afraid. The passengers in the subway car looked at me askance when I leapt aboard brandishing the camera with Jerzi's blood dripping from the corner, but after a few seconds, either out of disinterested urban narcissism or libertarianism, they turned back to their conversations, playbills, newspapers, lives. I was no threat to them.

The pale green of the rickety car nauseated me, so when the interior lighting momentarily clacked off while leaving the station I welcomed the relative darkness. I moved away from the door and shut my eyes against the returning light. When I next opened them, I was surprised to see the train pulling out of Times Square. I had not noticed the previous two stops. I had no idea where I was going. Panicked, I pushed my way out at the next station and followed a couple to what I hoped was a safe exit.

Instead I found myself amid a crush of commuters pushing toward suburban trains bound for Long Island or New Jersey. I extricated myself and tried to appear purposeful in my aimlessness (an artifice which I could not don at that time, but could pull on in an instant after a couple months of being on my own). Eventually I found an exit and ran up the stairs, out into the night.

• • •

Near the end of Book XV, the final book of *Metamorphoses*, Carlo filed another of his early photographs. It shows the military set up inside the massive Temple of Neptune, circa 450 BC, one of the best preserved examples of ancient Greek architecture. Members of the American Fifth Army briefly used the temple as a base of operations after the invasion. Jeeps are parked uniformly to the left of the temple and the setting sun appears through a forest of thick Doric trunks. One of Carlo's longest entries begins on the flip side of the photo and continues onto a blank page preceding the book's comprehensive index, to which Carlo referred often judging from its thicket of ticks, circles, and underlines.

> September 21. Paestum. I wish the waning moon was closer to new tonight so I could see Callisto and her son rising over this ancient temple like the Romans did when they stopped here for a day to breathe "mild Paestum's rose-gardens" (*tepidique rosaria Paesti*). They were taking Aesculapius, serpentine god of medicine, to found his temple on an island in the Tiber. I would love to save lives like the medics do. Even the grunts probably save more than me. All I do is watch. The sight of the dead and dying is terrible and I'm forced to focus *[see end bk xv]
> * on it through my lens. Sure I can put the camera down when I need a break, or close my eyes, but it's everywhere. All I hear and all I smell is death. It is hard to close my nose and ears. A lieutenant who's seen a lot of shit told me to breathe through my mouth. I try. Get the shot without getting shot, they tell us. I try. I read some article where Capa said to get closer. Again I try. These past few days I made a lot of horrifying photos, including one of an Allied plane falling into the surf (filed at II 320: "*volvitur in praeceps longoque per aera tractu*" where Jupiter shoots down Phaëthon who has set the earth on fire with his father's chariot) and one of a young German, not much older than me, climbing dizzily out of his tank which had been shelled. He started vomiting blood and his brains spilled out of a gash in his head (filed at XII 238: "*sanguinis ille globos pariter cerebrum*" where Theseus kills Eurytus). I

just shot them without thinking. Who would believe I'd ever see such things in real life? Neither photo would have been released probably so I decided to keep them. I don't know whether that will get me in trouble or not. It's worth the risk though. I have to do something. [filed at XV 708]

• • •

When I emerged shaken from the station tunnels, the high, open brightness, epitomized in the shining spire of the Empire State Building at the end of the deep urban canyon to my right, dazed me. I turned from it, crossed the street, and slipped, unobserved I hoped, into the shadows of the Romanesque post office. (The third movement of the Seventh is marked *Schattenhaft*, meaning shadowy, and for most of those six years, I seemed to adhere to that designation, either corporeally, mentally, or both.)

Down the long block in the dark I cautiously walked. At the end, on the far corner of the intersection, sat a diner, neon signs bright above a brushed metal facade. I needed sustenance to make it until morning so, still jittery, I decided to spend some of the money from Jerzi's violin case. (I purposely left the empty shell beneath my table upon leaving, never again to be tapped by his toe.) I limped inside.

It was after midnight, but the diner was bustling, drunken couples glaring or gazing at one another, drunken groups shouting nonsense between bites. At the counter two cops got coffee. One booth along the outside wall was empty, and as I headed toward it, aching to put down my burdens (in every sense of the word), several stares made me acutely aware of the blood still on my forehead. I dropped my bag and the violin case on the banquette and went to wash up. I kept the camera in my hand.

As I rinsed my newly emancipated face, I silently rehearsed my answers should anyone ask who I was, what I was doing, where I was going, when I got injured. (No one ever asked why.) I'm a newspaper photographer. Had to work late, officer. Someone threw a rock at me because they didn't want their picture taken. Sure, it can be dangerous, but you have to try and get the good shot.

Back at the booth I ate, then paged through Carlo's copy of *Metamorphoses*. I was distracted. I looked without seeing. The books were just something to have in front of me after flipping through the newspaper that I had grabbed off the counter. I completely missed the lizard that night, which was undoubtedly for the best. When I did finally spot it some days later, I was in the library reading room. I screamed loudly, eliciting several ocular reprimands from the silent patrons and a whispered warning from a security guard.

I sat in the diner until almost four in the morning. I did not want to go even then, but everyone who was seated when I arrived had left already and I worried I had overstayed my welcome. (I soon learned that I could sit in any diner, and even several hotel lobbies, all night if necessary.) By that time I had drunk enough coffee to keep me awake for a week, which was good, because as my anxiety had abated in the relative comfort of the diner, my body had begun to ache, to acknowledge its fatigue. I had not settled on a spot to spend the night, so I decided to listen to the lies I had told to my reflection and pretend to be a photographer.

Once outside, I crossed the street and milled behind the giant post office, where I assumed business would be starting up soon. Even when trucks did start to pull in and out, there still was no comfortable spot for me to be. I nervously circled the block again and again and again. (Thirty-two times, 927 steps per revolution, *donec delirium agitatum*.)

For a seemingly endless series of moments, I played at waiting for something, for someone. It was exhausting. I was sweating from nerves, chilled from the night, and startled by each movement or sound. And then I realized that not only could I not take a photo with the camera, I couldn't even open it. I remember maniacally laughing at the hopelessness of my plight, but the sound of my voice frightened me too, so I retreated into silence again, taking some solace in the thought that at least I knew how to use the camera as a weapon.

• • •

When years later I went to Italy to search for Carlo, I stood on the beach south of Salerno where Operation Avalanche had landed. It was wide and flat, deserted in both directions. Carlo shot one of my favorite photos on that beach, but in his depiction the expansiveness is interrupted by mammoth piles of Army supplies and the smooth surface cratered by shelling. In pits in the sand stand Italian men, prisoners I presume, although there are no visible means of restraint, no barbed wire or guns or guards. The men are not soldiers. They are well-dressed to a man and generally appear old, if not elderly. Despite the heat, each of them wears a jacket, many with a vest or a sweater underneath it. Most wear ties. I'm guessing their attire was dictated by necessity, not sartorial sense. Their homes had been abandoned (at best) or destroyed (more likely), and they probably were wearing all they owned at that point. Some are crowded two or three to a hole, smoking, chatting, watching the sky. One pair even plays cards on the edge of their pit, *Scopa* from the looks of it.

Right of center, the obvious focus of the photograph, stands a man alone in his own hole. He looks directly into the lens, which seems a hallmark of Carlo's photographs in these books; even in combat situations he often managed to get the subject's attention, if they were still alive. The man draws a cigarette away from his mouth with his left hand, a watch visible on his wrist. He is just starting to exhale as evidenced by the small puff of white smoke hovering around his lips. His right hand is in his trouser pocket. He wears a hat.

On the back of the photo are two short notes. The first, in ink, says: "Cadmus sows the serpent's teeth and founds a new nation, although hopefully more than five will survive this civil war. [filed at III 103]" The second, penciled in later, is two words: "*Mio suocero!*" My father-in-law.

• • •

Wandering for almost twenty hours since leaving the diner, I was in a stupor. I stopped on the street for a few moments when it felt safe to do so. I popped in an Automat for a coffee or a snack. But I never stopped, period. I didn't know what was propelling me. I thought frequently of returning home but rejected it each time. To help keep myself awake, I scoured the sidewalks for change as I walked, lunging hungrily for each coin I spotted. Picking up a penny, I recalled that the opera season opened on Monday. (Jerzi had promised to take me since the company had been touring on my birthday.) It was Friday. Standing-room tickets for the first week would go on sale in the morning and crowds of people would be waiting overnight to buy them. I had no desire to see Jerzi, but I doubted he would have recovered from his shock at my clouting him and decided to risk a potential confrontation. Penny in pocket, I headed for Lincoln Center.

When I got to the plaza, there was not yet a line. Sitting by the fountain trying to focus on my next move, a familiar couple, whose names I could not remember, appeared out of the shadows and waved hello while walking past. I said hi and they asked if I was waiting for Jerzi. Hoping they didn't know his location, I lied and said yes. They said a group was gathering at the hotel across the street and I should wait there. It was either abandon myself to another night on the streets or accept their offer. Standing up again my legs ached. My anxiety level rose dramatically when they mentioned that the first week included three works by Puccini, one of Jerzi's favorite opera composers. It didn't matter though. I had chosen. And I was too tired to change my mind, so wearily I followed.

I waited out the night, trying at first to respond when someone addressed me, but generally keeping quiet and listening for Jerzi's voice. Drowsiness eventually won out over wariness and I closed my eyes to rest.

When the crowd moved to the Met at six in the morning, I had to be awoken. I walked over, signed in, then went back to sleep. Opera fans being an eclectic lot, no one asked why I was carrying a small suitcase and a thirty-year-old Speed Graphic. (I overheard one man waiting on line say the camera was probably from World War Two, thus confirming what I already thought I knew.)

Tickets went on sale at ten in the morning, and I caused a fair bit of consternation by leaving the line at five minutes to. Someone shouted after me as I walked away. I turned and lied again. Jerzi was supposed to buy my tickets, but he had never shown up. I had no money. (Which was actually close to the truth.) The couple who initially had stopped me on the plaza said they would lend it to me and get repaid by Jerzi on Monday. I said I didn't feel comfortable with that arrangement, but they said phooey and one of them held out six dollars, motioning me back into line with the bills, repeating over and over, "I won't hear of it," "I won't hear of it," as he waved the money back and forth like a fan. I bought two tickets. I knew I would never attend the performance.

• • •

Another early photo captures perhaps Carlo's most gruesome

image. He filed it in the story of Actaeon, a man who accidentally stumbles upon the goddess Diana as she is bathing. Because Actaeon sees her naked, Diana changes him into a stag, which is then hunted down and devoured by his own hounds, thirty-five of whom Ovid identifies by name. The tale begins with the line "*Quod enim scelus error habebat?*" or "For what crime had mere mischance?" Carlo took issue with Frank Justus Miller's translation and wrote several variations in the margins. He seemed to settle on the equally alliterative and, with its double dactyls, much more poetic decameter, "What wickedness is had in wandering?" because he circled it and wrote *melior* alongside. The words on the back of the photo say as much as any description of mine could:

> October 13. Outside of Napoli. Packs of wild dogs roam everywhere. We come across them a couple times a day since getting here a week ago. They devoured these two corpses (*mersisque in corpore rostris*—plunging into the body snouts, *dilacerant*—tear to pieces). I think they were a man and a woman. Based on the smell, they were dead for a while. I don't know how they remained uneaten for so long. Some of us were joking when we drove up. "Boy they look hungry." "I wonder if they're rabid." "She looks like she'd take all you could give her." We laughed. Why I don't really know. [filed at III 259]

Cracks in Carlo's armor such as that introspective final fragment begin to seep more frequently into his notes once the Allies moved past Napoli. Not until the very end, however, when he is so anguished that he goes AWOL, do his musings become wholly philosophical or nonsensical. At that point he stops notating details altogether when cataloging photos. No dates. No locations. No specific indication where he feels a photo belongs in the books. His handwriting is barely legible, little more than a scribble in some instances. He rambles. And while the changes in themselves are revealing, they are frustrating because they prevent me from knowing for certain whether I am following his *Metamorphoses* in the order in which it occurred. But I'm jumping ahead. Refocus.

• • •

After buying the tickets, I fled the plaza to wrestle with my conscience in private. I was simultaneously disappointed that I had lied and intrigued by the fact that I had been given money. (I soon turned it into more, too. I went to the Met on Monday, hours before the house opened, and found a couple visiting from Barcelona who hoped to see Placido Domingo's debut in *I Vespri Siciliani*. I sold them my two tickets for twenty dollars. I didn't actually attend a performance for more than a year.)

I quickly realized that I was too tired to assess how I felt about this moral dichotomy, so I listened to the proud peccant part of me and left my guilt-ridden righteous self at Columbus Circle. I continued down Broadway, the air hot and stagnant. I imagined my unintentional benefactors were aware of my deception and trailed somewhere behind me, waiting for the best moment to attack. I gathered momentum both from the perceived pursuit and the weight of the Speed Graphic as it pulled my left arm lower, dragging me forward as I continually looked back.

There was nothing there, but for the next six years, I felt followed. It was certainly imagined, merely an *ombra*, but without it I never would have survived, I would have given up and died dozens of times. (Maybe it was just the music in my mind—throughout the *Scherzo*, one group of instruments finishes the phrases and runs of another, propelling the movement—chasing me along toward its conclusion.)

I began to walk faster, ignoring as best I could those around

Times Square urging me persistently to check it out. Check it out. Check it out. I passed Madison Square Park, and when I entered Union Square, the weekend pedestrian traffic disoriented me and I faltered, lost the thread of Broadway, emerged on Fourth Avenue, and just kept heading south.

The crowds dwindled and then vanished all together. When people reappeared, they weren't couples or families strolling, they were bums, they were homeless men, and all they did was idle. Looking up from my feet, dirty, drunken faces greeted me, many menacingly, others with an amused toothy grin. Most begged for money through fetid breath. One grabbed at my wrist. I tensed and drew back the camera. He took the reaction as a prelude to violence and yelled something that I didn't comprehend due to the panicked buzzing that had returned to my ears, the same deafness that had first appeared when I was leaving Mamma.

Glancing back I saw the man had stood up and started advancing toward me. Without checking for traffic, I stepped into the street and was startled by the screech of tires to my left and the blare of a horn. I jumped and turned to see a cabbie screaming and pointing at me.

Instead of returning to the sidewalk, I ran. Two more drivers had to slam on their brakes to avoid me meeting my father's fake fate. The bums jeered from behind. I kept running.

After a few blocks I eased my pace. My head ached dizzily. My arms were tired from the weight of the camera and the suitcase. I needed to stop but fear forced my feet forward. The close call crossing the Bowery made me realize that scared as I was, I would need to use my eyes, to look up, to see.

I tracked back and forth along streets teeming with different races and ethnicities, searching desperately for something that seemed familiar. It was so different from my restricted world in Corona where, despite a recent influx of darker-skinned immigrants, nearly everyone I encountered was of Italian descent.

These streets were extreme, all dissonance and desolation. There was no middle ground. Voices rose ardently. Below the din, tension simmered. Violence showed itself confidently. Occasionally I did sense laughter, but largely I tried to ignore my ears, the main avenue people were using to assail me. I shut them up, focused my vision.

On some blocks, masculinity seemed strewn about as boys in shorts ran shirtless in the streets and men with fierce eyes stood sentry in breezeways, jostling each other in an almost intimate fashion. On other blocks, there was no one and nothing but decay, but garbage, but blight. Most buildings ran flat-faced right up to the sidewalks, edging me toward the gutter. If it was a populated block, people stared down from opened windows or hung above me perched on exposed fire escapes or sprawled on the concrete stoned out of their minds. It often seemed that every upright person approached me, walking so close that I could feel the heat off their skin, and offered to sell me something, dope mostly. I felt I would be lucky to emerge at the end of each block's gauntlet.

The deserted ones were worse because there was still a stealthy peril lurking somewhere though I couldn't see it. On some streets irrelevancy seemed to cloak me and I passed without harassment. I would almost relax after those blocks, only to have that complacency vanish with a flourish as I turned the corner and faced a new challenge. The heat catalyzed the ebb and flow of chemicals through my body, depleted after two days without much nourishment or sleep. My heart pumped exhaustion into constricted arteries. Fear had eaten all my energy. Internally I edged toward a cliff. There was nothing left.

I turned away from a roiling park on the far corner. A block-long school ran opposite a building that looked as if it had been bombed. I hurried beneath the classroom windows, turned away from the school's main door, walked half a block, and stopped.

I looked left and I looked right. Four- and six-story brick

tenements, except for number 526 (on Fifth between A and B), a walk-up set back from the curb. I was delusional, so I don't put much stock in the images I recall from that day. Myself on the sidewalk, suitcase resting atop the black metal rods of the railing to ease the soreness in my shoulder. A woman in her first-floor window looking out at me, maternally in one light, with a lewd leer in another. The door, free of loiterers, propped invitingly open with a cinder block. The top-floor windows boarded. Silent children playing on the patch of concrete between the building and the railing.

In a voice-over I hear Jerzi shortly after his move to Lefrak talking about his super's vigilance in keeping out squatters since all the units weren't occupied yet. He is supplanted by a siren. I squeeze the suitcase's handle with my right hand and the Speed Graphic with my left. I think of Carlo. I start a prayer to Mamma's god before I stop myself and swear. I turn right to leave but my feet don't go, my legs don't work. Not in that direction they won't. There is nothing in that direction. Facing the door again, I fall forward and walk with a fatalist's indifference to the eight steps that lead into the building.

Once inside I climbed more stairs, turning left at every landing, continuing up. A child of five or six years old ran around the corner at one point, startling me so much that I dropped my suitcase and swallowed a scream. He didn't stop. I glanced down the hall and spied a girl about my age disappearing, breasts, shoulders, back, blonde braid, into a lighted doorway. I kept climbing.

When the stairs ended, I stood in a dark hallway with four doors, two on either side. A dull haze seeped from under two of the doors, behind the one to my right a radio played. I heard booted feet marching below but then realized it was actually my heartbeat. I tried futilely to get the ventricles to contract more gently. I started to swoon. I shut my eyes and walked in complete darkness past the music. I smelled stale smoke on my right and turned left. I peeked out through tears veiling my vision, saw I faced a door. Resigned I pushed it open with my suitcase. Opening my eyes fully, I prayed to someone (Mamma be damned) that the room would be empty.

Lines of sunlight shining through the slats covering the broken window-glass cut the floor into irregular fragments. Next to the sill leaked a radiator. In one corner sat a wooden chair with no seat. Newspapers piled in columns. A doorway on the right opened onto a darker darkness. Nothing else. I stumbled inside, dropped my bag, and set down the camera. I closed the door behind me. There was no lock so I dragged the chair over and wedged it beneath the knob. Then I laid down, put my head on a stack of newspapers, closed my eyes, and slept.

• • •

Carlo's commentary on a photo of an Allied cemetery illustrates his evolving attitude. Crosses have sprouted in a freshly tilled field. In the foreground, two GIs dig yet another grave. One of them is bent to the task, his back to Carlo, while the other looks into the camera lens, spade resting on his right shoulder like a baseball bat. Beside the hole is a muddy, once-white mattress cover containing the dead soldier waiting to be interred, *ultimus inter pares*. The contrast between the black fertile soil and the white cumulus clouds and crosses is intense, as if Carlo used a polarizer making the photo. The clouds almost glow, the crosses hover. More of the words on the reverse belong to Ovid than Carlo. They refer to the aftermath of the plague of Aegina in Book VII. Both authors are bitter:

> Everyday. Everywhere. "And by this time there is no reverence for the dead ... There are none left to mourn the dead. Unwept they go wandering out, the souls of children and

of parents, and of both young and old. There was no more space for graves, nor wood for fires." We're all young here it seems, on both sides. Children really, acting out for the adults who see themselves as gods. The result is continuous reinvention of death.

• • •

When I awoke the next day, neck stiff from my too-tall newspaper pillow, I was torn between a fear of leaving and the hollow ache of hunger. Despite doubting whether I could ever recapture the fortitude to return, the latter proved more powerful. I stood my suitcase alongside the wall so it would be unseen by anyone peeking in, put all my money in my pocket, picked up the Speed Graphic, and crept down the hall, past the radio music, and out.

I spun quickly to fix the front of the building in my mind and noticed, to the left of the stairs, a tree. It rose almost as high as my boarded-up window and grew out over the sidewalk and street. Somehow I had not seen it the day before, a fact which made me wonder what else I was not seeing. I turned and walked west, away from the school that blocked the street at the east end of the block. (Fifth Street was interrupted to the west as well, by the Village View Housing Co-op, but I always went in that direction, maybe subconsciously to avoid the school since I was technically truant. Whatever the reason, that school along Avenue B, as well as the glow of fires burning beyond it, acted as a barrier, kept me from exploring in that direction, and likely helped me to survive.)

On Second Avenue I found a cheap lunch counter and ate so much so quickly that I got a stomachache. As I walked it off, I realized my right side was sore from the hard floor and resolved, as difficult as it might prove, to find something on which to sleep.

I walked the streets, more nervous than the day before, and

spotted an unattended van with blue moving blankets piled by the open back door. I boldly strode up to it and grabbed three blankets, which I cradled the best I could with the camera in one hand, and ran. I didn't stop until I was in my room, chair back beneath the doorknob. Then I peered out a gap between the plywood slats covering my window, watched the street, waited for the moving van to drive up.

It never did, but while waiting, I noticed my tree blowing in the breeze. A maple. Finally convinced I was not going to be caught, I left the window, folded the packing quilts into a futon-like mattress and spent the next three days burrowed inside it, alternating between fitful sleep and waking terror, imagining the doorknob turning and the shadows encroaching. I only emerged to go sell the opera tickets and find food to drive away the hunger.

Foraging later in the week, I gave myself one additional mission, to find someone to buy Carlo's camera. If I got enough money I would leave the squat I thought, although for where I did not know. I ended up in a store on 17th Street that I later learned was a mecca for New York's photographic community, so venerated in fact that I may have even browsed next to Carlo one afternoon, blind to his identity. They were not interested in buying the camera, but they offered to show me how to operate it. I think they felt sorry for me when I told them it had belonged to my dead father.

Over the next two days I learned about Carlo's camera from a bearded man whose name I've half forgotten, Richard, I think. In the process I gained a tremendous amount of respect for anyone, Carlo begrudgingly included, who shot with a Speed Graphic, especially in combat. Despite the name, it is not designed to do anything fast. It is ponderously slow to operate. It is heavy, as I had realized when it first landed on my head. It is built to make one high-quality photo at a time. It is best operated from a tripod, which is not always possible, particularly in a war. It is awkward to hold and initially it's hard to figure out where even to position your hands. Images are framed and focused through different eyeholes and there are two different shutters you can use.

They gave me an exposed piece of sheet film to practice loading the holder, and for two nights I sat in the darkness of my lampless squat and repeated the task over and over until it was unconscious. I was told Carlo would have been issued an adapter to hold multiple-exposure film, but I saw more practicality in buying a plastic back that fit snapshot-sized Polaroid packs. Months later, after converting my apartment's closet (the darker darkness didn't go very deep, in that place at least) into a simple darkroom, I acquired both a roll-film adapter and a newer 545 back that made nice prints from single four-by-five-inch sheets.

Over the next month, ennui and hunger prodded me to use what I had learned, and Carlo's camera began to provide me with an income. Three or four days a week, depending on the weather, I snuck out early while the neighborhood was relatively inactive and walked until I found a store that sold film. Then I stole some, almost always only one pack in case I got caught. (I confess that I once came across a bored clerk who, with a nod of his head, led me to know he knew what I wanted and he didn't much care, I could walk out with all I could carry.) I never stole from the same store more than once a month and I never stole period from the people who taught me about Carlo's camera. (They gave me a free pack of Polaroid film the day I bought my adapter.)

Once I had stolen the day's film, I stayed out until I had sold the whole pack, usually twenty-four pictures, charging one to two dollars a shot, the price varying over the years and with the subject doing the paying. I worked train stations where children departed for universities, where boyfriends and girlfriends parted after quick weekend visits, where in-laws left after vacations, where lovers bid teary-eyed adieus as their trysts ended. (One time a man who seemed to think his wife had sent me screamed "get lost" and started after me as I ran.)

I went to Saturday matinees at performing arts venues, which was especially lucrative in the run-up to Christmas when proud matrons, many formerly dancers, took dolled-up granddaughters and nieces to see the Nutcracker for the first time—or the fifth.

If I still had exposures left in the evening, I went to Lincoln Center (risking a confrontation with Jerzi that never happened) or Carnegie Hall (closer to my subway line in winter and a shorter walk in nicer weather) to capture successful couples who looked like they were celebrating with a night out. In summer, when the concert halls were largely closed, I went to parks and found people wanting to document their happiness.

I even roamed the city at random and discovered that, for reasons I still don't understand, people love photographic proof of what they are doing. Maybe it is simply fear of forgetting.

Once the film was shot, I ate, usually in an Automat or cafeteria where I could get the best value.

Returning home late at night that first winter, a day's earnings stowed in my shoe or zipped in the pocket I had sewn into the gusset of my jacket's left armpit, I felt uneasy. A few times I stayed out all night, thus learning the aforementioned lesson that some hotels had lobbies where I could sleep undisturbed after wandering in from the street.

I was taking care of myself, and over time I ended up earning almost a hundred dollars a week. I even sold a few prints to gallery owners and artists I met in the neighborhood, but it wasn't enough. I was biding my time, for what I did not know. When springtime came and the light began to linger longer, I fantasized about saving enough money to go away, to shake off my cocoon, to escape the darkness that was settling ever deeper inside me. But it was not yet time. I hadn't changed enough.

• • •

One of Carlo's photos shows a soldier who died in close combat after getting trapped behind enemy lines. He had been missing for several days. Once the Germans ceded the hilltop and pulled back, the Allies moved slowly up the slope. The body lay behind a big rock near the summit. Carlo took the shot while the soldier who found the body was bent over it in grief. The uniform makes clear that the dead body is that of an enlisted man, a fact which makes the blood-covered Latin words at the beginning of Book V where the photo lies even more shocking. "*Bis adhuc octonis integer annis.*" Twice more eight whole years. After the brief narrative on the back, Carlo provided a one-word gloss of the bloody phrase, one word that he wrote an uncountable number of times, one word in big letters and small, one word over and over and on top of itself so many times that amorphous blobs of ink were created in places. "Sixteen."

Another photo shows a soldier who died after stepping on a "bouncing Betty" or S-mine (*Schrapnellmine* in German). The mines shoot up into the air after being triggered and explode at waist level, spraying metal rods and ball bearings. They aren't always lethal, but they maim, blowing off part of a limb, ripping through guts, genitals. In the picture, the soldier lies on the ground, left leg missing below the knee, both hands gone. There is a pool of blood around his waist, which is covered by a tattered uniform. The photo is filed at the end of Book X where Adonis dies from being gored in the groin by a boar. Carlo wrote on the reverse:

> Artillery fire is unceasingly loud. It shakes the earth. My tinnitus is getting worse, but the doc says it's all in my mind. Another mine. Another victim. They're everywhere. This kid was born eight months after me. Wasted beautiful life.

Carlo's almost frustrated commentary on the death of that nameless kid is nonetheless still detached, especially when compared with his handling of another S-mine victim, his friend and driver Seco.

Signal Corps cameramen were assigned to three-man crews comprising a stills photographer, a motion picture photographer, and a driver. Seco was a member of the 36th Infantry Division, Texas National Guard. Carlo nicknamed him from the Italian "*secondo me*" or "according to me," a phrase Seco apparently uttered nearly every time he started to speak.

There are three pictures of Seco in the books, only one other person appears more often. In the first, the whole crew pose in their Jeep, top down and doors off. The word *Cerberus* is painted beneath the Jeep's windshield. I assume the reference to the "three-headed watchdog of Hades," as Ovid's index identifies him, originated with Carlo and the other two "heads" nodded along with the nomenclature. The photo is filed just pages after the Astraea photo. Jove has decided that an early incarnation of the human race is too evil, too impious, and too savage to survive so he decides to end "wild fury's reign," which Carlo blood-highlighted in Latin, "*fera regnat Erinys.*" In the margin he wrote, "A motto for our time." Rather than use thunderbolts and risk the heavens catching fire, Jove opts "to destroy the human race beneath the waves and to send down rain from every quarter of the sky." It is Ovid's Noah's ark moment.

In the photo it is visibly raining and the sky is dark gray. The shot is grainy from the low light. The anonymous photographer stood directly in line with the presumed path of the Jeep, which appears to be rearing like a wild stallion. Looking closely with a loupe, it is possible to see that the blurry back two wheels are buried deep in the mud. Seco stands, hands on the top of the windshield, pulling a look of faux fright—bugged-out eyes, O-shaped mouth—appropriate to a silent-film extra whose stage-coach just got robbed. The motion picture cameraman, who is never named in the two volumes, stands in the back of the Jeep holding an umbrella over his camera, which is mounted on a tripod. He gapes in mock fear at the same spot as Seco. Only Carlo remains seated, barely visible behind the reflection of the rain-spattered windshield. He has pulled his jacket over his head and his face is (once again) unreadable. On the back, he wrote:

> October. The Great Flood. Somewhere wet. Clearly Jove had seen enough of this war and me along with him. It had rained for so many days that I lost count and wasn't able to take a shot, just watch as the dying continued without a care for the weather. It's a little easier to take when the sun isn't shining. Why should birds chirping and blue skies accompany death? Despite it all, we try to have some fun when one of Seco's buddies from back home drives by. He gave me this copy. [filed at I 259]

Seco was killed five or six months later, in March or April 1944. Based on what Carlo wrote then and what happened in early June, just before he went AWOL, I don't think the S-mine was directly responsible for Seco's death. It hurt him badly, likely fatally, but didn't kill him. Carlo killed his friend, as an act of mercy.

Near the end of volume one of *Metamorphoses*, in the tale of the Calydonian boar, is a close-up of Seco from the chest up, eyes closed, a look of peace on his face. Cradled in the hollow below his Adam's apple, his dog tags gleam so brightly that it isn't possible to make out his real name, just the letters SAN and the number 20, indicating a Guardsman. Carlo underlined two phrases on the *recto*: the reportorial "his entrails poured out amid streams of blood and the ground was soaked with gore," and Theseus's epithet for his dear friend Pirithoüs, "O dearer to me than my own self, my soul's other half." Highlighted in blood on the Latin side is "*madefacta est terra cruore.*" Soaked is the earth with blood.

On the back of the photo, these few words are printed neatly: "My friend Seco. He did me a favor, so I did one for him. Forgive me. *Requiescat in pace*. I hate this place."

• • •

Days I did not photograph were usually spent sitting in the New York Public Library, either below the sempiternal blue skies of the Rose Reading Room on Fifth Avenue or in the comfort of the Donnell branch on 53rd Street. I was concerned about not having finished high school. Initially I had an eye toward getting an equivalency degree and attending CUNY, but when the city imposed tuition in 1975, just as I was ready to take the GED, my plan became unachievable, so I abandoned formal education for good.

The first month after I ran away, I studied only *Metamorphoses*, reading it over and over from cover to cover. Then I focused on Carlo's photos, first trying to determine the correct chronological order of his experiences, then trying to understand the man who became my father but left before he could act the part. That immersion generated other questions and I began to read more widely to try and answer them.

Out of a desire to know more of the backstory for Ovid's tales, I read Homer and Virgil, but somehow didn't get around to Dante until much later. (Not until she mentioned him to me.) I picked up Great Books editions at random as they were easily accessible along the outer walls of the reading room, and eventually worked my way through many of those volumes. Much of it was lost on me I confess.

On the lighter side, I reveled in Tolkien's Middle Earth and returned there again and again. I checked out Sjöwall and Wahlöö's Martin Beck books after seeing *Mannen pä taket* at Film Forum in 1977 and from there it was on to Raymond Chandler. I have stayed a steady reader of mysteries, police procedurals, true crime stories, anything to distract from my own issues and allow my mind to focus on the troubles of others.

I often borrowed the books I read, both from libraries and bookstores. This borrowing was technically theft since I didn't have a library card or disposable income, but since I always brought back the books when I finished reading them, I exonerate myself. (Cleared of one charge.) Although sometimes I did sell them back to the store where I had stolen them if I needed quick cash. "It was a gift from my mother who drinks so much she didn't realize she gave me the same book last birthday" usually softened even the most hard-hearted clerk.

I visited the periodicals rooms to check on how the city, the country, and the world were ailing. I read histories, I browsed the encyclopedias on the reference shelves. I flipped through dictionaries and, enchanted by Carlo's love of Latin, acquired an antiquated grammar. I got *gratis* a lesson in Roman civics and turn-of-the-century ethics from the book's archaic exercises as I slogged through the cases, declensions, and tenses. Nominative: *ancilla est*, "she is a slave girl." Accusative: *quis populum liberum cohibere audet*, "who dares to repress a free people?" Genitive: *dominus bonus ancillae*, "the good master of the slave girl." Dative: *ancillae nigrae*, "for a black slave girl." Ablative: *de ipso edicto nihil dicere volumus*, "we want to say nothing about the actual decree." Vocative: *O miles!* "O soldier!" (O me!). Locative: *belli*, "in war" (O Carlo!).

Latin led to an interest in other languages when I came across them, but while linguistics fascinated me, I never carried my studies through to fluency.

When I came home, I tried to be tired so that I could fall asleep despite the nightly rounds of gunfire and violence. I stuffed cotton balls into my ears. I read in dim light until the vertical hold I had on the page began to blur the words intoneanother and the type face faded.

Exhaustion wasn't always enough. The night before my eighteenth birthday two policemen were shot to death across the street from my building, a harrowing occurrence that disturbed my sleep for weeks.

Latinate nightmares often interrupted my repose, revealing that even when I had finished focusing on Carlo, he remained on my mind. The most common dream was me being crushed in a variety of ways, but crushed with an object so massive that its pressure was distributed uniformly over my entire body, fingertips, hips, chest, temples, knees, neck, eyes, and toes. I would be Hercules and, wearying, my legs would buckle while I temporarily cradled the *caelum* on the back of my neck. Or I was Sisyphus and would slip when once again starting to push my *saxum* up the steep slope. The worst was when I was Caeneus, smothered with mountains and forests thrown by Centaurs, their leader crying out "for wounds, let *pondus* suffice."

I would awaken drenched in sweat and shaking, believing I was buried alive. I had to will my resurrected self to sit up, to inflate my body to its proper dimensions. Then I would lay back and focus on nothing, wishing that I knew what to do.

Now I know those dreams were just foreshadowing, insinuations of the pressure building up around my core (this middle movement with all its increasing agitation), building up before I detonated.

• • •

I classify the photos Carlo kept in Ovid into three categories: the visceral, the philosophical, and the lyrical. The first group makes up the majority of the photos and largely depicts the agonies of war. The second group, taken mainly after Seco's death, includes the photos after Carlo deserted. They capture his mental disillusion and descent into violent despair. The third group has nothing to do with the war intrinsically and is the most interesting for me on a personal level. Those eight photos (not counting the one that exists outside the book) tell the story of Carlo's love for—and eventual marriage to—a young girl he calls Lucia. Lucia is not my mother.

No character named Lucia is mentioned in *Metamorphoses* incidentally, and the only other non-Ovidian name that Carlo used in his notes was Seco. Lucina, which does appear in the index as a moniker for both Juno and the goddess of childbirth Diana, means "she who brings to the light." Lucia could be an alias, but I doubt it. Who would he be trying to protect?

Regardless of the name's genesis, to this day I cannot listen to Edgardo sing "*L'universo intero è un deserto per me senza Lucia*" (a good tenor makes me weep on the without) near the end of Donizetti's *Lucia di Lammermoor* without thinking of my father's heartache. This does not always make me sad, it is just a statement of fact.

Carlo and Lucia's story begins chronologically with the "*Mio suocero*" photo of the man standing in the pit on the Salerno beach. It is probable, although I have no way of verifying it, that Carlo knew his future father-in-law before he knew either of his future wives, Lucia or Mamma. What is certain is the fact that the wedding which caused Carlo to write *suocero* was not my parents'. Mamma came to America in 1947 as part of the Alien Fiancées and Fiancés Act, an extension of the War Brides Act enacted at the end of 1945, but she and Carlo did not marry until four years later. (That was the story I had been told as a child. As I started to unravel the truth from *Metamorphoses*, I confirmed it by getting a copy of my parents' marriage license, filed May 13, 1951.)

So unless Carlo recalled the photo of the man in the pit eight years after he shot it, got out his Ovid, read through to find the picture, and then joyfully scribbled two words on it—a succession of events that is extremely dubious—he married Lucia in Italy during the war. Indeed their marriage is alluded to in another photo in this subset, which will be treated in its turn.

Lucia herself is introduced in a photo Carlo took with his Speed Graphic and taped to the inside of the back cover of volume one, bracketing his own portrait from the front. The picture shows a girl of sixteen or seventeen taking a break from sweeping a bedroom on the second story of a house. The scene is visible only because the roof and most of the wall facing the camera are gone, blown away by a mortar shell. On the left of the room is a chest of drawers with a cracked mirror miraculously still hanging above it. Along the back wall a small bed is visible. The girl holds her broom, a besom fashioned from a bundle of birch twigs, in front of her body with both hands, her chin resting lightly atop the handle. She stares down at the camera with black eyes. Her head is tilted to her right. Soft black curls frame her face and hang just past her shoulders. She smirks mischievously as if she could either ditch the broom and leap laughing down onto the photographer or else straddle its handle and fly away. Her skin is so white it looks like it was carved from Volterran alabaster. On the facing flyleaf Carlo wrote:

> Lucia stands apart from the mythical realm, outside of reality, *super bellum*. [NB: That phrase could mean either "above war" or "beyond beauty," both are accusative.] She is more playful than any nymph, more innocent than any virgin, more deserving of veneration than any goddess. I wish I could keep her from the ceaseless sorrow that plagues Tramonti.

For many reasons this passage leapt out at me when I first saw it. Aside from the effusive expression of love, the sight of my last name written by Carlo's hand was shocking. I never knew the origin of my surname and assumed it belonged *ab ovo* to Mamma.

Here, however, Tramonti refers not to Mamma or Lucia, but to the small town and its eponymous *comune* in the hills north and west of Salerno. Lucia (and likely Mamma, but I will get to that) lived there during the war. I doubt their last name was the same as their hometown, so when Mamma arrived in America, an immigration official must have renamed her, intentionally or not, after her *luogo di nascita.* Thus was my matronymic born.

Carlo kept one photograph from a visit to Amalfi with Lucia. She doesn't appear in the picture, so there is no proof of that claim, but it would be uncharacteristic, as far as I can tell, for Carlo to falsify an anecdote. He didn't lie like Jerzi. There is no indication of how long they had known each other at the time of the trip. The picture, likely shot with whatever second camera Carlo carried, is not of much interest from either a documentary or an artistic perspective. It is a touristy shot of the streets of the town taken from the hillside. There are no warships visible in the Tyrrhenian Sea so the photo was probably taken after November 1943. Of greater importance to me is what he wrote on the reverse, which reads like a page from a schoolgirl's diary:

> Lucia and I went to Amalfi today and walked to the mausoleum overlooking the city. (371 steps, we counted!) She wanted to hold hands the whole way and we did it, which was not easy at times because the route often narrows as the passage goes through archways between and under houses. A storm blew in as we climbed and we just made it, dashing under the portico as a heavy rain came down. We watched the city get washed clean below us. I told her that I was in love with her and she kissed me. Thirty minutes later the rain stopped and the sun returned. *Che giorno!*

The tone is shockingly different from almost everything else Carlo added to Ovid. Equally incongruous is the placement of the photo in volume two midway through Book XV. That final chapter begins with Numa, the second king of Rome, traveling to Greece to visit the philosopher and mathematician Pythagoras, a meeting which, apropos or not, is apparently apocryphal according to a notation Carlo made at the beginning of the section. Pythagoras expounds on many topics, but concludes with a litany of things that change—time, life, seasons, bodies, elements, rivers, oceans, cities, animals. One of the specifics he cites is the phoenix, the immortal bird that is reborn every five hundred years from his father's body.

After rebirth, the phoenix disposes of his old nest. Carlo underlined the passage describing this rite: "When age has given him strength, and he is able to carry burdens, he relieves the tall palm's branches of the heavy nest, piously bears his own cradle and his father's tomb through the thin air, until, having reached the city of the Sun, he lays the nest down before the sacred doors of the Sun's temple."

I can make no sense of Carlo's decision to place the Amalfi photo by this passage. "City of the Sun" could conceivably refer to the mausoleum on the hillside where there are "tomb[s]," but the connection is tenuous for someone who is usually more concrete. Perhaps Lucia's father died and was buried in the mausoleum. Perhaps one of her siblings. Maybe Carlo moved the photo here in a clumsy attempt to make her eternal. (Maybe it was a message for me, presciently made, like Mahler's Seventh, prior to my conception.)

Whatever his reasoning, there is no indication that he was ever happier during the war, or indeed during his life, than on this particular day when he declared his love for Lucia.

• • •

Though my new neighborhood was informally referred to as

Loisaida, by and because of its majority Hispanic population, the residents of my building were Ukrainian. They were different generations, but all from the same small village and distantly related. Even though most of their compatriots had moved further west or north, the landlord for 526 had not been heard from for more than a year, so they just stayed on, rent-free, and maintained the property as best they could. They all knew I was living upstairs and did not have a problem with it.

From Marko, a tough who lived at the front of the first floor with his parents, his wife, and their two children, I learned how my apartment had become available. At the beginning of June, a fire began in the room across the hall from mine. It was empty at the time, but the other three units on the floor were occupied. No investigation was held to determine the cause of the fire, but if it was intentionally set, perhaps at the behest of the absent owner, the would-be arsonist's attempt to burn down the building was snuffed out by the presence of the police precinct-captain's teenage son, who was dating a girl who lived on the second floor, possibly the braided one I had spied on my first day. The captain apparently didn't approve of the non-Irish lass and so had his son followed whenever he visited her. When the off-duty officer parked down the block saw smoke coming from the building, he radioed the fire department, which arrived in record time for the neighborhood and quickly doused the nascent flames.

Because of smoke damage, the third floor was temporarily uninhabitable, so those residents moved away to live with family on Seventh Street. They never returned and the rooms remained unoccupied. Until Vanessa appeared.

At first she was alone. Then Glenn joined her. After a few days he left. Then Ken came. And went. Then Mike, then Kelly, then a second Mike, and then Jeff, who lasted the longest she later told me, staying all of eight days. He had gone for good a few weeks before my arrival and Vanessa had been alone since.

She was sixteen when we met, with coltish legs that she showed off beneath short skirts, bad acne on her forehead that she hid behind brownish bangs, and comically crooked teeth that she kept covered at all times. A sometime mediocre strumpet who was unable to differentiate between her personal life and her work (viz. Ken, Mike, Jeff, *et alii*), she would go stand on 12th Street whenever she felt lonely and give a couple of hand jobs for a few bucks, her shame at her dental imperfections preventing her from making more money. She wasn't interested in intercourse with customers, so sometimes they got invited home, q.v. *pueri citati.*

She was from somewhere "in the north," exactly where she never said, but I would be surprised if it was more north than 95th. She never lacked for money, no matter how infrequently she hooked, so either her artist friends paid her for occasional nude modeling, which would have been surprising given the way the neighborhood worked, or she had another source of income. I think she was just a rebellious rich kid who ran away from what she saw as overprotective parents, but stayed in touch with someone at home, maybe a sibling, who continued to funnel her money.

Anyway, we became friends, Vanessa and I, not necessarily because we had a lot in common, but because she didn't like to be alone.

Initially our interaction was limited to nodding silently to one another on the way to and from the toilet at the end of the hall. Because she was often nearly naked, I tried to keep my eyes down and at the same time descry her silhouette through the darkness.

Then on October 19, one month after running away (I stopped for a piece of carrot cake on the way home to commemorate the anniversary), I opened my door to find Vanessa on my bed. The night can hardly be called amorous (that would come more than ten years later and make up my second *Nachtmusik*), but regardless, I can recall the scene in its entirety.

"Um, what are you doing here?" I said.

"I'm really sorry but it's so cold and my radiator apparently doesn't work or they haven't turned it on or something and I just thought maybe we could hang out, but you weren't here so I decided to wait because it was warmer in here and you usually aren't out very late. Maybe it's the wind?" She could string together words in her nerviness.

"What's the wind?"

"Why it's warmer here. Cuz the wind isn't blowing through your boards."

Wind or no, she was right about the temperature. It had plummeted and I had been cold the entire day, miserable since the sun set.

"Well, that's fine, but from now on maybe wait until I'm here before you come."

"For sure." She smiled. "I have a bottle of whiskey if you want some. Do you want to listen to my radio? I'll go get it, if you do."

"No, that's okay." So soon after my break with Jerzi, music was *noch verboten*.

"Well, do you want a nip? Are you are a photographer? Who do you work for? You can photograph me if you want. My name's Vanessa."

"I'm Milo." Nervous as I was, I still had my manners. "Nice to meet you." I shut the door and walked toward her, realized I still held the Speed Graphic, put it on the floor, and bent down to shake her hand. It was warm and she shuddered at my cold, dry grip.

"Brrr. You should definitely have something to drink. And put your hands between your legs or sit on them or something. That's what I've been doing."

I focused on her legs. They were shapely but covered in green tights and a gingham skirt that stopped above her knees. She was sitting on her feet, which I could see had on thick, gray men's socks with red toes and heels. While conscious of the fact that a girl was in my room, it still had not occurred to me that something might happen between me and that girl. I sat down on the floor beside the bed.

"Well, don't sit there, silly. The floor is cold. Sit on the blankets with me. Where are you from, Milo?"

"Poland." It was the first thing that came to mind. I have no idea why I said it aloud. I started to sweat even though my teeth were trying to chatter.

"Poland, far out. When did you come here?"

"I was born here. I mean, I'm not from Poland. I don't know. I mean I knew someone from Poland, but not any more. I'm from here. New York. City. That's where, here is where I mean, here I was born." I reached out my hand for the whiskey bottle, largely to shut myself up. The extent of my tippling was the occasional sip of wine on special nights at Nonna's, so I didn't know if whiskey would help or hurt my situation, but I needed to do something differently.

"Cool. You're funny." And she took the bottle back from my hand and smiled again, her mouth still closed, lips still covering her teeth.

We talked for a while longer, awkwardly at first but then more freely. She was confident. I was happily drunk and sleepy. Near midnight we both grew quiet.

"Can I stay in here, Milo? It would be warmer. And we can fool around if you want to." I didn't really know what fooling around would entail, but I got excited hearing her say the words.

"Okay. That's fine. I mean, you can stay here, sure." Even if I had wanted her to leave, I felt that saying so would have made her cry. "I won't do anything though. I mean, you don't have to, to stay. That's not the reason. You can just stay."

"Oh, it's alright, I kinda like you." She giggled, then rocked back pulling off her two socks in one smooth motion and wriggled slowly out of her stockings. Her skirt stayed on. She slid beneath the top blanket. "Come on. Take your pants off. It'll be warmer with the body heat. And more fun."

Modesty prevents me from listening to the conclusion of this duet, but I will quickly recall the thrill of kissing someone at long last (my heart beating so nimbly, *piccolo Paukenschlägel* pounding *fortissimo* tremolos upon atrial timpani), my hands and elbows not knowing their proper places (resulting in pulled hair and pinched skin, *staccato* trumpet squeals), the warm wetness of her wondrously soft legs (between which I would lazily lie once we were better acquainted, my fingers playing up and down their ivory lengths), and my failed fumbling attempts at actual coitus (she eventually rolled on top of me and, as cold air rushed around us, put me inside her, making all music cease).

In the morning she took me out for eggs and coffee and then bought me a winter hat, reversing our gender roles by playing Rodolfo to my Mimi, and initiating my curiosity regarding the source of her funding.

No regular relationship ever began between us, not like I imagined one between two people who were dating. I didn't love her, which probably sounds mean, but I did care for her a lot. During those six years in Manhattan, she was the only person I got close to in any fashion. I doubt she considered me her boyfriend. If she did she never said it. I felt more like a security blanket. She came over when she was bored or scared or cold or when no one else was around. We usually had sex, but not always. She occasionally cried afterward, but when I asked her what was wrong, she wouldn't say anything, just nuzzle into my neck, tears puddling in the cavity above my collarbone until they spilled out.

We always stayed in my room, with one significant exception.

It was after the opening of the International Center for Photography exhibit and I went to her first, bursting through her door as soon as I got up the stairs. I had never needed someone as much as I did that night, and having her near me, even when I couldn't find the words to speak, probably kept me from running back to Mamma in Queens. So thank you, Vanessa. I didn't say it at the time.

• • •

Three photos chronicle Carlo's newly declared love for Lucia, two of which are tainted by his concerns with the ongoing war. In the first, she is barefoot in the middle of a dusty road leading out of Tramonti. No one else is visible. The bombed-out house where she was sweeping sits on the right. (I have since stood there, too, and imagined what Lucia saw as my father photographed her. The house was razed and replaced, the new building looks nothing like the old.) She wears the same dress as in that first photo. Since both prints are black-and-white, it is impossible to discern actual colors, but based on the shocking brightness of the dress in this photo compared with the first, I'm willing to guess the dress was yellow and Carlo used a red filter shooting the second shot. Lucia's shoulders are not bare now but covered with a dark shawl. Her left arm is thrust straight out in front of her, finishing a farewell wave to the cameraman or catching a kiss he blew to her. Carlo writes:

> "O envious wall … why do you stand between lovers?" [filed at IV 70] At first I was against placing this photo here with Pyramus and Thisbe because I didn't want anything to come between Lucia and me. But something already has. Our wall is the war. I won't let it keep us apart for long. I will come back for you, Lucia. Come back to you. You're my reason to

> fight the death I see now even in my sleep, the death which destroyed so many great romances in these books, the death that I return to, leaving my love behind. Good-bye for now, *la mia* Lucia.

Sometime later Carlo did return, and the photo which he made then is among his most remarkable, if for no other reason than it is the only color photo in *Metamorphoses*. I still struggle to explain its existence, and yet there it is. Did Carlo buy the film from a friendly magazine photographer and keep only one shot from the roll to emphasize his *Heilige Fräulein*? If so, how did he process the film? Unlike with black-and-white, he could not have developed color negatives in whatever mobile darkroom he and the *Cerberus* crew used when they couldn't get back to HQ. (And by this point it is unlikely Carlo returned to HQ often.) Did someone else take the photo, then send it to America to be developed, have it sent back, and return it to Carlo when next they met? Did Lucia present it as a present? (Do dewy-eyed Italians hear heteronyms? This line of questioning is irrelevant.)

In full color, Lucia's simple beauty is jarring. Behind her the sky seems a plasticky matte blue. Her eyes and hair are luscious black, her pale skin young and unblemished. It must be early spring because a garland woven of sweet violets and snowdrops sits atop her head. She wears a deep-green sleeveless shift with white lacework along the bodice. She leans back, long legs bare below the knees and crossed at the ankles. Her elbows rest on a lichen-covered stone wall. She looks like Titania's fairest cousin.

The story referenced on the reverse of the photo is a disturbing one. Cephalus has escaped from Aurora, who abducted him, and returned to Procris, his wife. Though he never responded to the goddess's adulterous advances, they make him wonder whether his wife has remained as faithful as he has. She swears to her fidelity, but Cephalus doesn't believe her and jealously murders her.

Maybe Carlo had legitimate reasons for not trusting Lucia, or maybe his doubts were born out of separation and its attendant ignorance. He could even have been projecting his own guilt onto her. Irrespective of the incentive and lacking any other information, I find the subject of the photo uncharacteristically detached from where it was filed. Inapt allusion aside, the annotation is important because it holds the first overt expression of Carlo's wavering faith. He begins it with a quote from Cephalus, which he underlined on the Latin page facing the photo:

> "Her beauty and her youth made me fear unfaithfulness; but her character forbade that fear ... we lovers fear everything." And I do fear losing Lucia. It is a time of thoughtless action. Why think of consequences when so often there are none? We die and are judged by a culpable God. Going back to the war last time and leaving her was almost more than I could take. I couldn't stop thinking about her, except when I feared dying. And even then, if it got really bad, I eventually thought of her and life without her. Before the war, I dreamed about someone like Lucia. Now I have her and am so close to being happy. I don't know what I would do without her. More almost than the war, that possibility terrifies me.

The only photo in the Lucia group that ignores the war in both composition and annotation is the third photo after their trip to Amalfi, the photo that obliquely implies she and Carlo were married. Neither of them are in the shot, which shows simply a tree, albeit a spectacular one. It is a massive pine of the kind that grow in many Mediterranean countries, their tall branchless trunks supporting high canopies formed from only a few sturdy limbs. Their pinecones can grow as large as a trombone *Dämpfer*. Any one of these trees is impressive based on its size and structure, but I have never seen another like the one in Carlo's photo. It has a double trunk which begins at ground level and twines around as it climbs, ending up back where it started after a three-hundred-and-sixty-degree embrace. If not for the lack of scorching, you could imagine that lighting had struck the tree and spirally cleaved it clear to the earth. Carlo took the picture from the base aiming up. The two canopies cannot be resolved even under a loupe. (I have looked for this tree all over Tramonti and never found it. Perhaps that isn't surprising, an unsuccessful search for a specific tree on multiple tree-covered mountains, but I have continued to try.)

The photo is filed in the story of Baucis and Philemon, who died in each other's arms and were changed into two trees growing from a double trunk. The simple plea on the back reads:

> Now may we be as blessed as Baucis and Philemon were, to spend our lives in each other's constant company until death takes us together. "*Nec coniugis umquam busta meae videam, neu sim tumulandus ab illa.*"

The Latin is translated on the page behind the photo as "May I never see my wife's tomb, nor be buried by her."

Sadly for Carlo, his prayers were not answered. Lucia did not survive the spring.

• • •

In the two months since I ran away, the International Center for Photography exhibit with my father's photo had remained fixed at the forefront of my thoughts. I folded and unfolded the congratulatory letter addressed to "Dear Carlo" so many times that it ripped where the creases intersected. One night in a fit of anger, I tore off the number Nonna had written on the top corner and burned it. Because I had dialed the number so often from pay phones all over the city, it was a futile attempt at banishment. (I will never be able to forget that number, it is etched into my mind.)

Several times I threw the letter away, but I always ran back down the block in a panic to retrieve it. There it lay, crumpled on top of the trash, right where I had tossed it. I put it beneath my moving-blanket mattress, but it disturbed my sleep, resting below me like the princess's pea. I taped it to my closet wall in the darkness. No matter where I put it, the letter cast its shadow on me. Whether making pictures, sitting in the library, lying with Vanessa, or staring into space, it oppressed me. The exhibit loomed.

Would Carlo be there? And if he was, would I recognize him? Would he have a name tag? If I did identify him, how would I react? Could I possibly bring myself to approach him? If I did approach him, would I tell him that I was his son? How would he react? If I told him who I was, what exactly would I hope to accomplish? Would he even care? What relation would he bear to the man I knew solely through the impressions gathered from the one hundred fifty-four photos in *Metamorphoses*? (Most frequently given answers at the time: maybe, no, maybe, frightened, no, yes, frightened, no idea, no, some. If I had to answer today: no, yes, no, I plead the fifth, yes, sort of, I plead the fifth, plead the fifth, plead the fifth, none.)

The Saturday of the opening, November 16, 1974, I awoke early, washed my face, and was out the door before I noticed my nerves. I habitually tapped at Carlo's books, tied together and shoved into the left pocket of my outsized navy-blue corduroy suit coat, which I had found on the street a couple of weeks earlier. (When I later read *Oliver Twist*, I realized I had unintentionally outfitted myself *à la* the Artful Dodger at the outset of my criminal phase, *avec* his rolled-up sleeves *mais sans chapeau.*) I stopped for coffee and challah on Second Avenue and then walked eighty-six blocks north before turning left on 94th Street to head over toward Fifth Avenue. My stomach roiled.

There were three exhibits that day, and whether out of terror or some other motivation, I opted to view the one with Carlo's photo last. The first comprised a series of photographs that Henri Cartier-Bresson made during a visit to the Soviet Union. Not knowing anything about photography at that point except what I had seen in Carlo's souvenir shots, Cartier-Bresson's work struck me principally as something completely different. I was awed by how well he conveyed the vastness of Russia. Skies looked limitless. No one appeared crowded. Only emptiness was abundant. The subjects of his photos almost never made eye contact with the camera. He captured them looking down or to the left or with their backs to him. In Carlo's photos, the subject was almost always optically tethered to the lens. Cartier-Bresson merely observed, while Carlo seemed to consciously make himself a part of the photo, albeit in a way that did not appear to me to have altered the event.

I lingered, losing myself, happily delaying the focus of my visit. I was especially taken with the image of a young girl captured while hovering in mid-stride, running down a sidewalk past cherry trees in bloom. Another favorite showed a beautiful female brick layer whose face and frame looked far too delicate to be handling so casually the massive brick in her hand.

And then suddenly I had procrastinated enough. I needed to know immediately whether my father stood somewhere above me in that building.

I skipped the "Eye of the Beholder" color photography exhibit and pushed my way upstairs to the Classics of Documentary Photography. I scanned the space and saw the backs of scores of heads staring at white walls hung with photos framed in wide white mats. Deep breath. Start at the start.

Photo after photo by Robert Capa (whose brother Cornell

had signed the letter to "Dear Carlo" held by my shirt pocket), Lewis Hine (whose images of children I found particularly affecting as I studied them over the next several weeks), more from Cartier-Bresson, others whose names I choose not to recall. The crowd flowed from one room to the next.

My mind taut to receive the affecting blow, the letdown of non-Carlo photo after non-Carlo photo passing before my eyes lulled me. Maybe it was a mistake. I braced myself again, only to read an unfamiliar name on the next white placard and relax once more before repeating the process again. Despite these precautions, I was strangely unprepared when the gentleman ahead of me slid slowly to his right and CARLO ESPOSITO appeared before me. "Still I Weep (1944)" was typed above my father's name.

I shuddered, knowing what I would see before I saw it. I glanced around. No one was paying attention to me. I looked.

A woman's upturned face twists in pain, imploring God for release from that which He hath wrought. Her hands, raised, rend her hair. Tears cascade down cheeks from swollen eyes. She is slack-jawed and exhausted from the agony. Lying in front of her, along the bottom of the photo, is a young girl. If she lay alone, one might assume from her physiognomy that she was asleep. But her dress, rumpled and splotched with dark patches of blood, and her mourning mother reveal the truth. She is dead. She is Lucia.

After several moments, I slowly lowered my gaze from the blown-up eight-by-ten on the wall and pulled Carlo's books from my pocket. I slid off the string and opened volume one, flipping carefully through the pages until Book VI where I found the photo I was seeking, the concluding photo in Carlo and Lucia's tale. Better than any other photo in *Metamorphoses*, I believe it captures the horror of war.

The photo is filed in the story of Niobe, who saw her seven

daughters and seven sons killed. Niobe turns to stone while weeping over her children's deaths and is whisked away to a mountain peak where "even to this day tears trickle from the marble." On the back of the photo I held in my hands, Carlo had written two words "*flet tamen.*" Translation: Still [she] weeps.

I looked in disbelief back and forth between the photo in my hands and the one hung on the wall. They must have been shot moments apart, as fast as Carlo could reload his camera. Most of the differences are minor. In the photo in the book, the lighting is perceptibly brighter, as if a crowd had shifted outside the frame. The older woman grabs Lucia's dress, not her own hair. And she looks into the lens, not above it, a distinction which supports my theory that one criteria for photos in *Metamorphoses* was that the subject connect with Carlo eye to eye.

It was not the cosmetic changes that stunned me, however. It was the other difference, a significant and a revelatory one. In the picture in *Metamorphoses*, there is another person in the shot, a young girl. She kneels in the upper righthand corner, by the head of the dead Lucia. She has one hand on Lucia's brow and stares into space beyond the camera. It is Mamma, recognizable across the years. She is in complete shock, and even though it is a photo, she doesn't appear to be breathing. She looks like she is made of stone.

That picture had frequently moved me to tears the past two months as I searched *Metamorphoses* for clues to Carlo's disappearance, but now, looking up at the same image, except with Mamma missing, I started to sob uncontrollably. Not at the photo necessarily or at the fact that Lucia's mother's sorrow was so much more palpable in isolation, but because Mamma was gone. Literally taken out of the picture. It was the first time I had truly felt her loss.

After a minute or two, I composed myself and looked up at the wall again, at the placard with my father's full name. He had titled the photo "Still I Weep," in the first person, not the third, referring to Niobe or Lucia's mother. Here was clear proof that the source of his pain was the same as it was thirty years ago, and it had nothing to do with Mamma. Or with me. Carlo still wept for something he had lost during the war, long before I existed.

I felt sorry for him and I felt sorry for Mamma and I began to cry again. How had they felt as they said good-bye? Were they angry with each other, as I had been with Mamma when I left? Had she gotten pregnant on purpose, without telling him, in an attempt to get him to love her? How many times had she lain alone in the dark, hands on her pregnant belly, knowing that she would have to continue to carry that burden on her own?

A burden. Was that how she saw me? Was that why she found someone or something—Hupka or God or the *Pietà* or religion—to replace me? She had found that something, found comfort, and she wasn't alone anymore. But I was.

My anger returned. I selfishly thought of my losses. The fact that my death would not be mourned. *No pietà per me*. Who would shed a tear? Walking back to my empty apartment, I could get beaten to death—as had happened the previous night to a junkie two blocks from where I lived—and no one would know, no one would care. How horrible to have nobody, to die an anonymous death in a foreign city. (Not that yet. I retract the sentiment.)

I shoved the books back in my pocket, wiped my eyes with my sleeve, turned and ran out of the gallery. On the street, I kept running, and I ran with abandon, knocking strangers out of my way, running until my legs burned, until my lungs ached and labored with each panting gasp, until I pushed open Vanessa's door and threw myself on her bed, pulled her down on top of me and held her, as tightly to myself as I could squeeze. (And the cellos and basses played B-flats, *pizzicato*, super *fortissimo*, so hard that the strings smack the wood. THWACK!)

• • •

A crack of thunder transports me back to reality. I was disembodied for a moment. The wind howls steadily. The café is dim, almost empty. The mother and her child are long gone, only an old man gazing absently at his cigarette smoke and a couple sitting silently (he reads while she writes freely on unruled paper) remain. The proprietor glares in my direction, perhaps wondering how much longer I will be requiring him to stay. Maybe he wants to be home before the storm, its growing ferocity now audible, bursts over Split. I'm uncomfortable, but I must finish with this movement. Then I will change locations to conclude my reckoning.

• • •

Metamorphoses holds one other photograph of Mamma, and my belief that she and Lucia were related is largely based upon it. The posed photo shows a family sitting down for a frugal wartime feast. A shallow bowl of broth waits in front of each of them. Also on the table are a loaf of bread, a bowl of zucchini, a jug of wine, and some kind of meat on a platter.

At the front of the frame is an unidentified elderly woman with a scarf tied under her chin. Opposite her at the head of the table sits *il suocero*, wearing the same suit jacket he did in the detention pit on the beach. To his left sits an empty chair, likely Carlo's, and next to that Lucia. To his right sits his wife, the woman from the Niobe photos, and then Mamma.

She has the same blank look on her face as the girl Carlo likened to Astraea. I have spent hours examining the two faces under my loupe, and have reached no conclusion as to whether they are the same person. If Mamma is the child standing barefoot in that puddle, if Mamma watched as her mother was stoned and beaten to death behind her, then, then I just don't know. And maybe that is what has prevented me from reaching a decision on the issue.

I can see only three reasons for such a relatively elaborate meal during the time that Carlo and Lucia knew each other. The first is Christmas, but I eliminate it peremptorily because of the flowers that appear not only braided into Lucia's hair, but also in bloom in the background. The second possibility logistically is Easter, which in 1944 fell on April 9. The Allies were still behind the Winter Line then, but since Signal Corps photographers often went off on their own for long periods of time, Carlo could have traveled to Tramonti without being missed. What would have been missed on Easter, however, were *uove*, or eggs. No *Pasqua* celebration would be complete without them, and their absence from the table, even during the war, disqualifies Easter. The only event that fits the facts of the photo is a wedding. And while it is odd that the groom does not actually appear in the frame, perhaps Carlo kept the practice shot and Lucia's family the official commemoration.

On the reverse are two phrases, both written in pencil. The first is an Italian expression written across the top, "*Circondata dall'affetto dei suoi cari*," which means "surrounded by the affection of her (or his) loved ones." It is a literal depiction of the scene and not particularly illuminating, except in classifying Mamma as a loved one.

Below that, and written in haste, is "*quantum mortalia pectora caecae noctis habent!*" The text is from Book VI, where the photo is filed, and in English reads "what blind night rules in the hearts of men!" Carlo's scholastic translation, neatly printed in ink in the margin, runs "how blind night manages the mortal mind!!" The double exclamation points are penciled in, emotions from a later date.

The line, regardless of how it is rendered, refers to Tereus, who was married to Procne but lusted after Philomela, his sister-in-law. It is one of Ovid's longest tales and full of the extreme actions that make his stories so entertaining centuries later. After a visit to his wife's family, Tereus agrees to take Philomela home to visit her sister whom she hasn't seen for several years. He has other designs, however, and upon reaching his homeland, he imprisons Philomela in a hut, cuts out her tongue, and rapes her. Eventually she escapes and finds her sister. They get their revenge by murdering Tereus's son and cooking his flesh for the unknowing father's supper. After Tereus realizes what he ate, he goes mad and chases Philomela and Procne out of the palace, where all three are changed into birds.

As a metaphor, the story is one of the more powerful Carlo could have chosen. It implies that Lucia and Mamma were sisters, which means the Astraea photo would likely have no relation to Mamma. If Ovid isn't supposed to be taken so literally, Mamma could still have been Lucia's cousin and come to live in Tramonti after losing her mother.

There is no evidence that Carlo had feelings for Mamma while Lucia was alive. Maybe after her death, Carlo needed to be surrounded by *suoi cari*. Maybe he asked the family if he could take Mamma back to America to give her a better life, to get her away from such terrible memories.

Or maybe his motives were not so selfless. Maybe he forced himself on Mamma, tried to make her his mute mate, his Philomela? Did she ever want him or did she view him solely as her savior? Could he ever love her when he never stopped crying over the loss of Lucia? (I'll never know these answers now.)

• • •

I needed to physically find my father, but I had no idea how to go about it. Admission to the photography exhibit was by voluntary donation so, with no *noblesse* obligating me, I returned *gratuit* almost every day. I stood before Carlo's photo for hours, scrutinizing both it and its audience, hoping its creator would show. Some days I became lost in the mourning mother and forgot Carlo completely. Other times I searched solely for phantom traces of Mamma in the vacant spot where I knew she had knelt. Often I fixated on Lucia, trying to reanimate her, hear her, feel her, make her move. I saw the photo so vividly—even outside of the gallery—that I began to believe silver halides had replaced my retinal rods and imprinted a reduced metallic image on the concave ceilings of my eyes.

One afternoon my concentration was broken by a man approaching from behind me. I turned quickly but knew immediately 'twas not he. Too wide a face, too old, too stout. Seeing he had startled me, the man introduced himself. Cornell Capa, founder and director of the center. He had noticed my "obsession" with Carlo's photo and wondered what motivated it.

Without thinking to lie, I blurted out that he, the photographer, was my father.

Seemingly not surprised, Capa said, I see. You should be proud of him. He is a good photographer.

Noting his use of the present tense, I responded that we had never met.

He said sorry and, perhaps unsure how to continue, somewhat abruptly left.

During my next visit, Capa and I talked a little more. I learned explicitly that Carlo was alive. And he was still a photographer, a revelation that I received with some surprise. He was even a member of, and occasional contributor to, Magnum, the photographic collective founded by Capa's brother Robert, Henri Cartier-Bresson, and others after the Second World War. Carlo's submissions almost always came from different locations, but Capa hadn't heard from him for more than fourteen months, explaining why the congratulatory letter was sent to Nonna's. Carlo's current location was unknown.

This final piece of information crushed me. Out of desperation I decided not to trust Capa completely. He had to know. Hadn't his letter to Carlo thanked him for his submission? If Carlo had not submitted anything, who had entered the photo? Nonna? (An intriguing possibility. Was her design to draw him out?) Maybe Capa withheld information from me not out of malice, but because his loyalties lay with his fellow photographer, not with the young man whom he had just met. Maybe Carlo had mentioned me. (Please, I almost prayed.)

With an eye toward bribery, I briefly considered showing Capa the copy of *Metamorphoses* in my pocket. But I decided those books were too personal to let anyone else see. I did however tell him the origin of the Speed Graphic that I held in my hand during most of my visits. He acted interested and offered me free enrollment in the workshops that the center taught. I attended several and found them invaluable, learning more than I ever could have through experimentation or from books. Shortly after the exhibit changed, I stopped going to the classes, believing (correctly) that Capa would be key to eventually tracking down Carlo, and not wanting to take advantage of his generosity.

Before they took "Still I Weep" off the wall, however, I got Capa's permission to photograph it. I arrived early, before the center opened, and he let me inside. Then he left me alone. In the gallery, I stood the Speed Graphic on a tripod, as it was intended, and pretended I was in Tramonti in 1944 making the original shot. I changed the aperture, snapped the shutter, read my light meter. I imagined the action outside my viewfinder. Stray villagers stand around. A chilly wind blows and they huddle closer. Carlo tries (and so do I) to focus through his (my) tears. (*L'universo intero è un deserto per me.*) *Cerberus* idles to the side, ready to transport us back to the hell of the war. I wait, hoping that Mamma will magically walk back into the frame.

Where did she go? She was ten or eleven years old, capable of processing only so much emotion. (I should know.) Had she run off to hide? To mourn by herself? Was she just scared? Was she thinking of her mother's murder? Had she walked behind the lens to help the photographer? (Carlo? Hupka? Me?) I couldn't find her. She wasn't coming back.

To my lens. I inserted my film. It was time. He couldn't bear to listen to Lucia's mother's continued wailing. I bent forward and looked into the past, at the same scene—through the same pieces of ground glass—that my father had seen. Then we took our shot.

I made a four-by-five print from the negative, exactly as Carlo would have done, and hung it on my wall. When I left the country, I stashed it in *Metamorphoses* next to its sister picture, where it still resides today.

• • •

Carlo never specified what killed Lucia. And even if he knew, he was likely too grief-stricken to record it. A mine or mortar fire, an errant bullet or disease. She was dead. Why would the cause concern him?

He did take one last picture of her, though she can't be seen. It is a shot of what looks to be a small funeral procession, a wooden cart carrying a casket turns beneath a simple wrought-iron arch. The camera must have moved when the emulsion was exposed because the resulting print is badly blurred, almost like it was shot in a fog and the lens was dewy, wet with Aurora's tears.

Nothing is written on the back of the photo, which is filed immediately preceding the cemetery-in-the-field photograph, but Ovid's text is altered on the pages enfolding it. On the English side: "What were my feelings then? Was it not natural that

I should hate life and long to be with my ~~friends~~? LUCIA!" Opposite them, the Latin words *vitam odissem*, "hate life," are smudged with blood. There is of course no proof that the burial is for Lucia, but it is a logical assumption.

The fallout from her death and its effect on Carlo's increasingly fragile mental state is not in doubt. Signs can be found throughout *Metamorphoses*. Words and phrases alluding to it, including *furit* (to be mad, wild with rage), *saevit* (to rave, rage), and *lacrimas* (tears), are encircled each time they appear (eleven, ten, too many). *Chaos*, *Erinys*, *nox*, *tenebras*. Chaos, Fury, night, darkness. All highlighted in blood. Sometimes her name is written, all capital letters, LUCIA, in the margin alongside a passage about death.

Carlo's heart was riven, his grief and his blood spattered on the pages. He was trying anything he could think of to cope with his anguish.

• • •

Beginning in July 1975, I slowly let music return to my life. It wasn't an intentional decision. I went to Central Park before a concert performance of *Madama Butterfly* on the Sheep Meadow with no intention of listening to the actual opera. I planned to sell some photos and leave prior to Jan Behr entering the pit. Since the area was so sprawling, I had no fear of bumping into Jerzi, who I knew would never miss Renata Scotto singing Cio-Cio San.

He had taken me to see the opera eight years earlier during my spring break, and while early on I was deeply moved by the score, particularly the wedding-night duet, the local-girl-marries-military-man story started to hit too close to home. I hadn't read the program because we had arrived just as the lights were going down, but by the time Teresa Stratas sang "*Un bel dì vedremo*," I knew that her husband would not return. The Humming Chorus confirmed my instincts, as it was too achingly beautiful to presage anything but sorrow. Watching Suzuki kneel next to the fatherless child while his mother, the bereft Butterfly, stood over them reminded me of all the nights Nonna had sat silently next to me on the couch while Mamma, waiting for I-knew-not-what, had stared out the window. I was no longer looking at the stage as Butterfly gave up her child and committed suicide.

When I got to the park a little after five, I promptly got distracted by the sunbathing opera-goers, many wearing not much more than their underwear. Vanessa, who often disappeared for a week or two with no notice, had been gone for several days and I yearned for attention. I hid behind the comfort of the camera and went to work.

The crowd seemed enchanted by the perfect weather, as New Yorkers often are when the sun shines down with a quiet warmth as opposed to the dense heat it sometimes dumps onto the city, and I didn't have to approach anyone. People begged me to take their picture, and then chatted amicably as they pulled out their wallets.

After photographing a couple sharing an elegant picnic dinner, complete with champagne and *truffes au chocolat*, I was whistled over by two slender brunettes smoking cigarettes. I finished up with the alfresco epicures, collected my five-dollar fee, and went over to where the girls lolled. They were enrolled in summer school and were reciting their French lessons, all exaggerated accents and attitudes, perhaps mocking the picnickers. They put down their textbooks and proceeded to vamp for the camera, languorously teasing each other, almost undressing completely, and generally making me blush for nearly an hour. I shot an entire roll of film on them. Once they had possession of the pile of instant prints, they threw me thirty dollars and dismissed me as a nuisance.

I was used to rude treatment, but their exhibitionism produced such a tangle of emotions in me that leaving the park I started to stumble and had to sit down beneath a tree. I was still there, lost in my thoughts, when Puccini's *vigoroso* violins awoke me from my stupor. Fifteen minutes later *la* Scotto made her entrance, and her cool, clear intensity kept me planted for the first act. During intermission, I realized that the music had helped me see past my feelings, helped me forget about the slight. I resolved to stay for the second half. The subject matter still struck a chord, and I certainly cried, but I relished the return of the familiar feeling that had been missing from my life for more than a year, the feeling of music breathing through me, telling me in notes what I couldn't express to myself in words. I left before the final act, still not ready to accept the abandonment of the child, but with my ears reopened.

After the performance, I began spending some of my free time listening. I went back to the Met a handful of times that next season, although each trip I hesitated on the plaza, turned away from the entrance, and walked up and down the rows of the band shell for several minutes, fixated on possibly seeing Jerzi. Once I heard the final chimes, I raced inside to find my place in the dark. Eventually the music began to win out against my past, notably the time I bravely bought spots to hear Joan Sutherland and Luciano Pavarotti sing two performances of *I Puritani*. Jerzi must have been out of town, because he was absent both nights, but the shows were worth any confrontation that could have come, so magical they may even have reconciled us had he been in attendance.

I also resumed the musical education that Jerzi initiated. While he had introduced me to numerous pieces, I wanted to immerse myself, to develop a deeper appreciation. I chose one composer at a time and listened to his compositions from start to finish. Faced with the fecundity of some geniuses, Mozart or Haydn to name two, I often balked and tweaked the curriculum, choosing to tackle a more manageable subset, such as the piano concertos or the symphonies or even the string quartets.

I listened in that fashion for more than a year, either at the Lincoln Center library or the Donnell. Then, during the fall of 1976, I made a fateful decision. In considering which composer to focus on next, I would imagine myself back in Jerzi's basement, where I mentally browsed the shelves. In this instance, however, something blinded my sight (perhaps the hands of time were tired of waiting) and I could only listen, listen as he admonished me. That is not for you. It rang in my ears. That is not for you, not for you, not for you, for you, for you, for you, you. Naturally I chose Gustav Mahler.

Looking into his *oeuvre*, ten complete symphonies and a handful of song cycles, it seemed as if it would be a fairly quick class. It was not. My studies of his music continue today, are ongoing at this moment.

For no other reason than defiance, I tried, as much as was possible at the time, to choose recordings on which Jerzi had played, starting with Bruno Walter conducting the New York Philharmonic in *Symphony No. 1*, January 1954, from Carnegie Hall. The eerily droning flageolets hooked me, though seemingly random pronouncements from winds and horns left me at sea as for what to expect. Once the harps had their brief moment in the third movement, I was caught. Mahler's musical emotions spoke poignantly to me and I knew that I must heed what he had to say. (Although the grandeur of the finale told me that the First was not my symphony, specifically.) When I read that the first movement took its main theme from a *lied* composed earlier, I checked it out and saw how Mahler had first tried to express through words, "*und da fing im Sonnenschein, Gleich die Welt zu funkeln an*," what he later felt he could say differently, maybe more effectively, with orchestration only. Music names them for us. Only in notes. I heard. And I was ready to listen.

Whereas with Beethoven's symphonies I had finished my study in two weeks (a full day to each of the first eight and four days devoted to the Ninth), I moved much slower with Mahler. The scores were more complex. There were more vocals to consider. And frankly for me, the music had more to say. Not that it was better, necessarily, as it is hard to be better than Beethoven, but I knew from the beginning that I was intimately connected with this music.

I lived with the first five symphonies for seven weeks. I stuck with Bruno Walter conducting Jerzi for the Second, a fractured recording process that took two years (1957–8) to complete because Bruno had a heart attack after the first session. (I listened over and over to Emilia Cundari urging me *zu Gott*, wishing that was truly my destiny.) For the Third I was forced to do without Jerzi because all the library had was a 1961 Bernstein-led performance. (O ethereal *Langsam* of the Third! would that you were mine. But I could never have obeyed, loved only God, "*Liebe nur Gott in all Zeit!*" All I wanted was the love I would learn of from Alice!) Back to Walter, and Jerzi, for a 1945 Fourth (Desi Halban singing the child's view of heaven, *Das himmlische Leben*, that I knew I'd never get to see) and a 1947 Fifth (the same recording I had first heard in Jerzi's basement the day we memorialized Robert Kennedy).

In December 1976 a stubborn storm settled over the city, refusing to move out to sea despite an insistent western wind. At the beginning of the month I studied the Sixth, Bernstein and the Jerzi-less Philharmonic from 1967, and two weeks later I was still psychologically shaken. (Not as shaken as I would be years later when I found a bootleg of the Sixth that did include Jerzi, conducted by Dmitri Mitropoulos. It was creepy in a way which I don't have words to describe, but listening I felt as if Jerzi was lying in front of me bleeding, staring up with an evil grin in his eyes. I returned the records the next day.)

Where am I? (Shake him? No, shaken.) Yes, I was shaken by the Sixth. The orchestral blast at the end had caused me to jump forward in my chair, but that shock was not what rattled me. No, what rattled me was my response to the massive chord. You see, once I heard it, I knew what it meant. Not specifically, because I still did not know that the Seventh premiered on my birth date. And I knew nothing of the Rainier test. (That would come later as I dug deeper into my past.) But I knew I was related somehow to that blast. I had heard it before. The kettledrums seemed to reverberate somewhere within me. And the little *pizzicato* plink at the end, such a Puckish Mahlerian wink, didn't conclude anything for me. It beckoned, drew me forward toward the symphony of my life.

But I didn't follow. Not at first. For days I resisted. Out of fear? (To be out of your brother's bluster, Boreas?) Maybe, I don't know. But I stayed alone in my room, telling Vanessa whenever she came over that I needed to think. In reality I was attempting the opposite, namely to *not* think, but to absorb all I'd heard, let it gestate naturally, without dwelling on it.

And then, on December 22, I was ready. I would continue to grow.

• • •

Not gifted with the skills of Arachne, I fear losing the *Scherzo*'s elusive narrative thread, so a moment ago I took a break and went to rinse my face. The washroom sink had only a cold water faucet—H for *hladno*, not for hot—with a knob on top that you push down to operate. The water flows only as long as it takes the knob to pop back up, however, and this knob's pop was frustratingly resilient. I had to force it down with both thumbs and hold it there while cupping my hands beneath the spigot until they cradled enough water to splash on my face. I repeated this ablution several times and then noticed there was nothing with which to dry myself, so I stood staring at my dripping visage while the water evaporated. It was the first time I had looked at myself since fleeing Zagreb. (Afraid of what you would see, maybe?) I appeared so gaunt and tired that I had to convince my mind it was me looking back.

My eyebrows have become unruly, growing at wildly varying angles and speeds. The eyes themselves, washed-out and rheumy, used to be hazel where now they look beige. I haven't shaved for a couple of days and a dense black stubble shades my pale cheeks and chin. Nothing has ever grown below the shadow of my sharp nose so my upper lip always stays smooth.

Unable to abide the sight any longer, I wiped off the excess water with my palms and slicked back my hair, even though each strand was already in its proper place. They never stray, they just grow gray, one by one by one by one.

• • •

I am not going to comment here on listening to the Seventh (Bernstein, *sans* Jerzi) for the first time, because everything I am writing today is the result of that experience. Hearing it, knowing what it meant (and I knew from the downbeat), has colored all I do, including how I interpret my past. I will add, because I find these things fascinating, that the day of my initial hearing was the same day in 1907 that Mahler and his wife, Alma, arrived in America. He was forty-seven, the same age I turned today. He was contracted to conduct *Tristan und Isolde*, *Don Giovanni*, *Die Walküre*, *Siegfried*, and *Fidelio* for the Metropolitan Opera's season. He carried with him the score for the Seventh, which he was revising. And he carried the trauma of the death of his daughter Maria Anna, from scarlet fever and diphtheria.

Putzi, as Mahler called her, was not even five years old when she died, on 12 July 1907. Her funeral was two days later in the Vienna suburb of Grinzing, near the *Wienerwald* where Mahler loved to walk. She was openly regarded as his favorite child, and yet scholars claim that no letters survive revealing his thoughts on her loss. Bruno Walter, his closest confidant at the time, wrote that Mahler was "a broken man," outwardly displaying nothing, but inside dealing with all he could handle. Alma, not the most reliable biographer, wrote little about the death of their child, but what she did emphasized an exaggerated account of Mahler's diagnosis with heart disease, a diagnosis coming so soon after the blow of losing *Putzi* that it "marked the beginning of the end for [him]."

Lacking any direct account of Mahler's feelings at the time, biographers writing about *Putzi*'s death usually mention the *Kindertotenlieder*, or Songs on the Death of Children, which Mahler had composed several years earlier based on poems by Friedrich Rückert. Some writers, Alma included, have even foolishly suggested that Mahler presaged *Putzi*'s death with those songs.

"*Ach, zu schnell erlosch'ner Freudenschein!*" runs the last line of one *lied* (fulfilling my biographer's duty). "Alas, too soon, my light of joy extinguished!" That at least could be considered prescient.

How did Mahler actually deal with *Putzi*'s death? Did he cradle her for the two days before her burial? Did he hold her cold, dead hand? Could he tear his gaze away from her frail body illumined in the darkness? Is the smell from a single corpse as omnipresent as the smell that surrounded Carlo during the war? How long can you watch a tiny chest that doesn't rise and fall, irrationally hoping it will start to move with tiny breaths? (*La mia Lucia!*) Once you exhaust your reservoir of tears, do you stop crying or *fles tamen*? Can one actually weep dry, airy despair? Do all parents feel the same at such times? Did Lucia's mother think the same terrible thoughts as Mahler? As Mary, who cradled her crucified son on Golgotha?

These lines of questioning can't continue. There are no answers for most of them as the witnesses can't be produced. Except for Mahler. The scholars are wrong. He did leave a record of how he felt. And I have it.

• • •

New York City suffered a massive blackout in the summer of 1977. It began on the night of July 13 and lasted more than twenty-four hours in parts of the city. I was listening to the *Goldberg Variations* when the record slowed its rotation and then stopped. Glenn Gould was intoning his way toward the end of the *Canone alla Quinta*, and I knew that after the next track I would have to get up and flip the record to begin the second half. My lamp was already off, in a futile attempt to neutralize the sweltering heat, and I thought for a moment that the eccentric pianist had somehow managed to sneak away from his keyboard for a drink. (I still tense up when listening to those final notes, wondering if Glenn will walk away again.) Losing power was a common occurrence in my squat though, so I realized what had happened and got up, put the tonearm on its rest, slipped the record into its paper jacket, replaced the cardboard cover I had fashioned for the phonograph, and climbed into bed. Falling asleep, I didn't detect any departure from the normal nocturnal noises of the streets.

Still without electricity when I awoke, I decided to investigate. Sidewalks were crowded but businesses were closed, metal gates pulled down. Some windows were broken, all darkened. I saw a few stores being robbed, but this was ordinary enough on the Lower East Side, so I just looked the other way and walked as quickly as I could.

A man sold popsicles out of a cooler in the doorway of a corner bodega. There was a line of ten people. By the time I reached the front, I had learned the whole city was without power. He was selling his stuff before it melted or was stolen.

I shut my eyes and listened. It had been an abnormally hot summer and I had been aware, whenever I went walking, of the continual drone of overhead air-conditioning units. That day however the urban buzz was missing its electrical component. It was as if an orchestra tuning on the A had lost all its violas. *Voila!* I looked up and saw dozens of faces staring out, hoping for relief. Aurally conscious of the absence of electricity, the white noise felt almost oppressive. I put my head down and headed toward Lincoln Center, because that's where I went when I didn't know where else to go.

• • •

Carlo claims to have kept a pet *lucertola* beginning in late February 1944. While the skittery wall lizards are found throughout Italy, I cannot imagine how he managed to keep one as a pet. Carlo named his lizard Stellio, from the Latin *stella*, or star. The word *stellio* does not appear on the left-hand Latin pages of *Metamorphoses*, but in an English footnote to a story about Ceres, the goddess of agriculture. Searching for her daughter, who has been kidnapped by Pluto, she comes across an old woman who kindly offers her a drink. She accepts, but a "coarse, saucy boy" standing nearby mocks the grieving goddess, calling her greedy. Ceres is quick to anger and turns the boy into a lizard. Ovid explains that the starry, bright spots on the lizard's back are eponymous, simply, "i.e. *stellio*, a lizard or newt."

Several bizarre anecdotes involving Carlo's *lucertola* are recorded throughout the second volume of *Metamorphoses*. Stellio supposedly lived in an extra film pack adapter—basically a thin, metal box—that Carlo carried in his jacket pocket. At night, he fitted the adapter to the back of his Speed Graphic;

adjusted the focal-plane shutter, really just a slotted curtain, to its widest setting; and removed the slide, thereby releasing the lizard into the bowels of his camera, where he had already placed insects for it to eat. (I've never gotten up the nerve to ask a professional photographer what effect such an interjection, if it had actually occurred, would have had on the functionality of the camera.) In the morning, Carlo somehow wrangled Stellio back into the film pack, replaced the slide, and detached the adapter, all without killing or maiming the lizard.

Carlo also transcribed pseudo-Socratic discussions he imagined he had with Stellio. Sample:

> C: Do the ghosts of all the dead soldiers I have photographed live inside my camera?
> S: Indeed they do. Chained and wailing in an inconsequential heap on the camera's ceiling. A pile of tissue-thin Prometheuses. Their tears keep me awake all night. Force me to cling to the sides or feel them raining down on me.
> C: How do I process them? Get them out?
> S: Shed your own layers.
> C: And then they will be delivered?
> S: Then they will have access to your soul.
> C: Will you find peace if I take on your burden?
> S: You would crumble under the load.

I believe Carlo created Stellio's consciousness to assuage his tortured mind. Or as a consequence of said mind. Or both. He needed to feel responsible for nurturing life, as well as documenting death. And he needed to disembody his doubt, his faithlessness.

I am uncertain whether the actual dead lizard in *Metamorphoses* is that of Stellio-the-pet. Flattened *lucertole* lie on every Italian road that has automobile traffic, and a tank with its wide treads would have been an even more effective killing machine, so Carlo could have scraped a dead lizard off the ground whenever he wanted.

If he did develop an attachment to one specific *stellio*, one which he cared for and talked to and then watched die, the act of burying the body in his books is another example of his inability to let go of the past. (Still he weeps.) Such a loss would have furthered his collapse. Carlo could not move on because he held too tightly to his dead. And each new death that he witnessed, each loved one who left, widened the cracks, his sanity slipped further away. He didn't lose it completely, however, until he was the one who did the killing.

• • •

Juilliard students sat solo or grouped in trios or quartets on the benches north of the Met. Couples crowded the Milstein Plaza steps. My walk uptown had been dizzying. The whole of Manhattan seemed to be on the streets, luxuriating in an impromptu day off, while on the boundaries of my hearing, sirens faded in and out, shifting frequencies as Doppler dictated. Smoke from burning buildings in boroughs north and east spiraled on the horizon, glimpsed between the shimmering skyscrapers.

Wanting to get away from crowds, I skirted the rippling reflecting pool where basking teenagers dangled their feet, and went down the cold, sunless stairway to Amsterdam Avenue. Outside the lower entrance to the music library, a man in jeans and a short-sleeved denim shirt smoked a cigarette. I approached him. (Our meeting was not documented, taking place before the era of the omnipresent security camera, but if it had been, the video may have been of interest to anyone prosecuting prior crimes, either his or mine.)

I assumed that he, like me, was a potential patron, a powerless nomad looking to escape the heat. I was wrong. He was nothing like me.

I asked him for a cigarette, and as he handed me his pack, he remarked that I looked familiar. I shrugged and said nothing, handing the pack back. After accepting a light, I said thanks and started to walk past him, but he called after me.

"You tryin' a get in the library, you can't. Not open today."

I stopped and turned toward him.

"Are you sure?"

"I'm security. So yeah. I'm sure. I know all." He smiled broadly, but the cigarette clenched between his front teeth made the warmth seem sinister. He took a drag.

He explained that he usually worked at the Fifth Avenue branch, but because of the blackout, he had been sent here to cover for someone who hadn't shown up for work. I thought of all the books I had stolen from the Rose Reading Room and began to fidget, nervously clenching and unclenching my grip on the carrying strap of Carlo's camera.

"Even closed buildings need security today, right? You a photographer?"

"Sort of. But I just take pictures of people. Like souvenirs."

"Souvenirs, huh." He laughed. "You go out last night an take some souvenirs?"

"No. I didn't know. I just went to bed."

"Well, you wouldn't a found too many people to memorialize," he drew out the last word, five syllables, each sounded separately. "Was a bunch a fuckin' animals out there."

He held my gaze as he said it, seeking a reaction. If his attention had wavered, I likely would have left, not because the assessment was said with malice, it wasn't—in fact it came out almost dubious, the unstated subject we, despite its incongruence—but because he was intimidating. And not in the way authority normally was intimidating. His swagger was more akin to that of a potential menace I would identify on the street and then avoid by quietly crossing to the other side. But I had walked right up to this one. I was nervous. Even though we stood in the shade, I became conscious of the sweat rolling down the sides of my face. I waited for him to release me, but he continued to talk.

He lived alone up on 106th Street but had been down at the P & G when the power went out. As the extent of the blackout became known, he finished his beer and started to walk home with a woman who lived in his building.

"People were everywhere. Comin' outta buildings. Restaurants. No one wanted to be inside. At first it just seemed like a big block party. Talkin'. Drinkin'. But the more uptown we went the more fuckin' nuts it got. Breakin' glass. And people jumpin' outta windows with TVs. 'Lectronics. Food. Anything they could carry. And it wasn't just one person. It was like four. Five. Ten at a time. Kids runnin' all over the place. Women. It was loud. Sounded like we were walkin' into a war zone. Gunshots echoin' everywhere. Finally we decided this was just too good to miss. Ya know? Here." He held out his open pack to me again, still not letting me look away.

"Can I … ?" And I motioned with the unlit cigarette, causing him to finally stop scrutinizing me as he dug his lighter out of a breast pocket. As he was replacing it, I exhaled and looked down at my feet. Breathed deep.

"What would you a done? You ever steal anything?"

I looked up, and regretted it immediately, as once again I felt trapped, examined, as if he were searching my face and my answers for a weakness. But I answered. Truthfully.

"I sometimes … My film. Usually I take that. But just one roll at a time."

"You think there's a difference between what you do and what we did last night?"

"Maybe? You didn't mean to do …" Not knowing what he wanted me to say, I hesitated, and he wasn't going to wait while I deliberated.

"Look, this was a free pass, kid. A chance to make my life a little bit better. I gotta job. But I do what I gotta do. I tried to be a cop but couldn't afford the academy 'cause I gotta kid I hadda support. So I dropped out and started doing this. Then after two years, my old lady just took off. Took my son. Never told me where."

I wanted to say I was sorry, tell him about Mamma, but he wasn't done.

"Listen. There were all kinds a people out there last night. I saw people I know are teachers. I saw a woman I know has three kids. I saw a lawyer knock a guy out cold to get the bottle a vodka he was reachin' for. Lawyer coulda bought fifty of 'em. But we were never gonna be the ones arrested. We're the people you don't expect to see runnin' outta buildings carryin' cash registers. Jewelry. So we become invisible. Right or wrong, that's the way it is. That is this city. The cops are just as fucked up as the rest a society. Maybe even more because they have the power. And they abuse it, just like the rest of us. I saw a cop last night stick two guys inna trunk of his car. And then put the stereo they had stolen in the back seat." He punctuated the last two words by poking the air with his cigarette. "You think that was gonna go to the precinct? That was goin' in his livin' room. Don't think that there ain't times you gotta look. The other. Way. You do what's necessary. You gotta lie? You. Lie. You gotta steal? You. Steal. You got a lot of growin' up to do if you don't know that."

"I didn't … I don't. I know. I ran away. I know that sometimes, sometimes …" I faltered.

"You ran away? My parents died when I was nine. My granny raised me. But what, you just decided that you knew everything you needed a know? You didn't need a mom? You didn't need a dad? I tell you what, kid. You think I don't know you? You think I don't see you hidin' behind that giant camera and stuffin' books into your bag every time you leave the library? You think I don't pay any attention? You think I'm no good at my job?"

"No. I always …"

"I see you wearin' the same thing every time you come in. I know you probably don't have a pot. To. Piss in. You ran away. Well, if you wanna read a book when you're all alone at night. Wonderin' why mommy and daddy don't love you. Well then, be my guest."

I was shaking. Not out of fear anymore. Or anger. But because I felt flayed, laid bare, not just by his bravado, but by the fact that everything he had said was accurate.

"You're a kid. You're scroungin' what, ten bucks a day? Twenty?" He swung his cigarette in front of my face, as a censer. "Whenever you're ready a quit scroungin', you come find me. If you don't get caught, son, then you are not. A. Criminal."

I cringed, not at the epithet "criminal" but at the label "son." And he saw. He had meant it innocuously, but strange as it may seem, a man had never called me son. He had found the weakness he had been seeking. Satisfied, he nodded, picked a piece of tobacco off the tip of his tongue, and walked past me into the library.

• • •

About sixty pages before the *corpus lucertola*, Ovid relates a story that is essential to understanding Carlo's demise. The tale centers around Juno, the eternally jealous goddess who spends so much of her time punishing mortal women and their kin because of the liaisons of her husband Jupiter. In fact, Juno's entry in the index lists seventeen such instances of revenge, including the story of Bacchus's birth. Semele, his mother, trysts with Jupiter but does not live long enough to be punished, as she is incinerated *in flagrante delicto* after trying to mate with Jupiter in all his godly glory. Not wanting to lose the child, Jupiter retrieves the zygote from her burning womb and gestates it in his thigh. Once Bacchus is born, he is given over to his aunt Ino and uncle Athamas, who do not live happily ever after.

Juno, stung by Bacchus's very existence, enlists the Fury Tisiphone to drive Ino and Athamas insane. Tisiphone first hurls two of the *colubra*, or serpents, from her hair at the couple. But as the poisonous snakes slide over them, "No wounds their bodies suffer; 'tis their minds that feel the deadly stroke." Furthering their madness, the Fury douses the couple with a bloody concoction that includes "strange hallucinations and utter forgetfulness, crime and tears, mad love of slaughter." The results are definitive. Athamas snatches their son Learchus from Ino's breast, swings his small body in the air like a lariat and smashes his head into a rock. Ino flees with their daughter, climbs a high cliff, and jumps into the sea, the water churning white where they hit.

These pages are covered in gore, clotted and spotted with so much dried blood and hair and skin that many individual words are blotted out completely. Of course Carlo stuck a photo in there, too. It is a black-and-white shot of a boy, no more than ten years old, sprawled on the ground. I no longer need to look at the print to see it in my mind, I simply shut my eyes and there he is.

The child wears a light gray, long-sleeved shirt and short pants of the same hue. He has on no shoes, like seemingly every child Carlo encountered. He has boyish curly locks that match the matted hair in the book—as I'm certain his scalp would match the skin. His head is smashed, encircled by a halo of dark gray blood so radially constant that it evokes an Orthodox icon. A lubricious black rock rests near the head.

Only once did I pry the photo free from the blood to read

what Carlo had written: "Learchus learns my madness. Let *oblivia mentis* come! *Chaos vincit omnia.*"

• • •

My twentieth birthday was a cause for some reevaluation. The conversation the day of the blackout shadowed my mind, and that plus the arbitrary milestone of leaving my teens behind made me introspective. In the three years since running away, I had done nothing except subsist. I was no closer to finding my father than when he had been dead. I did not want to be a photographer, especially the trivial type I had become. And, perhaps most significantly, the novelty of hardship had lost its interest. I was tired of struggling.

But neither was I ready to concede. I never considered going back to Corona. I didn't yet consider seeking out the security guard to see what he had meant by his open-ended offer. In fact, I didn't reach any kind of a verdict that day. (The stakes were not as great as what I'm facing currently.) But I did resolve to try harder, whatever that meant.

For the next two months, it meant very little. In my defense, I wasn't helped by the things outside my control, all of which seemed to deteriorate. The city was bleak and broke. Thousands of teachers had been laid off. Budgets for emergency services had been slashed. And while these didn't directly affect me, they contributed to the general malaise of my surroundings. Everything seemed dirty and forgotten and unloved; and the dirt, the neglect, the abandonment made the city a more depressing place to live.

Vanessa moved out, without leaving a note. I went across the hall one morning—it was frigid outside and that made her frisky—and everything was gone. Even her radio. She didn't have a lot, but she couldn't have carried all her things alone. Someone must have come to pick her up during the night. I don't know how I missed them. I could have helped. I was surprised she didn't say good-bye. We did share a lot.

Libraries were open less often, because of the continued fiscal decline, although I had already been avoiding the main branch, afraid of being arrested, and the music library, not wanting another lecture. As a result, I spent most of my time alone, most of it in my room. I built the darkroom in the closet and developed the prints I hadn't gotten to in the spring and summer. Since Vanessa had left, I tried to sell some nudes of her to local artists, but she had modeled for most of them personally and they'd gotten what they wanted from her.

Finally, a focused campaign to stop shoplifting, which had launched in the city's major department stores at the onset of the decade, was now running rampant. It seemed every mom-and-pop store had hung a sign telling me that I was being watched. In the weeks before Thanksgiving 1977, I got chased out of so many stores, including once by a gun-toting old man who threatened for two blocks to shoot me before I lost him down an alley, that I considered throwing Carlo's camera into a dumpster and being done with it. I kept it, its *numen* too enchanting, but I forced myself—finally—to find another job to supplement my income, take the pressure off of making pictures.

The first work I found was guarding Christmas-tree lots on the sidewalks from midnight until 6 a.m. It was not a terribly taxing task, but it paid well, despite the fact that I never once sold a tree. I rested and read under a tarp, trying to stay warm while distinguishing the sounds of rustling trees from that of trees being rustled. I also found temporary holiday employment sitting behind the counter at a used-book store on Broadway where no one seemed to buy books, only loiter.

I did other jobs that didn't last much longer than a month, but in early March, I began working in a diner, doing everything from helping unload deliveries to busing tables. The owners were an elegant Greek couple I knew only as Mr. and Mrs. Moulakis. They appeared to have their hands in several Hellenic pies throughout the city and would often send me to a different restaurant, either one they owned or one to which they owed a favor, each day of the week.

After a three-day stint over Easter weekend at one of their diners eight blocks north of Lincoln Center, Mr. Moulakis approached me and said he and his wife liked my work "ethos," meaning I showed up on time, did my job well, and "went away." That's what they wanted from an employee. He said that they owned a rooming house on 94th Street just off of 10th Avenue where, in exchange for fifty dollars a month, I could rent a cold-water flat with a shower at the end of the hall.

I was elated. Six months since I had decided to make a change, and I was on my way out of the Lower East Side. And I hadn't had to compromise. I hadn't had to steal anymore. And I hadn't had to lie. I felt proud of myself. In my eagerness to move I actually splurged on a taxi, one of only two times I took a cab in the years that I lived in Manhattan. I didn't have to say good-bye to anyone. I just left.

• • •

All the photographs Carlo kept after the Chaos photo are filed in volume two of *Metamorphoses*, which is dominated by the Trojan war and its aftermath. It seems as if he knew that day, May 18, 1944, according to a subsequent annotation, marked a turning point for him. Before the child was killed, Carlo was simply a photographer, an observer. After it—concomitant with it really—he became a combatant, a killer. Which is not to say that the photo necessarily documents a crime. He was in the middle of a war, and I assume that even Signal Corps members carried a weapon. But whether or not it was legal, it haunted him, and his photography reflects the change.

In the first volume of *Metamorphoses*, and in the few early photos filed in volume two, Carlo's focus is relatively prosaic for wartime—the countryside, battlefields, day-to-day activities, his relationship with Lucia, and of course, casualties, including Astraea's mother, Lucia, Seco, and Learchus. Of those ninety-four photographs, all except one—the Wedding Tree photo—show at least part of a person. And most of them make eye contact with the camera, even some of the dead, who are framed to suggest that if their eyes would simply open one last time, the connection that Carlo was seeking could be made.

In volume two, there are just sixty photos, and if there are people in them, they are all dead or will be momentarily. While one person cannot die more than the next, one can presumably experience more pain while doing the dying. Volume two documents that type of death. No one dies from a bullet wound. They die from maiming, from mutilation, from torture. For the dead of volume two, death was a welcome relief from the continued pain of living. These photos include the soldier dismembered by the bouncing Betty and the German tank driver whose skull is split open.

Most of the shots in volume two, however, are unpeopled, abstract, almost artsy, including my favorite of Carlo's photos, aesthetically. It shows a cratered landscape, the foreground barren except for a few burned stumps and skeletal trees. The frame is divided according to the golden mean by crumbling stone walls that may once have been ramparts or fences or parts of a home. Carlo quoted *The Waste Land* on the reverse:

> Dead mountain mouth of carious teeth that cannot spit
> Here one can neither stand nor lie nor sit
> There is not even silence in the mountains

Beneath those words is rewritten a Latin phrase that appears highlighted in blood opposite the photo: "*Et sunt, qui credere possint esse deos?*" Translated it reads: "And are there those who can believe that there are gods?" Based on the color of the blood and a stray hair that managed to remain stuck in it all these years, I have concluded that Carlo made this photo as he was fleeing the scene of the boy's murder.

• • •

My new home was comforting. And while the building was overcrowded, my living in it was legal, so I felt confident that my room would remain mine. I worked more often, in more different ways, than at any point since running away, and I was actually saving money. But despite no longer scrounging, I still lacked a *raison d'etre*. I found one on May 10, 1978, when my desire to seek my father was reawakened, fully refreshed from its hibernation.

That afternoon I sat down at the diner to have a cup of coffee and glance through the paper. The *Times* headline, which customers had been discussing all morning, blazed across two-thirds of the front page: MORO SLAIN; BODY FOUND IN ROME; WEST'S LEADERS ASSAIL TERROR. The accompanying photo showed the "bullet-riddled body" of the former Italian Prime Minister Aldo Moro, lying in the trunk of a small car, his neck bent sharply to the left so he would fit.

Moro, the *Times* reported, had been kidnapped fifty-four days earlier by the Red Brigades, a Communist-leaning terrorist group. He was shot "at least ten times" and left in the little red car on a side street near Rome's Jewish Ghetto. The article, which continued on page A16, also included a chronology of the ordeal. One of the dates highlighted is March 18, when the kidnappers issued their initial communiqué stating that Moro would undergo "a people's trial." Because of an editing oversight, that date's item is printed twice, although there are some textual differences, cf. the Red Brigades "affirm" responsibility in the first version, then they "claim" it in the next. The last sentence of both is identical, however, describing a photo showing Moro "in front of a flag of the Red Brigades."

Reading the phrase the second time, my eyes drifted back to the top of the timeline where the photo was reproduced. It is a grainy black-and-white shot of Moro from the chest up. Behind him hangs a banner with the words *Brigate Rosse* surrounding a circle with a white star inside. Moro wears a white shirt, open wide at the collar and, perhaps because it was only the first or second day of his captivity, is almost smiling, a look of bemused resignation on his face. He stares straight into the camera. Our eyes locked and the shutter in my mind was tripped. I blinked and tore my gaze away, dragged it to the bottom of the photo. Credited to United Press International, no photographer specified. But I didn't need the name. I knew who took the shot. I ripped out the whole page and stuffed in my pocket.

When I got out of work, I walked for a long while, up around the park and down, through neighborhoods in which I probably shouldn't have walked. When I finally got to my room that evening, I sat and stared into Moro's eyes, trying to see what he saw. Was it really Carlo in front of him? After all, lots of people look at the camera when they are being photographed. I compared the photo to all the shots in *Metamorphoses*. For days I tried to convince myself that I was wrong. But I couldn't.

And it didn't matter. I had needed something to spur the search for my father, and I had found it. We believe what we want to believe. I didn't need proof. What I needed was money, and a lot more than I could make taking Polaroids or cleaning dirty dishes off of tables. I would have to do something else. Whatever it took.

• • •

In April 1908, the Metropolitan Opera traveled to Boston for a series of eight performances, three under the baton of Gustav Mahler. He and Alma were set to return to Austria in May, but his mind was already on home, having realized that while he enjoyed many aspects of life in America, he was—and always would be—Viennese. Walking up Washington Street after the 8 April evening performance of *Die Walküre*, Gustav's mind still reverberated with the aching strings of Wotan's farewell to his daughter, still burned with the flickering piccolo of Loge's eternal fire. He would have to clear his head before going to bed.

The waxing quarter moon drew his eye to the illumined, ivy-covered steeple of the Old South Meeting House. Seeing it standing tall and solitary against the cool night sky, he took leave of his companions and turned west at the next block. He would allow himself a quick stroll through the Commons before returning to his rooms at the Parker House. Since being diagnosed with a weak heart, he had been careful not to overexert himself, especially after conducting a work as taxing as *Walküre*, but that night he needed to walk.

Once in the park, he rambled, sticking to the relatively flat ground to the east and south. He ruminated on the performance of the principles. Marta's pathos, particularly on "*Der diese Liebe*" and "*ihm innig vertraut*," had shaken him. Anton had gotten to him even more poignantly on "*Leb' wohl*" and "*der freier als ich, der Gott*." One freer than I, the God. Such a complex sentiment. During the ensuing farewell and all the way until Wotan's kiss stole away Brünnhilde's divinity, he and Anton had been in perfect sync. He had sat on the orchestra, ornamenting the God's *abschied* in a whispering *piano*, permitting them to rise to *forte* only once, on the agony of "*unseligen*." Unfortunate. Ill-fated.

He thought of his little *Putzi*, but immediately stopped. He still could not always handle the emotions, and now, in the middle of the night, was not the time to test himself. He looked up and across the expanse of the park. Near the top of Beacon Hill, twin, towering elm trees framed the gold-domed State House. He made for them, walking briskly, taking long strides as he used to do, striving to free his mind from the haunting memory of his daughter.

When he had almost reached the top, something flitted across the grass to his left. Startled, he stopped, his breath caught in his chest. Looking around, he was aware only of his heart beating *energico, sehr rasch*. It had certainly been a cloud moving swiftly past the moon, he told himself, but the timpani pounding away in his chest made him wonder if the shadow had lodged inside him. It was late. He should get back. Tomorrow was *Don Giovanni*, more death and reincarnation. He turned right and headed down the hill, trying to ignore the feeling of defeat that crept after him at having abandoned the summit, as abject and low as it was.

Reaching the bottom of the slope, a cool mist clouded the night. He turned up Tremont Street at the church and through the haze saw the Parker House at the end of the block. Almost there, he relaxed his pace and glanced to his left through the iron fence of the burying ground with its squat slate tombstones. Feeling more at ease and not ready to battle Morpheus just yet, he passed under the archway and entered the cemetery.

A verse from *Die chinesische Flöte* (The Chinese Flute) floated to the forefront of his consciousness: "*Im Mondschein auf den Gräbern hockt eine wild-gespenstische Gestalt.*" "In the moonlight on the gravestones crouches a wildly-ghost-like-eerie form." The book, which he had purchased his first day in Boston from a small German bookseller, comprised Hans Bethge's translations of Chinese poetry. It was already imprinting itself on his mind. As he walked the foggy footpaths, his mind was an olio of Li Po's graveyard image and Wotan saying farewell to his daughter forever and the looming shadow of the murdered Commendatore.

Suddenly he stopped in fright. Standing in the darkness before him, bestride a blocky granite grave marker, was *Putzi*. It was she, wasn't it? He imagined that he screamed but all remained silent. He stood frozen for several moments and then slowly started to lift an arm, just to adjust his glasses. *Putzi* appeared to giggle at the movement and opened her eyes wide. She looked around, waved quickly, whispered "Papi," and was gone.

• • •

The final photographs included in *Metamorphoses* are thirty-three enigmatic shots of apparent nothingness, all filed in Book XI. For thirty-two of those shots, nothingness is exactly what Carlo got. The photos have no artistic value, no studied chiaroscuro, no geometric tension, nothing. They are blurs, light leaks, almost accidental exposures.

If they were made purposefully, as I believe they were, maybe he was trying to capture something that moved too quickly for him, an animal or someone chasing him or an aspect of the landscape seen at night out the window of a train. Or maybe it was some phantom he imagined he saw. Stellio's ghost. Or Learchus. Or Lucia. Conceivably he could simply have been using up all his remaining film, but why would he have then kept the results.

Regardless of his motives, none of the pictures has a description on its back, no clue or quotation to lead the viewer (only ever me) to enlightenment. And the photos are not dated either, so I cannot even swear that they were taken after *The Waste Land* photo. Given their location and the deterioration of Carlo's mental capacity, however, I am confident they were. In fact the only embellishment visible upon first glance, is a number stamped in red Roman numerals on the front, top left of each photo. I have no idea how these were created. Nothing like them appears anywhere in *Metamorphoses*.

The key to the set is photo XXXIII. The first time I really studied *Metamorphoses*, I picked up that shot, flipped it over a couple of times and decided it was an exposed film, a casualty of a hasty Stellio feeding session maybe, and replaced it where it rested, among the pages describing a visit of Iris, the goddess of the rainbow, to the home of "sluggish Sleep." It is one of the most fantastic, imaginative passages in Ovid's magnum opus. Perhaps the only section comparable for escapist *mise-en-scène* is the cave of Envy in Book II, "filthy with black gore," "full of a numbing chill," where the goddess sits eating snakes.

I returned to photo XXXIII often, not to look at it, but to read about the "deep recess within a hollow mountain" where the chamber of Sleep lies. Poppies and other soporific herbs grow by the entrance, which is unattended so that no guard can holler "Halt!" or "Who goes there?" (Thankfully my guard went quietly, too.) There are no doors because doors can creak. "Mute silence dwells." The only noise comes from the gentle waves of the Lethe, which invite slumber (as they did in my initial liminal life).

Somnus, the god of Sleep, child of Darkness and Night, reposes on a soft, black couch with a black blanket. He can hardly lift his eyes or his head. He is surrounded by "*somnia vana*," translated as "empty dream-shapes." In neatly penciled marginalia likely born in a classroom lecture, Carlo elaborated:

> *Vana* is not just empty in the sense of containing nothing, it means much more, it is *sans* meaning, fruitless, in vain (from *vanus*, its root). And isn't that what our dreams really are, meaningless forms which can never be realized. What a wistful characterization and wise.

I clearly recall the moment I first saw him. It was long before the blackout, and I was seated along the middle aisle in the Rose Reading Room, poring over volume two. At the instant I turned back the page and exposed the photo, a cloud blew past outside, allowing the sun to shine down through the great arched window above me for the first time all day. The ray that was released reflected off of both the photo and the table, blinding me momentarily. So bright was the glare that I bent forward and closed my eyes.

When I began to reopen them, they addressed the photo from an oblique angle. And in that inky darkness, I finally saw, staring back at me for the first time, two eyes, the two eyes that had been hidden from me for so many years, hidden over the couch, hidden on the ship, hidden behind *Cerberus* and the rain. Two eyes in the uniform black matte. Carlo's two eyes. I grabbed the picture and looked at it closer, but I saw nothing. I tilted it at an angle, shielded my gaze with my other hand. There again in the shadow, just discernible, they popped back open.

I detected a face surrounding them. The unmistakable visage of horror. The eyes opened wide, trying to gather every stray photon bouncing around the gloom. The mouth agape. Outside the face and neck, nothing else is visible. He is spectral, no body below, no surroundings, just a wisp of fear floating in the dark. I turned over the photo and on the back, so faint that I forgave myself for missing it so many times, was a word. It wasn't written with any writing implement, but was scratched into the backing, maybe with a dirty fingernail. HELP.

I shivered and the sunlight disappeared. I flipped back to the front of the photo, searched askance for my father's eyes, found them once more, and began to cry.

• • •

My initial effort to track Carlo after seeing the Moro photo in the paper took me back to the International Center for Photography, which I had only visited a handful of times since photographing "Still I Weep." I had not seen Capa during any of those visits, but happily he was at the center the day I returned. I told the young man at the desk that my father was a Magnum photographer and I had a question for Mr. Capa about his latest submission.

I was worried he wouldn't remember me, but when he came out, Capa greeted me by saying, "The boy who takes pictures of pictures." I was relieved. Without getting into specifics, I explained to him that I had come across what I suspected was a photograph taken by my father, and I wondered if he had been heard from lately.

Coincidentally or not—and I firmly believe the latter—my timing was fortuitous. Capa said Carlo had sent in a few rolls of film several weeks earlier, photos of the political unrest in Italy. Italian politics had been particularly unstable and violent since the late 1960s. Hundreds of people had been murdered, the Moro assassination being the most high profile, and bombings and other acts of terrorism were routine. The violence would continue into the 1980s, earning the era the sobriquet *anni di piombo*, or Years of Lead, because of the number of bullets fired.

I asked Capa if I could see the photos and he showed them to me. They were pretty spectacular shots of a far-left demonstrator shooting at a policeman. Carlo had established some good contacts, Capa said, and he expected photos would be coming in regularly. He agreed to leave word for me at the diner whenever new film arrived.

With Carlo placed under makeshift surveillance, I turned my attention to financing the search. I pretended at planning some big heist for a couple of days but really it was just steeling my nerves. I knew that there was nothing that I could legally do to earn enough money to fly to Italy and still retain the fiscal freedom of movement to chase Carlo. So on my first day off I returned to the Rose Reading Room. It took four trips before I ran into the security guard.

I thought about concocting an elaborate story to explain the nearly eleven months that it took me to seek him out, but in the end I knew he would see right through it, so I walked up to him, said hello and got it over with.

"I'm ready."

And that was all it took. He told me to come back at closing time on Tuesday, when the library was open late, and we would go to meet the man who could solve all my problems.

The morning of the meeting, I had second thoughts, but Capa called me at work to tell me that a new roll of film from my father had arrived. I was resigned to my fate.

I was introduced to a man who looked much more like a librarian than a criminal. He, or one of his acquaintances, I never learned which, trafficked in stolen manuscripts, maps, anything that came on paper. Initially I stole supposed first editions from bookstores around the city. Once a week I met with either the security guard, who never gave me a name (and I never asked) or the librarian, and gave them what I had. I quickly learned that any book I could steal easily was not very valuable. I made only a couple hundred dollars by the beginning of 1979.

After I expressed frustration at the pace of my income, the librarian told me to think bigger. He said most university libraries were blindly trusting of students and loathe to report anything stolen from their collections because of institutional obstinacy regarding theft. They either didn't want to believe it happened or didn't want to devote the resources to stopping it. Even the Morgan Library did not have terribly tight security once you gained access. It was the only advice he ever gave me but it was enough.

The next week at our meeting, the security guard handed me a student ID. (Obviously a forgery, but no one ever noticed this fact. Someone—the guard, the librarian, an acquaintance—could get any document, with any name, at any time. I never asked where they came from. And I never had to pay for them. They were just provided when required.) I took my new identity uptown to Columbia. In the next year I stole from every university library in New York City, Boston, Philadelphia, and the state of New Jersey. I stole from historical societies, museums, and antiquarians. I stole maps, sketches, letters, photographs, manuscripts. Once I had stolen, I never returned. My bank account, set up in Europe with the assistance of the librarian, began to grow much more rapidly. He told me I had *fingerspitzengefühl*, meaning I could sense valuable things with my fingers, despite knowing nothing about the objects.

By March 1980 I was ready to leave. I had tickets for the middle of May, the eighteenth actually, to honor Mahler's death day. I had enough money to follow Carlo for several years. And I had a passport. And even though that passport is long gone, the name that was on it remains my name today. Whoever forged the document misread what I had written, however, so instead of the meaningless anagram of Mahler I had chosen, I became—perhaps more aptly—Miles Ambler.

Then, ten days before I was to depart, as I sat scanning the papers for any photos attributed to Carlo, Bruno Walter's name in a headline caught my eye. It was a tiny article in the middle of the Arts section at the bottom of the page. It stated that Walter's memorabilia, including the original draft manuscripts for the first and third movements of Gustav Mahler's Seventh Symphony, would be on display at the Lincoln Center music library beginning at the end of the month.

I had read about the donation of Walter's estate more than two years earlier and had inquired about seeing the manuscripts. I was told that they were being archived and I would have to wait. I figured that once that had happened, I would never get access to them without being a composer or musicologist. Gradually

I had forgotten about their existence. Now they were going to be on display and I had to see them. I delayed my flight until the summer.

But the wait was interminable. By the time the Walter exhibit finally opened, I was regretting my decision to stay. It was only the end of May, but the weather had been hot and dry for weeks, putting people in mind of the sweltering summer three years earlier, the summer of the blackout. I was done at the diner, I was done stealing, I was packed and waiting. I was idle.

Then the exhibit opened and I became distracted. I went to the library whenever the gallery was open. The manuscripts, lying in shallow glass cases, were open to a different page each day, and each day I studied that page, following along to the soundtrack in my mind, seeing what had changed, if anything, from Mahler's original intent.

One morning, early in the run, the third movement manuscript was closed. As I stared disappointedly at the nearly blank cover, the blue-penciled phrase *"III Satz Entwurf"* hovering aslant above silent empty staves, I noticed ghostly lettering seemingly trapped beneath the surface of the page. I reached my hand out and remembered that there was glass in the way only when my fingers hit the top of the case.

Even though a guard sat continually outside the gallery, a research librarian often checked on the exhibit, so I anxiously waited, wanting to ask someone about the letters I seemed to see. Finally late in the afternoon, one came. I asked him about the hazy text. He said it was indeed there, I was not just seeing things. Mahler had written all over the title page, he said, but then covered it up with another sheet of paper on which he had written the simple appellation "III movement draft."

I asked whether anyone had tried to read what had been written beneath, and he replied that there were plans to remove the pasted-on sheet, but there had not been time enough before the exhibit opened. Rather than keep the entire document from the public eye, they postponed the examination of the covered-up note. Likely they were just scribblings, he said.

I dreamed about the hidden message that night and two days later, on Thursday, July 24, 1980, I completed my metamorphosis. Walking on Amsterdam, minutes before the gallery opened, I saw dozens of police cars down the block, parked behind the Met. Initially I panicked, my guilt suffusing me, they were onto me, the security guard had turned me in. But seeing no actual officers, just their vehicles, I convinced myself that I was not the reason for their presence.

Still I was on edge as I approached. I spied a lone man standing against the building, outside the library door. I didn't trust my eyes. I felt like I had gone back in time. There, in the same spot he had stood the day of the blackout more than three years earlier, was the security guard. When I got close enough that he looked up and nodded at me, I knew that day would be my last one in America.

• • •

Mahler never mentioned the incident in the Granary Burying Ground to anyone. He referred to it cryptically, and without elaboration, in a letter to Bruno Walter the ensuing summer as a "*panischen Schrecken*," or panic terror. Throughout that letter to Walter there are other small clues to the actual nature of the experience. The terror was not, Mahler wrote, the "hypochondriac fear of death" that everyone imagined it to be. He had stood "*vis-à-vis de rien*," face-to-face with nothing, and "there are perhaps no words at all" that could explain it.

As soon as he had recovered his faculties, he fled the cemetery and raced across the street into the Parker House. Once in his room, he sat down at the desk where earlier in the day he had been looking over the draft copy of the Seventh Symphony, specifically the third movement. He probably grabbed the first writing implement he could find, which was the blue pencil that he had been using to emend the orchestration, and right there on the oblong title page, he recorded the events of that evening, much as I have recounted them. (I translated them long ago with the help of an acquaintance because my German *ist nicht gut.*)

Beneath the narration, he wrote something else, something quite remarkable. From a historical and compositional point of view, the trail it leaves to *Das Lied von der Erde*, composed largely during the summer after his first stay in America, is beautifully clear. From a paternal point of view, there are times I actually feel very guilty for having it solely in my possession, wishing I could give it to one of his distant relations. (In my defense, I had to keep it, it is my souvenir.)

The last thing that Mahler wrote that night is a letter to his dear *Putzi*. It is written on the far right of the page, beneath the underlined "*Mein Abschied*." His farewell reads:

> *Meine liebende Putzerl,*
> I know now that you await my farewell wishes, so I have decided to send them to you at last. But why did you disappear so quickly and leave me all alone, O beautiful child? I would have loved to look at you a little longer. The darkness of your glance reverberates still in my heart. I cannot express in words how deeply I feel your loss. All of my prayers, all of my longing, must remain unfulfilled, however, because I know you shall never return to me, shall never again sneak down into my composing hut to share our secrets of a morning, shall never accompany me on walks through the flowers and grasses in the golden sunlight. It is late and sleep calls me now and I will go, but know that soon I will return to Wien, to my homeland, and while the thought that you will

not be there to greet me is almost unbearable, I know that the beloved Earth will blossom forth as it does each Spring, and everywhere life will begin anew. It must begin anew. For me and for you too, *Putzi*, in eternity. Forget your happiness and youth in this life and learn life anew once more.

I will think of you always, my sweet child, always and forever, forever, forever …

Your loving papi,
Gustav

• • •

Carlo's final words in *Metamorphoses* are a dialogue with Stellio. It starts with him culling lines from Ovid's text near the end of Book XV and continues in the form of a non-dogmatic Catholic mass, with Stellio as lector and Carlo the congregation, written on the endpapers. The imagined service supposedly took place on May 28, 1944, which was Pentecost, and indeed several readings associated with that feast are used, as is the *Veni creator spiritus*, a primary Pentecostal hymn. (That hymn is also the one that Mahler set to music in the first movement of his Eighth Symphony, the premiere of which took place on the date that was so recently so fateful for me.)

In the conversation, Stellio refers to his own murder ten days earlier, the same date the child called Learchus was killed. This fact convinces me that it was Learchus who killed Stellio on May 18, 1944. (Incidentally that date also marked the thirty-third anniversary of Mahler's death, thirty-three being the age of Christ when he died and also the number of photos it took to capture Carlo's eyes. And when I was supposed to flee before I … all of this means nothing. I retract it.)

The initial sentence in the dialogue is underlined on the English side and prefaced by a capital S (Stellio, Satan, salvation, not me, I'm small). It reads: "In the marketplace and around men's houses and the temples of the gods, dogs howled by night, the shades of the silent dead walked abroad and the city was shaken with earthquakes." Carlo crossed out "city" and wrote "*Roma*" in the margin. The Allies liberated Rome without much of a fight on June 4, so if Carlo is taken literally—*id est* if Rome was truly shaking, more likely from shelling than an earthquake—then the dialogue could have been created on the actual Pentecost.

The next line underscored is on the opposing Latin page and preceded by a C (Carlo, Christ, condemnation). It reads: "*non tamen insidias venturaque vincere fata praemonitus potuere deum, strictique feruntur.*" Translated: "Yet even so, the warnings of the gods were unable to check the plots of men and the advancing fates."

This pattern continues for the next seventy-five lines, with S and C claiming Ovid's sentences, phrases, sometimes just individual words. C always speaks in Latin, S in English. Their discussion touches on fate, the apotheosis of Caesar (whose soul is carried to heaven by Venus), and sons supplanting their fathers. Honestly it doesn't make a lot of sense to me and I am not going to recopy it here, when so much more can be gleaned once Carlo used his own words.

On the last Latin page of the book, Carlo drew a (blood) red rectangle around the line "*quique tenes altus Tarpeisas Iuppiter arces,*" or "Jupiter, whose temple sits high on Tarpeia's rock." The left side of the rectangle extends below the base. In the center he placed a considerable dot on *Tarpeisas* and to the right he wrote DB. On a military map, this symbol designates the command post of the enemy's defense battalion.

I believe the diagram indicates that Carlo had holed up near the Tarpeian Rock, a steep cliff on the southern side of the

Capitoline Hill, where convicted murderers and traitors were thrown to their deaths. By using the symbol for the enemy's command post, he is saying that he is under attack from within, that he was his own enemy.

The text of the mass is below. I added the parenthetical annotations years ago because I grew tired of looking them up each time I read through it.

S: In the name of my Mother, I her Son, greet the new arrival.
C: So be it.
S: Peace be with you.
C: And just who are you?
S: And God spoke all these words, saying I am the *lucertola* Stellio, which my mother Ceres hath created out of wrath. Thou shalt raise no other child after me.
C: Amen.
S: I am unclean to you among all that creep: whosoever doth touch me, when I be dead, shall be unclean until the evening.
C: *Dies saeculorum.* ("Daylight without end.")
S: A solemn reading from the Proverbs 22:15, "Foolishness is bound in the heart of a child; but the rod of correction shall drive it far from him."
C: *Qua patet orbis.* ("As far as the world extends.")
S: Further wisdom from the subsequent chapter, "Withhold not correction from the child: for if thou beatest him with the rod, he shall not die."
C: *Agere sequitur credere.* ("Action follows belief.")
S: "Thou shalt beat him with the rod, and shalt deliver his soul from hell."
C: *Animum debes mutare, non infernum.* ("You must change your soul, not your hell." Bastardization of Seneca's

paraphrase of Horace.)
S: In Acts 2:19 we have the story of today, the Pentecost, wherein the Lord doth sayeth: "And I will shew wonders in heaven above, and signs in the earth beneath; blood, and fire, and vapor of smoke."
C: *Videlicet.*
S: "The sun shall be turned into darkness, and the moon into blood, before the great and notable day of the Lord come: And it shall come to pass, that whosoever call on the name of the Lord shall be saved."
C: *In luce Tua video Lucia.* ("In your light I see Lucia.")
S: Ten days ago did I up to Heaven ascend and there from an adoring host did I hear this homily. Two trees did grow beside a mountain, and on the shorter of these trees did feed a bug. A baby bird came along, verily it was its very first *volatus*, and not knowing what to make of the bug moving in the bark, it pecked. It pecked again and eventually the beak of the bird brought about the death of the bug. Then suddenly there came a rushing mighty wind, *in esse* not as in Acts, and the trees began to creak. And the bird was sore afraid. Finally the bird tried to fly away, but at that moment the trunk of the taller tree snapped, for it had grown too tall in its desire to reach Heaven. As the tree fell, it clipped the bird on its right wing and the bird fell to the earth. Yet the Lord was merciful and the bird was not dead. But the bird could not fly, and it was as a grasshopper hopping around. Then a man came along. He saw the tree was fallen, and he wept for his father's father had planted the tree. When the man was weary of his crying, he looked down and saw he was in deep mire, as was the bird. So the man bent over the little bird and placed it on solid land. Then he picked up a rock and smote the bird. Again and again he smashed the bird,

breaking its bones, flattening its organs, until the earth ran dark red with blood. Then he took the fallen tree, sawed it with a saw, carried it to his home, and he burned it.

C: *Fuoco! Feu! Feuer!*

S: A sassy child I came into this world and from a sassy child did I depart. The Lord gave him life, he took mine, and you took his. The next permutation is? What sayest you?

C: *Abattoir.*

S: Some of Psalm 104 for our Pselebration: "Thou takest away their breath, they die, and return to their dust. Thou sendest forth thy spirit, they are created: Thou renewest the face of the earth."

C: αλλά εβασίλευσεν ο θάνατος. ("Yet death reigned" from Romans 5:14)

S: "O come, let us sing unto the Lord: let us make a joyful noise to the rock of our salvation." Salvation. Retribution. The Lord just likes singing.

C: Of the rock that begat me I am mindful and hast forgotten God. (Deut. 32:18)

S: The rock hath begat thy punishment. Be mindful.

C: I hast forgotten all.

S (chanting): Come Ceres's spiritus/Enter in my mind/ fallen upon the ground/the heart thou hast made cold/ so comforting.

C: *Infirma nostri corporis/tortus firmans perpeti.* ("To our bodies frail/give eternal torment.")

S: Drive the foe further away/Grant us peace forever.

C: *Ductore sine te praevio/vitemus omne puerum.* ("And without thee our leader/we will avoid all children.")

S: Ceres my mother is glorious.

C: "*Et Filio, que a mortuis.*" ("And the son, that has died.")

S: And this eternal confortion. [sic]

C "*In saecula, in saecula.*"
S: Amen.
C: *Sera.* ("Too late.") *Cado ego, non consurgo. In tenebra consido, sine Lucia, sine luce, sine te. In aeterna.* (Micah 7:8 bastardization. "I fall, I will not rise. In the darkness I sit, without Lucia, without light, without God.")

• • •

I approached the security guard. He smiled, genuinely this time, and pulled out his pack of cigarettes. He pointed to the Speed Graphic and mockingly asked if it was souvenir day. I said yes, and asked why he was here given that there was still electricity in the city. He said that a violinist had disappeared during intermission of the Berlin Ballet performance the previous night at the Met. They were searching for her right now.

I was about to respond when a police officer walked up. The two of them talked for a moment and then the guard turned back to me. The woman's body had just been found, he said, bound and naked at the bottom of a ventilation shaft. She had been pushed into it from the roof and fallen six stories to her death.

I was stunned, appalled that something so gruesome could happen in a place that I loved so much. I started to sweat and realized I was squeezing the handle of the Speed Graphic, clenching and releasing my grip. The guard said that he had to attend a security meeting for a few minutes, something about press inquiries.

I already knew what was going to happen. My ears were buzzing and my vision went blurry.

If I was around when he got back, something, something.

I nodded. Sure. Yes. A minute.

I watched him walk away and once he turned into the tunnel under the Met, I dropped my cigarette and entered the library. To the right was the guard's desk, obviously empty. I passed it and went into the gallery. I was alone. I looked around. Across the lobby, beyond the glass doors through which I had walked, Bruno Walter's name stared down from above his eponymous auditorium.

The frenetic beginning of the last movement of Mahler's First sounded from the speakers in the ceiling. It was the 1939 version, conducted by Walter himself, the earliest recording of that work. I walked around the gallery listening. I knew I had time. For fifteen minutes I paced. I recalled my first night on the streets when I circled the post office. I heard Walter grunt on the recording, spurring on his orchestra. I shook my head. It was pointless to try. I had known when I came in.

I checked the lobby again. Still empty. I could never come back, I knew, but that didn't really matter. I had to read what he had written. Whatever it takes. I circled around again to the display case that held the manuscript of the Seventh Symphony's third movement.

Horns were blaring. Kettledrums rolled. The winds blew on high. This was me, I was the music, living it at that very moment that I raised the Speed Graphic over my head with both hands and closed my eyes. Then I smashed the camera down into the plate glass to the far left of the score. (BOOM!)

I opened my eyes, loosened my grip on the camera, and let go of it. I never touched it again. But it wasn't really mine to begin with.

I knocked loose the pieces of broken glass with my wrist and grabbed the manuscript, brushing it off. I carefully rolled it up and walked, *nicht eilen*, not hurried, out of the gallery, turned left, and pushed through the library doors. I stumbled, blinded briefly by the sunlight, and walked right off the curb into the street. A car honked in the distance and I looked left.

The security guard wandered up the sidewalk toward me. He didn't run, but he knew. I stuck out my hand to ward him off and a cab that was driving past pulled over. My arm had cuts all over it. Blood dripped onto the road. I started to laugh. I opened the cab door and climbed inside.

Someone called my name, my old name. Milo. Milo. Milo. I didn't respond to that name any more. Milo was gone, destroyed. I swooned and slammed the door shut as the cab sped away.

4. Satz.
NACHTMUSIK.

Andante amoroso.

As my birthday ebbs into evening, my spirits wane as well. I don't feel any closer to raveling my life, let alone escaping this day unscathed. Recounting the intricacies of my nature is one thing, but taking direction from them is quite another. Perhaps there is no purpose in this exercise. Down with Jerzi! (Take responsibility. Stop blaming. The real problem is continuing to avoid Zagreb. My actions. My judgment. I brought on the *bora*. It's my trial. "*Der Hölle Rache kocht in meinem Herzen*." *Der Himmel Urteil in meinem Seele*. No tongues, not yet. Keep it together. The Queen of the Night can't take the stage because this second *nachtmusik* must be spent with a she more meaningful to me.)

I finally surrendered my seat in the café, allowing the owner to close, hurry home to his loved ones, if any awaited him, to ride out the storm. I returned to my room alone. It was a twenty-minute walk to the east, past the pedestrian district. I followed the most direct route, briefly traversing the crowded sidewalks of *Kralja Zvonimira*, turning down *Petrova*, and climbing the narrower quiet lanes until I emerged onto *Matije Gupca*.

Upon entering the building, the elderly woman who rents out the rooms corralled me in the hallway as efficiently as she had following my debarkation in the bus station. She steered me into her tiny kitchen and poured me two successive shots of homemade *šljivovica* in memory of her husband, who died five years ago today. I considered telling her we could commemorate my life instead of his death, but decided against it. I ungracefully extricated myself, left her to her memories and her tears, and took the ten stairs to my room, with the brandy burning the back of my throat.

Three hours later I awoke disoriented, uncertain whether it was twilight or dawn. I righted myself, remembered the café, and panicked at the expiring day. I grabbed my books, a couple of maps, and a handwritten letter folded neatly inside its envelope; put them in my coat pockets, envelope carefully concealed between Ovid's twin volumes; and hurried out, destination unknown, to finish my birthday recollecting.

I have ended up here, a bar in a different part of Split from where I sat this morning. I initially walked away from the sea with the hope that I could escape the brunt of the *bora*, but to my surprise, the winds had died. (Was I tried *in somnus*?) In fact it is eerily calm. *Nachtmusik noch einmal von vorn*. Still the skies slate and low, still the unrealized rain. No, the storm has not passed, my judgment not in the past, nor passed. Rather it is resting up for its final assault.

The false fair weather allowed me to walk a bit farther than I would have had I been seeking immediate shelter, but I'm glad of the extra exertion, and this tavern is quite suitable for my needs. The walls describe a warren that seemingly hides countless nooks and private rooms. (It reminds me of the tunnel leading to my Rainier tomb. I mean womb.) They're wooden walls, stained, likely from decades of cigarette smoke, although they could be painted, it's hard to discern in the dim light, which is provided exclusively by varicolored candles placed directly on the wooden tabletops. After winding my way around several turns, I selected a spot with a rectangular table, a single chair facing the passageway, a blue candle burning tall above an unfrozen wax lake.

A waiter has just set down my *slabo pivo* and left me a menu as well. It is cool here in the cozy gloom. Rejoining my subterranean shade rooting around in my *mentis antrum*, we seek one thing, the two of us: a last respite. I can't revisit my search for Carlo in the early eighties after arriving in Italy nor can I think about the despair I fought through those subsequent years. I am sick of Carlo. (Fight it off. Fought him off? Avoid that argument while you still can. Still cam. And Seco. The three-headed dog of Hell.

And the film man.) Film canister. That's what I'm looking for.

I search around on the cranial ground, in the corners, and I listen. In a convolution I feel it between my hands. I open it up and remove the movie, carefully feed the film through and make sure it is caught up on the empty rear spool. *Whir*. The white light goes away and I await the viewing.

First I hear the solo violin calling out, *amoroso*. And here she comes, that sweet, deceptive clarinet. Her transposed voice looks different on the page than it sounds in the ear. I'm following the score too. And the script. My nose sniffs. I'm touching and tasting it. All the senses engaged for just this movement. After drawing my attention with an introductory phrase, her first, lilting trill arrives, a batting of her eyes. It is written as a B on the staff—B for batting—but that is not the note that is heard. What is heard, because of transposition, is an A. And A is for Alice.

• • •

samedi, 5 mars 1988

As the sun goes down, chilly air crawls over the city, settles comfortably atop the thin layer of snow that has insulated the streets since the day before. Flurries are falling again, illuminated briefly in the diffuse Parisian streetlights, but none live long enough to reach the ground.

Inside the Salle Pleyel, *the camera focuses in on a young man and a younger woman seated next to him in the blue-and-brown bedecked semidarkness of the* deuxième balcon, *row J. They sit on the* pair *side according to the French-language* plan de salle *posted on the lobby wall, which simply means their seats are even-numbered. Specifically they occupy 318 and 320. They are strangers to each other, their unfamiliarity apparent from the armrest between them, which remains vacant, untouched.*

She clasps hands with herself atop the coat in her lap. His arms are folded across his chest. Both stare fixedly down at Daniel Barenboim, who leads the Orchestre de Paris *in Schönberg's lush, stringy* Verklärte Nacht.

The man's eyes furtively dart right, once to glimpse her shoes, almost luminous, patent-leather Mary Jane pumps that snuggly cradle black-stockinged feet; and again to spy as high as her knees, hidden beneath a long, woolen pencil skirt with buttons down its front. His curiosity is uncharacteristic. He generally keeps his eyes to himself. In fact the only reason he noticed her was because he arrived before she did and, being seated on the aisle, had to stand to let her slide by. He didn't actually look up, he rarely does, but her worsted peplum jacket brushed against the back of his hand and whatever was underneath attracted him, felt magnetic, alive.

He tries to focus on the music, but his thoughts continually return to her. He can feel that she is enjoying the performance, too. Maybe he should listen closer, try to hear with her ears. But he did that for much of his life, and now he keeps his aural emotions close. Still there is a real energy coming from her and some force is making him feel like he should say something, do something, which he quickly realizes would be ridiculous at this moment.

He steals another look, this time up past her hands. Dark hair, the exact hue of which is impossible to discern in the darkened hall, hangs just past her left breast. Eyes and ears back to Barenboim. Was her blouse blue? The strings have turned lighter now, exultant almost, as the piece nears its end.

He peeks right again, almost against his will, staring higher still. Smooth profile, pale cheek. It turns. Caught! He looked too long. Overcompensating in panic, his head follows his eyes darting back to the orchestra pit, causing him to end up regarding his left leg. He sheepishly raises his chin and faces forward, doesn't notice her grin, and listens attentively until Barenboim lowers his baton.

As the orchestra leaves the stage for the interval, the young man embarrassedly hurries out to smoke with the rest of the audience.

The second half of the concert is Tchaikovsky's Fifth Symphony, a formative work in the young man's life. He returns to the auditorium early. He hopes, against his nature, to speak with the girl seated to his right. He practiced what he could say in the lobby. Upon reaching their row, his face falls. Her seat is empty. The others around him trickle in but she does not. Maybe to her the Russian work is too common, another iteration of an overplayed repertoire. She will not return. He pushes her out of his mind, thinks back to the basement where he first heard Thomas Beecham's 1939 version of the upcoming work. London Philharmonic. It remains his favorite interpretation.

The lights go down and the orchestra takes the stage en masse. One more check just to verify her seat is unoccupied. It is. The musicians sit.

And then he feels it, a touch, a tap on his shoulder.

Pardonnez-moi, monsieur.

The voice was barely audible, but he turns left and sees soft, kind, innocent eyes dilated by the dusky auditorium so that the pupils appear completely black. He is transfixed. Struck. He doesn't move, just stares. She repeats her plea, even more quietly as Barenboim has acknowledged the audience's applause and turned his back on them. Finally her words connect and he mumbles something incoherent in English, then in French, stands up and lets her pass. She silently takes her seat as the clarinet plays its first mournful, longing notes over the low strings. When she is settled, he looks over at her. She looks back. She smiles. And so does he.

Barenboim drives the orchestra like a runaway troika at the end of the first movement, wrings every ounce of melodramatic passion from them in the second, dances them through the playful third, and then, in the finale, rains down arpeggios of strings, unleashes majestic winds and horns, bathes the whole hall in such radiant sounds that the crowd erupts after the last note.

The two young concertgoers studiedly ignored each other after their initial eye contact, but now, as throughout the hall couples turn to each other, eager to share their impressions on what they saw, he looks to her to gauge if she had heard how he had. She beams widely like everyone around them and their eyes meet again. Too soon an elderly couple on the far side of her starts to push its way past and their connection is broken. She leans back to let them by, stands straight up against the back of her raised seat, and the young man tears his glance from her and slides into the aisle so the couple can squeeze out, and then more people are pushing past him and he is forced to take a tentative half-step up the stairs and then again—against his will—a full one, and suddenly he is gone, carried along in a cloud of smoke and haste toward a descending stairway, and he tries to look back but he can't see her and somehow he is already on the première balcon *and then in the lobby and then out in the cold, Parisian night.*

He waits for a minute, off to the side, but when she doesn't immediately emerge, he chafes at the thickening crowd. And he doesn't want to alarm her. So he pulls his collar up around his neck, wishes for a scarf, even the scratchy one Mamma made him wear in his childhood winters, and shoves his hands deep into his pockets. He turns left down the Rue du Faubourg Saint-Honoré. *He focuses on the fading echoes in his ears, struggling to keep the final motif in its triumphant major incarnation, rather than let it morph into the minor mode that began the night. Eventually he loses the fight. He gives up and listens to the discordant traffic.*

It is then that she walks out of the theater. She looks quickly over the few remaining stragglers but does not see him whom she seeks. She shrugs her shoulders and turns right to walk the short block to the Métro.

• • •

The film in my mind snapped and, momentarily blinded, I heard only the repeated *thwap, thwap, thwaping* of the negative against the projector's metal casing. Jarred out of my thoughts, I noticed that the waiter had set down another beer and a plate of food that I don't recall ordering. Maybe that was the sound I heard. He is already around the corner, and I am hungry and certainly don't feel like chasing him down to try and get an explanation. He doesn't seem to speak English anyway, or any other language I have ever heard. Not that I can speak in tongues, a few words here, a phrase or two there. (*Dis aliter visum.* Oh, bless the prisoner.) He certainly made no effort to comprehend my *hrvatski.* Maybe I shouldn't try anymore either. Where has it gotten me? There's no understanding. I'll just eat it. I appreciate the beer and am pleased that this pub appears to operate on the Eastern-European principle that says beer should be brought until the customer says halt, *za platim.* I don't want to keep interrupting my viewing to get more, and now that I have started, I shouldn't stop. Either. Drinking or watching. This movement was a singularity for me. But no matter how faithfully I try to re-create it, immerse myself, I can't. It's gone. Let her go. End this. No. Read on. Watch. Listen. Try to enjoy it. Remember the winds outside. Winds. Francesca da Rimini told Dante, "*Nessun maggior dolore che ricordarsi del tempo felice nella miseria.*" No greater pain is there than remembering times of happiness in times of misery. I may never have known that line but for you, Alice. Read on. Indulge the senses one last time.

• • •

À la mi-mars 1988

Our flâneur *passes his time in Paris. He lingers in a café in early light, pores over photos in the day's newspapers, but just the photos, no words, even in those papers whose words he could comprehend. He moves from* quai *to* quai, *out to the* banlieue *and back to the* arrondissement, *crisscrossing the* Seine, *either intimately familiar with the city or supremely unconcerned with where he ends up. Two spots get revisited daily: Fenelon College in the Eighth, where he paces back and forth for fifteen minutes; and the* Cour Napoléon, *where he climbs the scaffolding and peers down at the hole, now covered by I. M. Pei's steel-and-glass pyramid, which will be the new entrance to the* Louvre. *He sits in other cafés, reading, thinking, flipping through a pair of small red books. Late in the day a slight limp troubles his gait. After dining, he smokes* Gauloises *under the starless city sky and budding trees in the isosceles* Place Dauphine *at the west end of the* Île de la Cité. *Eventually he climbs a rickety, dark stair at the back of the* Hotel Henri IV *and sleeps. During the day he may have admired a gargoyle or an elegant display of* radis ou artichaut *or sniffed a ripe* Fromagerie *down the next block or turned because of the bell of a bicycle, but no person—no tour guide or shopkeeper, no dog walker or* bébé, *no* jeune fille en fleur—*caught his eye. He acts as if he is all alone. Or invisible.*

mardi, 22 mars 1988
10:20—LE JARDIN DU MUSÉE RODIN.
Our idle young man stands before The Gates of Hell. He crouches down, examines the chaotic mass of bodies being buffeted about at the bottom of the bronze cast. His concentration is such that he is unaware of the young woman watching him from a bench. It is she, the one who sat next to him in the Salle Pleyel *more than two weeks ago. Her long dark hair, dappled with strands that have lightened in the early spring sun, is loosely tied on the left behind her ear and pulled around her shoulder so it rests on her chest. She wears dark-green cotton slacks and lace-up leather boots. Her jacket hangs open allowing a glimpse of a white blouse beneath a fashionable blue scarf.*

He has focused his attention on a bas relief on the lower right jamb depicting a man tenderly holding his lover's hand while nuzzling her face. The woman on the bench stares intently as well. Her brow furrows slightly, crinkling her nose. She unconsciously chews her left lower lip. The man rocks forward onto the balls of his feet and looks up. Francesca and Paolo protrude above his head. Fugit Amor, *the identical stand-alone sculpture inside the museum dubs the couple. Fugitive Love. Paolo struggles to hold on to Francesca, to keep her from blowing away, from falling backward off the plane of the gates and leaving him alone. The woman on the bench stops gnawing her lip and pulls at it. Then her face relaxes, decided, and she looks around casually.*

Back along the path a small child stares down a yellow narcissus half his height. With both hands, he tries to get its blossom head to stay upright, to look back at him. He doesn't hear his mother's repeated calls of "Allons-y Alex."

We are alone, the young woman thinks. She stands and walks on the white clay pathway toward the Gates. When she is just a few feet away from him, the young man senses her presence and turns, still squatting, to look up at her untroubled, smiling face.

Well, now we're alone, so no one can separate us. We finally get to meet. I'm Alice.

Oh, hi, I'm …

(He reaches out to shake her hand but loses his balance and falls awkwardly to the side. Alice laughs a little and, shamefaced, so does he. He is flustered, but gathers himself and stands up, brushes the dirt off his hands, and reaches forward to greet her properly.)

Hi, Alice. I'm Miles.

11:15—JARDIN DE LUXEMBOURG.

Alice and Miles sit on a bench in the western part of the park. It is almost empty this time of day, and aside from the distant city traffic, the only sound comes from a tennis ball traveling back and forth between two friendly racquets.

There was never a field trip or anything? Or you never went with your parents?

No. I grew up in Queens and my school didn't take many trips into the city. Or if they did, I missed them because Mamma didn't let me do much. And I never had a father. Well, I mean, I did, but he died. Or I thought he was dead, until I turned seventeen. And then I found out he wasn't. Everyone was lying. It's sort of confusing.

I'm sorry, Miles.

Oh, it's okay. I'm used to it now. Or I've at least lived with it.

Did you ever try to find him?

My father? Yeah, that's basically why I'm here. But I've been looking for a really long time and I don't think I'll find him at this point. I don't know. I don't really know where he is anymore. I don't know if I ever did.

(They sit silently. The tennis ball bounces rhythmically left to right, right to left.)

So you're only here for another couple of months? In Italy?

Yeah. Unfortunately. I'm excited to graduate, but I'll be very sad to leave. Florence is such a beautiful city.

I went there once, looking for Carlo. My father. I loved it. Do you study literature? Is that why you knew so much about Dante's story of Francesca and Paolo? Which was impressive by the way.

Oh, thanks. That's how I pick up guys. Actually my major's history, but I'm getting a certificate in Italian and French. Although my French is terrible. I probably should have come here to study instead of going to Italy, so I could work on it, but I just like Italian more. And I love Dante. He's always been kind of a hobby, I guess.

That's a pretty erudite hobby.

I'm pretty *and* erudite.

(Miles laughs and she smiles sincerely.)

I should read him. I don't know why I never did. I mean, I didn't get a chance in high school because I didn't finish. Which is kind of embarrassing and I don't even know why I'm talking about it. Sorry. I don't usually talk this much. Do you want to walk somewhere? To the Pantheon?

Sure. I love it there. It's so peaceful.

(They stand up and head toward the *palais*.)

I went to the opera a lot.

Really?

Yeah. I guess that was my hobby growing up.

That's much more erudite than Dante, I think.

Is it? I'm not sure.

I've only been twice. Both in New York. Once we saw *Carmen* and the other time it was. Oh, the one ... shoot. The really famous one. Where she dies at the end?

They always die at the end.

It was a big set with a dancing bear. And three levels and it snows.

La Bohème.

That's it. It's in Paris, isn't it?

Yeah. That's a great opera, but I never saw the set you did. It opened the year after I left.

It's pretty extravagant. What's your favorite?

Favorite? I don't know if I have one. The first one I saw was on my tenth birthday, *Roméo et Juliette.*

12:30—LE QUARTIER LATIN.

Miles and Alice walk down the slick, cool cobblestones of Rue Mouffetard.

Have you read the poem?

I didn't know there was one.

Yeah, a poem inspired it. Well, a poem and Mathilde.

I was kind of preoccupied when I got there. I had a stupid phone call before I left my hotel so I didn't read anything. Who was Mathilde?

She was the sister of his teacher, Alexander Zemlinsky. They ended up getting married.

Who?

Arnold and Mathilde. It wasn't great.

The poem? Or the marriage?

The marriage. Well, both I guess. The poem isn't very good either. Or it's just different. It's by Richard Dehmel.

Never heard of him.

Yeah, he's no Dante. He was popular in Germany before World War One, but it's kind of an antiquated style or notion. The music is definitely better.

Do you like Schönberg?

Not a lot. I think his music's great, but I'm not always in the mood for it, especially his later stuff. Live, it's wonderful. Do you?

I liked *Verklärte Nacht*, but that's the only thing I've ever heard.

Oh really? You should try *Moses und Aron*. It's an opera. It's really intense but very ... I don't know. It's different.

(They emerge into a sunny side street and turn left.)

What's the poem about?

Two people, a man and a woman, walking at night. The night is *kahlen* and *kalten*. Bare and cold. She feels guilty because she slept with a stranger and got pregnant. She'd given up on happiness and basically just wanted to have sex and now she's met this guy, he's not her boyfriend or anything, but she seems to really like him. She says "*Ich geh in Sünde neben Dir.*" I walk in sin beside you. She thinks she's being punished for her for promiscuity or something. The guy thinks about this and says, don't worry about it, "*sieh wie klar das Weltall schimmert.*" See how clear the universe shimmers. That's very important, the shimmering of the universe.

(Alice titters.)

Then suddenly there's a warm glow between them and the guy says that the universe and the warmth will transfigure the child into his own, just like he'd fathered it. And then presto, everything's okay. They're happy and the night is *hohe* and *helle*. High and bright. The end.

Did you make that up?

No. Why? Does it sound like I made it up?

No. It's just. It's … never mind. You know a lot about him.

Just that piece. When he wrote it, Mathilde's brother, the teacher, was dating Alma Schindler. She eventually dumped him to marry Gustav Mahler. And Mahler is very, he's very important to me. I love his music, but it's even more than that. I feel a connection to it, to him, his music. It's kind of weird.

So Mathilde and Arnold and Mahler and … ?

Alma.

I know Mahler's name, but I haven't listened to him at all.

He said "The symphony must be like the world. It must contain everything."

And does it?

For me? Yeah. It's my entire life.

13:15—NOTRE-DAME.
Crowds of tourists walk slowly beneath the chandeliered aisles and through the crossing, examining the artwork in the side chapels,

gawking up at the rose windows. Few appear pious. To the left of the altar a choir in street clothes rehearses. At the back of the nave, Miles and Alice sit listening to the ethereal voices. They lean in close to each other, shoulder to shoulder. Occasionally one of them will turn and, with warm breath, whisper something in the other's ear. Their proximity began unintentionally, with a quick thought relayed in a hushed voice out of respect for any genuine worshippers. Now they both try to keep the conversation alive so their nearness will continue.

Do you believe in God?

No. Do you?

No. But I think if I had grown up here or in Italy, I might, just because God is so much more tangible, overpowering. Like this.

I didn't have any exposure to religion growing up. My mom's brother and his wife died in a plane crash, a couple of years before I was born. They got married a month earlier and were flying to the east coast to catch a connecting flight for their honeymoon. The plane tickets were my mom's wedding gift. She chose the flight they were on and everything. It haunted her. She wanted someone to blame.

My mom got obsessed with religion when I was six. Actually she got obsessed with an idol, which I'm pretty sure is a sin. Anyway, she started to ignore me, then she got kind of crazy, really religious. Like a zealot. I blamed God for taking her away from me, which was stupid, but I was a kid. I just stopped believing. I stopped paying any attention to her or anything she believed in.

Is she still really religious?

I don't know. I haven't talked to her for years. I ran away when I was seventeen.

(Alice looks at Miles who has raised his eyes to her face. She sees that she should ignore the comment for now.)

I don't think religion's as important for kids because they don't worry about anything. They aren't scared. They just live. But if you don't start believing as a child, it's too hard to start when you're older, when you might really need someone to turn to for support. At least that's what happened for me.

I was always scared growing up. I worried about everything.

Really? Do you still?

Sort of. I mean, yeah. I do. But I've got a lot of stuff to worry about.

Like what?

I don't know. Everybody does things they

probably wish they could change. Don't they?

Sure.

(The choir begins singing again, from the beginning.)

And my dad went crazy. So genetically I'm kind of worried, I guess. That painting over there keeps reminding me of him.

Which one?

Over there, below that arch.

I can't really see it from here, I don't have my glasses. What is it?

The Descent of the Holy Spirit. It's an episode from the Book of Acts where God fulfills some Old Testament promise he made. The apostles are in a room and they hear a big wind and then the Holy Spirit appears as fire and sits on top of their heads and they speak in tongues. It's the birthday of the church supposedly. It's called Pentecost. They celebrate it five weeks after Easter.

Which is soon. Will you still be here?

Yeah. I actually had a really hard time keeping my hotel room. But I'm there so often that the owner helped me out.

Why does it remind you of your dad?

That is a very long and very weird story. We should probably save it for later. Why do you think it's so hard for adults to start believing?

Because if you pay any attention to all the terrible things people do to each other, it would be a pretty sadistic god who created a world like this.

True. But you probably shouldn't say that in church?

(Alice turns her head quickly and smiles at Miles. They look into each other's eyes again, noses almost touching. The choir is singing full out now, something pitched very high, all sopranos and children. Miles closes his eyes but doesn't look away. They listen.)

Music sometimes makes me want to believe in God.

I can see that. Actually a lot of great art is more comprehensible if you credit divine inspiration.

I want to agree with you, but I have a hard time because I'm guessing that's what happened to my mom. I mean Michelangelo's *Pietà,* that was her obsession, is amazing, sure. But nothing else mattered.

Religion can make people act crazy. But it's

not religion itself, it's the believer. And to me, their biggest sin is the blinders, the selectivity. My mom only blamed God for the bad, for her sister. Nothing good got credited. Your mom ignored what her obsession was doing to you, to her family. It doesn't make sense to me. Or maybe that's the only way it makes sense. You have to compartmentalize. Believe in small things. God did this little thing. Thank you. Or I hate you. If you look at the world as a whole, I don't see how anyone could have faith in anything.

I know. But that faith would be so nice to have. So comforting. And I never used to think I would feel that way again, that I would want to believe in anything. But it's like you said, if you look at the world, or even aspects of it, or your life, without faith it's really hard to have any hope. In anything.

But God doesn't give you hope or faith, Miles. Those are the paths to God. Not the other way around. Dante gets quizzed on the virtues—faith, hope and love—right before the end of the *Commedia*, by Peter, James, and John. Love is actually the most important to them. In fact, Dante equates God and love, pretty absolutely. Love, in the form of Beatrice, the love of his life, literally leads him to God. She's his guide in *Paradiso*. All he has to do to move to the next level, the next heaven, is look into her eyes. And every time he does, he gets closer to God. At the end, God is described as the love that moves the sun and other stars, "*l'amor che move il sol e l'altre stelle.*"

That's beautiful. My Nonna used to say love was more important than the other virtues, too. "*Fede, speranza ed amore, Emilio, ma sempre amore.*"

Who was Emilio? Your grandpa?

Oh. No. He's me. That's my real name. It's weird though because honestly, the whole reason I'm here is because of faith. It's not like I can't have it. All my father left me, or all he left behind, not necessarily for me, was a bunch of photos in a book. I took those photos and created stories that to me, sort of define him. Give him a life. I don't know if they're true or not. But I believe them. I've thought long and hard about them. I didn't just make them up, however I wanted him to be. And they led me to one bigger conclusion about him. A conclusion I have absolutely no proof of. Just faith that I understood him. Understand him. And that made me believe that I'd find him in Italy. And it totally changed my life. I guess I could have believed it because I wanted to think the worst about him. But I don't think I did. And it's kind of okay anyway because the stories, or beliefs, gave me my father back. Gave me hope that I might find him. And then maybe I could forgive him. I don't know. Maybe he would want to see me. I mean, it's nothing like the faith in the Bible, but in a way it kinda is. It's the same word.

I don't have faith in anything.

I wish I didn't. I wish he'd never been resurrected.

(Miles opens his eyes. Alice is looking closely at him. She smiles.)

You probably shouldn't say that in a church either.

Yeah. Probably not. Let's go.

14:00—LES HALLES.

Alice and Miles walk across an airy pedestrian bridge over pyramidal skylights and Miles looks down. He has yet to visit the Louvre *today. He had planned to head there after the Rodin museum. He hesitates. He wavers. Then he looks up and sees Alice waiting at the end of the bridge. He goes to her and they find a bench and sit.*

What was that book you were looking at back there?

Oh, it's kind of stupid. It's a dictionary, a French-English dictionary. For chemists.

Are you a chemist?

No.

Was it a gift?

No. It's just, I come here so often and I wanted to work on my French, and one afternoon I was browsing the *bouquinistes* and found this for a franc or something ridiculously cheap, and I really like old things anyway, and it has a great grammar section, so I just decided to buy it. And actually it's a pretty good dictionary.

Can I see it?

(Miles takes a book out of his pocket and hands it to her.)

When's your birthday?

Why?

Miles?

Yeah?

I'm not going to hurt you.

What? Oh. I know, it's just that …

(Looking down, he feels her hand resting lightly on his leg. She leaves her hand there for a moment and then, as she prepares to pull it away, presses down perceptibly with all five finger tips. Miles's stomach muscles twitch.)

It's September. September nineteenth.

Alright, let's see. We used to do this on car trips when I was growing up. Nineteen nine. You have treat the date like Europeans do. Unless you always have thousand-page books around. One ninety-nine.

(She flips through the dictionary until she finds page 199.)

Let's talk about …

(Alice points a finger at Miles and smirks as she bites her lower lip then lobs the finger up in the air, like a *boule* aiming for a crowded *cochonnet*, and brings it down with a thud on the page.)

Jalousement. Well, that's appropriate I guess.

(Alice shakes her head, speaking more to herself than Miles. Then she looks over at him.)

When was the first time you were jealous?

(Miles thinks for a second.)

When Mamma didn't come home for dinner.

(He looks up at the black roof of *Saint-Eustache*, then over at Alice, who has put her hand back on his thigh. This time she leaves it there.)

What about you?

Mine's kind of silly compared with that. It

was in third grade when Lynn Gordin learned her multiplication tables before I did and got her name on the skills board.

Wow. That's pretty serious. How did you ever recover?

(Miles self-consciously laughs at himself and Alice shakes her head.)

No, I'm sorry. I'm not making fun of you. It's just that I never really talk to anyone anymore, about anything. Especially anything important. And you listen. It's been a long time. I've been in Europe eight years, and definitely not anytime then.

That's good to hear. Otherwise, I might be jealous.

14:25—PALAIS ROYALE.

Miles and Alice sit on a bench in front of a stately bed of spring flowers, yellow, purple, red. Miles leans over the back of the bench watching a butterfly.

That's a brimstone of some kind. Or a sulphur, in America. They're all over where I have been staying in Italy. I can't tell what kind though because it won't stop flapping long enough to let me look at it. I read one time that butterflies can see red, but bees can't.

(He turns and sits on the bench. Alice leans in toward him and puts her head on his shoulder. Miles freezes, tries not to feel awkward. He notices he isn't breathing and tries to start, but without moving his shoulder.)

I'm not saying bees can't land on a red flower. It's not invisible. They just don't know it's red apparently. I don't know if they have have names for colors. But, Monet could see like a butterfly at the end of his life. Or something like that. That was the point of the story. He had cataract surgery. Anyway.

(Silence.)

I'm engaged.

(Miles starts to sit up straighter, but Alice makes her head heavier, won't budge, so he stops. They stay like that, her head heavy on his shoulder, both of them staring straight ahead.)

Really? Um, congratulations.

We're getting married next spring. About a year from now. He went to school with me, but he graduated already. He's in America. And it doesn't. I'm not. I just wanted to tell you. His name's Felix.

(Miles feels Alice stop talking.)

Well. He's the lucky one, I guess.

(There are several seconds of silence and then Alice sits up and looks up at him and shakes her head.)

A Latin pun? Really?

Sorry. Couldn't resist. I won't do it again.

(She stands up with a smirk and reaches out her hand to Miles. He takes hers and she pulls him off the bench.)

So, as stupid as this sounds, this is just one day, okay? Until tomorrow morning. After that, we won't see each other again. Ever. Okay?

(Miles thinks for a second. Looks at her biting her lip.)

Sì. Okay.

(She lifts her hand that still grasps his and gently kisses the back of his wrist. Then she dramatically lets go and reaches forward to take the dictionary out of his jacket pocket.)

One day. Now pick another.

How about May 13. My lovely parents' wedding day.

Okay. Perfect. *Éprouver*. To test, to try, to experiment.

Well, their marriage was certainly a failed experiment.

(Alice laughs.)

And the day I was born, the United States conducted the first underground nuclear test.

Why do you know that?

Dumb luck. I was reading about the pyramid getting built at the *Louvre*, a few years ago, when they were approving the final design, and there was another article about the collapse of the test chamber after an underground test at this place called the Rainier Mesa in Nevada. One guy died, not immediately, but anyway, in the article they mentioned that the first underground nuclear test took place at that same spot, the Rainier Mesa, on September 19, 1957. Which is the day I was born. So I kind of connect them, in my head. The pyramid at the *Louvre* and the Rainier Mesa. And me. My birthday.

(They leave the gardens and turn right onto *Rue des Petits Champs.*)

I know it isn't really true, but … sometimes, when I'm alone at night and haven't talked to anyone for a long time, a few days or something, I start to think that I was actually born there. Underground, in the blast. Maybe I'm radioactive or something. Obviously I'm not. Literally. It just makes sense sometimes. Because there's no one around me.

(They walk in silence, counterclockwise around the *Place des Victoires*, passing up three streets before getting off on *Rue d'Aboukir.*)

So what're your thoughts on apro … ?

Éprouver? The only tests I've ever done are in school. Everything in my life has always been so planned. I was accepted to college when I was fifteen. Partly because my dad went there. And his dad. And his. It wasn't even a question. I guess I could've not gotten accepted. But. Now Felix. Who my parents love. There's never been any time for experimentation.

So am I? An experiment? Is that why you said that?

Well, no. That makes it sound stupid. Or cheap. But I guess, I can see you'd think that. But no, I don't necessarily see it that way. See us that way. It's hard to explain. There's definitely something about you. About us. I felt it the first time I saw you at the concert. And you knew it too, or maybe you didn't know it but you sensed it. You seemed like you knew. I don't know what it is. Maybe I'm a Geiger counter.

(Miles smiles. Crossing the *Rue du Louvre* they turn down *Rue Montmartre*.)

Felix was lucky. But sometimes I think that's all it was. His parents moved in next to my parents when we were eight. We went to the same school. We went to the same college.

Our parents were friends. I mean I do love him. But I also don't believe there's only one person in the whole world who can make you happy. It just seems that it would be foolish to miss out on getting to know another one of those people. If you think you might've been lucky enough to find one. So yeah. An experiment I guess.

I've never met one. Before. But I did, I felt something when you walked past me at the concert. I don't know how to explain it.

Me either. When you left at the end, I was so sad. I wanted to talk to you, or go get a drink, or go dancing, or something. I convinced myself it was just me traveling alone. Being lonely. But then when I came to the Rodin museum and you were there.

Standing at The Gates of Hell …

True, there was that. But you were there. And I thought … I didn't really know what to think. I guess I thought maybe it was fate. Which I didn't know I believed in.

So one day.

One day.

(Alice takes Miles's hand, interlaces their fingers and turns them left down *Rue Bachaumont.*)

15:50—BOULEVARD DE MAGENTA.
Walking north, Alice and Miles cross Rue la Fayette. *To the right at the end of the street is* Gare du Nord. *Alice carries a small paper sack from which she occasionally takes a date that she then bites in half, chewing one piece completely before putting the second half in her mouth.*

So, train station. Where do you want to go? If we could go anywhere?

We can go anywhere. I've got plenty of money.

Really? Goody. Where are you taking me?

You have no preference?

It's your money. You choose.

Then let's go to Leningrad.

I'd love to. It's supposed to be beautiful. And *Crime and Punishment* is one of my favorite books.

Mine, too. *Egli è delitto. Punizion son io.*

Huh?

He is crime. I am punishment. It's from an opera. *Rigoletto*. I think about those lines sometimes. About my father. He's the crime, I'm the punishment.

Okay, no acting out Dostoyevsky.

Check. Then we'll take a train across the Soviet Union.

I have a professor who did that. From Moscow to the Kamchatka Peninsula.

Perfect. Leningrad then Moscow. I just want to be on a train with you for as long as possible.

Really?

What really?

You said you want to be on a train with me for as long as possible.

I said I want to be on a train for as long as possible. I love trains.

You said with me.

Did I?

Yes.

Well, I guess that'd be okay, too.

I guess. Whatever would we do all that time? Would you get us a private car?

(Alice links her arm through his and coquettishly winks up at him. Miles blushes.)

Anyway.

(He shrinks away, shyly, not in anger.)

Once we got to the end, what would we do?

I don't know. Turn around and go back?

No. Sail to Japan.

And then Hawaii.

No. New Zealand.

Yeah. New Zealand. Perfect. And stay there.
Or could you buy an island?

Sure. But only a very small one.

Good. Because I don't want to have to wear
any clothes.

(Miles turns red again. Alice looks over at him. She chews on her lower lip, grabs a date from her bag, and holds it in front of his mouth.)

Open.

(He does. She hurries several paces ahead and then turns to face him, continuing to walk backward.)

So where did you get all this money, huh?

I stole things.

Oh! là là! Un criminel. Tres excitant!

21:20—PASSAGE DES PANORAMAS.
Alice and Miles sit at a table outside a small restaurant in the covered passage. Their server talks inside with the chef. No one else is around. An empty bottle of wine and a dessert plate sit between them. The plate has a smear of ganache *and a fork on it. A small amount of wine is in each of their glasses. They pass a cigarette back and forth between drags.*

How did you know so much about those cameras?

I know about the really big one because I took pictures with it for several years. Well, not that one obviously.

Do you still have it?

No. I left it behind. Old life.

That's too bad. You could've taken my picture.

Yeah, I don't think I'll ever forget what you look like.

You might.

I doubt it. Do you like photography?

Of course. My name is Alice.

Does Alice like photography?

"What is the use of a book without pictures or conversation?"

Huh?

That's the first thing that Alice says in *Adventures in Wonderland*. My parents named me after her. As embarrassing as that is to admit.

Really? After Alice in Wonderland?

Yes, really.

It's fine. That's a good book. Does it mean anything?

That they named me after a children's book?

No. The name Alice.

Oh. I think it means noble. Does it mean anything in French?

You mean in French chemistry?

Oui. In French chemistry.

(Miles looks through the dictionary.)

Nope. There's an alidade where you ought to be.

What's that?

An alidade.

Yes.

No, that's what it means. It's a thing. An alidade.

Oh. What kind of a thing?

It's that thing, it looks like a ruler with a telescope on it, kind of like an astrolabe. It helps locate things. It's used in mapmaking.

Another of your hobbies?

Kind of, I guess. More of an obsession. Or a safety blanket. I like to know where I am. On maps. So anything that can help with that. It's a good thing. So another plus for you, alidade.

(She looks at him for a long minute.)

Let's look under lice.

Lice?

Yeah. Like 'A' plus 'lice.' A, for 'under' or

'of' like '*à la belle étoile*,' plus 'lice.' Let's see. Here. '*Lice*' means 'lists, field, warp of fabric.' So you are 'in the warp of fabric.' Or 'of the field.' I prefer 'of the field.'

Yeah. Gimme that.

(Alice takes the book and flips through to the letter m.)

Well, you're not here either. You should be just before milieu.

That kind of fits. I'm never part of my surroundings.

Do you really feel like that?

Sometimes. But it's not always a bad thing. It actually helped me after I ran away. I ended up in a pretty terrible neighborhood and when I first got there I was too scared to leave my room lots of times. I was just squatting. I was afraid I wouldn't have the nerve to get back in or I'd get beaten up or someone would be in the room when I got back. So I just sat there. Until I got so hungry I had to go out.

That must have been awful.

Yeah. It wasn't the best plan either because my anxiety was exacerbated by being hungry and weak. I used to stand in the doorway, just before leaving and imagine that I was making myself invisible. It wasn't true, obviously, but I forced myself to believe it. Then I'd walk out. All confident. I wasn't allowed to hide or shrink against the walls or anything. Just walk like I imagined a normal person would. Except that no one could see me. I must have looked so terrified. But for whatever reason it worked. I never got chased or robbed or stabbed. Well, one time. Not stabbed. But robbed. But I saw all those things happen so much. And only once. I don't know. I just did what I had to.

Well, you made it.

Yeah. Some days I wonder how. It was pretty chaotic. I mean, not like Carlo saw during the war, but still pretty bad. My father was a photographer during World War Two. In Italy actually. That's the camera I had. His. It was a Speed Graphic, like we saw back in the other passage. He took all these pictures and stuck them in Ovid's *Metamorphoses*. Pictures of friends, soldiers, Germans, kids. Lots of them dying. I think it was his way of trying to control the chaos around him, mythologize it, order it, make it tell a story. I think he married someone, not my mom, someone else, before her, during the war. But she got killed. And then his pet lizard got killed.

Pet lizard?

Yeah. That really sent him over the edge. He took off. Like me actually.

You did what you thought you had to do, Miles. And maybe it really was the only thing you could've done. This is going to be weird, but we've had what, three bottles of wine?

Five?

Three. Anyway, so you know how science teaches us that everything tends toward chaos? Maximum entropy?

I didn't really get that far in science, since I dropped out and all. But okay, maximum chaos.

(Alice smirks. Miles lights a cigarette.)

Well, they didn't always think that. Back long, long ago, they believed that everything, matter, was made up of four elements: air, water, earth, and fire.

Got it.

Okay, well there was a guy, Empedocles, a Greek philosopher, and he said that those four elements interacted according to two forces, love and strife. I can't believe I'm talking about this. It's so stupid.

Have you listened to some of the things I've said today?

True. So love and strife go up and down, like a seesaw, one increasing and the other decreasing. At some point, it's all love, no strife—gimme that—and that's called harmony. But right as that happens, right at the very instant that everything's good, it switches. The teeter starts to totter. Strife starts increasing and love starts decreasing until there's no love left and only strife and that's called chaos. One hundred percent strife.

Why on earth do you know this?

Because I'm pretty and erudite.

Ha.

Actually because of Dante. Again. Virgil, who guides him through the first two parts, *Inferno* and *Purgatorio*, was a follower of Empedocles. So we studied him. To understand his mind. Actually everyone back then believed him. Well, not everyone, but a lot.

Like you?

Yes. I was really alive back then. But really, sometimes, when things are really, really bad, for someone or in some place, or when I am addled from nine bottles of wine, I hope that, for that person, or that country or whatever, I just hope that for them it may be a time of total strife. And eventually things will turn around. They'll get better. They have to.

(They both look down at the table, thinking their own thoughts. Miles picks up the fork and plays with the remains of their dessert.)

Anyway, if Empedocles is right, maybe your dad didn't go crazy. Maybe he just got caught in a place where everything was in chaos. The world and Italy and his life and the life of the family of the girl he married. Everything. All at the same time.

Yeah, I guess that's possible.

But look at today. Maybe today was a day when love was in the majority. We walked around all day and nothing bad happened to us. To anyone we saw. People just lived. Talking, walking, sitting, eating, driving cars, kissing. It wasn't abnormal, but that's what's so sad. We don't appreciate the harmony as much as we hate the chaos. We take harmony for granted. But when you think about it, it's astounding that it happens as often as it does. That it ever happens. People are so different. And there's so many of us. Chaos is so much harder to ignore. Strife demands attention. By its nature. It's jarring. Unexpected.

Violent. Love slips past unnoticed.

That is unbelievably sad.

(They sit quietly for a minute, then the waitress walks up and sets down two glasses of cognac, telling them that the drinks are complimentary. Alice and Miles look at each other, shrug, and raise the glasses to toast.)

This is certainly a prolific amount of alcohol we're consuming.

I'm not sure I've ever heard prolific used in that way.

It works.

(She sticks her tongue out at Miles.)

So that's what happened at the concert, maybe?

I got drunk?

No.

(Miles shakes his head and halfheartedly sticks his tongue out, only for an instant as he just ends up blushing. He takes a sip of his cognac.)

No. That harmony, or love, was trying to draw attention to itself. To get noticed. To get us to notice each other. That was the weird feelings that we felt.

So you did notice? You didn't say anything earlier.

Yes, I did. And of course I noticed. I waited outside for you. But I left. I didn't want scare you. That's why I was so astounded when I saw you this morning. I did literally fall over, remember?

I thought you were just drunk.

Ha. Ha.

So maybe harmony hires music to do its dirty work.

And that's why it's so meaningful to people. Why different kinds of people like different kinds of music. Because of all the different seesaws. Or because everybody loves different things. It makes sense. Music is the ultimate victory of harmony over chaos, even if it isn't harmonic music. I mean there is sound all around us all the time, but composers take groups of sounds, specific ones, and put them together to create such … such … whatever. Such beauty. Now I do sound drunk.

But why just music? Why not books? Or paintings? Books create harmony out of words. Painting out of colors.

You're right. All the arts serve harmony.

Love. It's just that music is the most immersive of them. Like Walter Pater said, "All art constantly aspires to the condition of music."

Who's that?

He was an English critic. Or writer. Something. At the end of the nineteenth century. I don't really remember. But that's what he said.

And what does it mean? Everything wants to be music?

Yeah. He thought so. And so did Joyce.

(The waitress appears with another glass and sets it in front of Alice with a wink. They exchange a few words in French and both laugh.)

What's that? What did she say?

She just said she's seen you here a lot, but she's never seen you happy. Or smile. Until tonight. I think she thinks you paid for me.

(They both laugh at this thought.)

Well, your harmony is appreciated.

Thank you.

What I was saying?

Something about Joyce and another dead guy want everything to be music.

Yeah, something like that. But Joyce did try to write *Ulysses* as a piece of music. Or maybe it was *Finnegans Wake*. I don't remember. But both of them are so musical.

(They both think. Share the drink.)

Wait. I know. I know why music is the epitome of love.

Why?

Because it allows us to feel emotions we can't understand or explain in any another way. Sometimes we don't even have words for them. But music names them for us. Only in notes instead of words.

(Alice sips the cognac and slides it across to Miles. Their fingertips touch lightly and they let the contact linger, both holding the glass.)

I like that. It's beautiful.

(Miles drinks from the snifter, puts it down, and lights a cigarette.)

Thanks. I didn't say it though. I mean, I did, just now, obviously, but I didn't write it. Leonard Bernstein said it while explaining music to kids during one of his Young

People's Concerts. He was actually using the Tchaikovsky symphony we saw as his example.

(Miles smokes. Trades Alice the cigarette for the cognac.)

Another strength of music is that words can be misused more easily. Misinterpreted. It is hard to do that to music. Sure, it can be co-opted. Or abused. But in the end, its interpretation is personal. The abuse comes from within the listener. An A played on a clarinet doesn't mean anything specific, like the word 'homicide' does. Once you add words to music, it becomes easier to twist it. Look at Wagner. No one could ever listen to his music, without the librettos, or the singers, or knowing anything about the composer, and think anything bad. You may not personally like the way it sounds, the way the notes are put together. That's fine. But it's the words, the sentiments possibly expressed by those words, the beliefs of the person who wrote them that get quoted, and held up, rightfully or wrongly, to bludgeon people with. Music is about emotion. Period. Words can be twisted. Like me, comparing my feelings about my father to faith in God. They're both faith. Neither has any proof. But my faith in Carlo being a terrorist is so different from a belief in God.

Your dad is a terrorist?

Oh. No. Well, maybe. Probably not. He might've been at one time.

That's weird. But I'm going to ignore it. No more Carlo talk. It makes you sad. Let's go walk. I need some fresh air.

(Miles meets her gaze, for the first time without flushing.)

Agreed. Light another cigarette.

Oui. Will you pick one last word?

Sure. What page?

Three twenty.

Why that?

It was your seat number at the *Salle Pleyel*.

(Alice stares, deep brown eyes wide. She bites her lip. Looks at the book. Turns its pages.)

Saisir.

What's that mean?

To seize.

22:00—RUE DE SURÈNE.

Alice and Miles have just turned off of the grand Boulevard Malesherbes. *They walk slowly, hand in hand.*

So you're quite the Proust stalker.

I come here a lot, without anything to do. You can only stare at the hole in front of the *Louvre* so long every day without people thinking you're crazy. I just love that you've read him.

But not in French. Yet. Maybe when I'm frail and old. Shudder. Why do you keep coming here? You never said.

Can I bring up my father again? As long as it is quick?

Yes. But quickly.

I don't know, obviously, but sometimes I really do think he's here.

Really?

Yeah. So when I said I thought he was a terrorist, I was kind of serious. And the fact that I'm here, in Europe, in Italy, Paris, all the other places, is because I took this leap of faith, or whatever it was, back in 1980, I guess. Or earlier. Maybe '78. Anyway, I don't think that he actually killed people then. I just thought he took a photo for a terrorist group. But then he actually sent in photos, to newspapers, for years. Always from Italy. It seemed like a good decision to run around chasing him. And I actually thought I'd find him. Every time he had a photo published, in the *Herald Tribune*, or some Italian daily, I'd see it, grab my suitcase, head to where it was taken. He'd be gone, of course. But there was proof of his existence. And it gave me hope. I was always just a step behind.

What happened? Did the pictures stop?

Yeah. For months. I was desperate. Trying to figure out what had happened. Which basically meant sitting and flipping through newspapers, trying to see if Carlo was in them. Once I remembered, or read, or reread, something about an attack on an Italian army truck, outside Salerno, near where I lived. One soldier was killed, eight injured. But Carlo had a connection to the area, and I convinced myself, again, he had participated. Somehow.

What was the connection?

Oh. Nothing really. He was there during the war. He met Lucia there. The wartime wife I mentioned. No evidence though. Again. Just my thought. And the Italian government's rounding up all these *Brigate Rosse* guys, who are still at large.

The ones who killed Aldo Moro?

Yeah. How did you know that?

I'm a history major studying in Italy.

Oh. Well, good point. That was actually the photo that started this whole thing. The kidnapped photo of Moro. Not him in the car. After he was dead. But the one right when they got him. I think Carlo took it. Anyway, so all these members are fleeing after the Salerno attack, going to Argentina and Paris. I don't know, maybe my faith isn't strong enough, but I wasn't going to fly to South America. So I decided to come here. And I'm stuck. I just go back and forth.

So you just walk around hoping to bump into him?

Yeah, it's ridiculous I realize. I've wasted my whole life looking for him. But I can't go back. Not to America. And I don't know what he looks like. I mean I've never seen him. And he's in his sixties. I have a picture of him when he was eighteen or something. I just imagine he'll be carrying a camera and wearing some sign that says "*Tuo padre.*"

Well. That could happen I guess.

Sure.

(They turn toward each other. Alice swings their clasped hands high in front of themselves.)

I don't even know what I would do if I found him tonight. Or tomorrow. There are so many emotions. But I actually have a plan. This summer there's a meeting of Magnum photographers here, at Fenelon College. Magnum's this international photography collective my dad belongs to.

So you think he'll be there?

I hope so. Sometimes.

When's the meeting?

The last weekend in June.

You're a little early, aren't you?

Yeah. Just a little. I guess I was looking for direction. Or I was afraid I'd get too scared and not come. I don't know.

(They walk quietly for while.)

I'm glad you're here.

Me too.

This is where he meets Gilberte, by the way.

Where they first become friends?

Yeah.

I love that part.

Me too.

I also like when she buys him the agate marble.

And says, "You may call me Gilberte."

And when she runs to him, with her arms open, that first day it snows.

I like her so much better than Albertine.

Really?

Yeah. They're both sad though.

They're both doomed.

His whole story is doomed.

Yeah. That makes it harder.

(They are heading away from the *Place de la Concorde*.)

I've had a really good day, Miles.

Me too. But. It isn't over, is it? I thought it was a whole day? Are you just tired?

I'm not saying I'm leaving. I'm just saying it's been a nice day.

Oh.

You're pretty interesting. For a runaway dropout.

(Alice giggles and Miles smiles.)

I actually only know about three things. Everything else is a lie. If you were around me longer you'd realize I was a giant fake. Holden Caulfield would hate me. But I'm trying.

(Alice turns him toward her with their clasped hands and puts her other arm around his waist. She pulls him in. Only when they are pressed closely together does Miles become aware of the music. Somewhere nearby a carousel spins or a street band jams or a record player broadcasts through an opened window. An accordion. A violin. A clarinet. A horn. Not exactly a waltz but close enough. It's beautiful in the cool, moonless night, the city light filtering through the lilac hedges and the still bare branches of the early spring trees.)

Miles?

Yes.

(He looks down and she leans in, tilts her head up, closes her eyes, softly kisses him.)

That's so you know it's okay.

23:40—CHEZ GEORGE.

A mass of bodies crowds the grotto bar under its low, arched ceiling. The music is not live and it is loud. It ranges from Edith Piaf to klezmer to Euro dance tunes. The space is hot and lit with candles and strings of bulbs and everything appears red. The revelers sway with the music, sing along, yet still somehow carry on conversations. Alice and Miles sit at a small circular table covered with glasses, bottles, and ashtrays. It sits on a tier a bit higher than the floor. Even though under normal circumstances their table could comfortably accommodate two, currently there are six people seated around it. It is impossible to envision how they could have negotiated the current crowd to reach their spot, and yet the sea of students, of drinkers, of lovers, willingly seems to part to allow the passage of anyone carrying a bottle of wine, a pastis, a tray.

This is so fun.

I've never been anywhere like this but I could stay here forever.

I think the guy sitting next me has the wrong leg.

(Alice turns and looks at a young man to her right. She says something and he expresses surprise and then laughs.)

Is this my glass?

I think our glasses are the same at this point.

I'll be gone when you get back to Italy.

I know.

It's too bad. It would be fun to walk around Firenze with you.

What?

I said I want to walk around Firenze with you.

You do?

What?

Nothing.

(The decibel level increases exponentially, and the whole place starts clapping as seemingly hundreds of voices begin singing along to *Hava Nagila*. It's one of the few songs that Alice and Miles sort of know the words to. Then suddenly the crowd gets unnaturally quiet, unnaturally quickly. A violinist stands in the entryway. He is older than everyone in the room, and he alone is now carrying the tune.)

Miles doesn't listen to the music. But neither does he ignore it. He just hears. He is ears. He was Mamma's Emilio. He remembers the heat of her body next to his on the soft Corona asphalt. Draped under her coat on a cold morning. Miles sees red like the butterfly he is and yet he doesn't stop. He looks through the viewfinder of the Speed Graphic at the mourning scene his father shot. He tastes the anise left on Alice's tongue. Her teeth still seem to bite his lower lip. The moist warmth of her mouth rings in his ear. The stale acrid smoke from cigarettes. He smells the sunlight left on her fair skin. The musky scent on the side of her neck and under her arms. The damp desire of their exhaustion. Sin.

He feels as Alice rubs her hand on him under the table. Her shoulder pushed into his chest. The back of her bare arm against his ribs. The inside of her knee above his fingers. The outside of her leg pressed firmly to his thigh. Her foot on top of his. Heat he feels. The heat of the room. The heat of the brightness of bare bulbs and candle flames. The heat of hundreds of bodies breathing. Alice's body. Hears singing. Laughing. Sighing. Aching. He's dizzy again. Then he sees Jerzi. Standing below the transom. Remembers him staring up at him through bleeding fingers, face bleeding. He reaches for a glass and tastes iron in his mouth. He is burning.

(Miles shakes his head and leans in close to Alice, his lips on the flesh of her ear.)

I almost thought he was my dad.

What?

The violinist. I thought he was … not my real, well …

(Alice kisses him. Stops him talking.)

• • •

Enough Miles. Enough Alice. Mice. Malice. Aimless. *Alles*. My malaise. I should just stop it. It's almost over. One more scene. Just watch it. What did Proust say? The audacious first step across "*le «blanc» indéfini de l'hésitation, de la timidité*," the indefinite «*blanc*» of hesitation, of timidity. Between desire and action. Feel. Don't think. That day made all the difference. It kept me alive.

• • •

4:40—CHAMBRE 27, HOTEL HENRI IV.

Miles lies alone, naked beneath a sheet. The door creaks opens and Alice walks in on bare feet. She wears a T-shirt that she takes off upon reaching the bed. She looks down at him, her smooth, long limbs almost luminescent in the light sneaking around the window curtain. She climbs into bed, nuzzles into his neck, arms tight around him, straddling his left leg.

We should go to sleep.

I know.

I don't want to though.

I know. It'll make it end too fast.

I'm so tired.

Me too.

This has been a pretty perfect day.

Maybe it really was the apotheosis of harmony.

I wish there'd be more.

There will.

There won't. Or they won't be the same.

For me either. But it cycles.

Yeah. It cycles.

(Alice raises up on her elbow and kisses Miles. Then she turns on her side and pulls his arm over the top of her, cradling it between her breasts, squeezes his hand tightly. He presses against her, as close as he can get.)

Thank you.

For what?

For everything.

Me too. For everything.

Buon nuit.

Buona notte.

I think I love you.

• • •

Sunday, 19 September 2004
22:10—UNKNOWN BAR IN SPLIT

1 june 1988

Mon cher Miles,

Hello! Well, I have arrived back home—finally—but it was sure hard to say *arrivederci a Firenze*. I flew into JFK on Friday and it has been in the high 80s every day since. It's nearing 90 as I write this letter to you and there are not enough leaves on this tree to provide comfort for me. There's no shade. I'm wearing a sundress and still broiling hot. It's supposed to cool off starting tomorrow, which is a good thing because my parents arrive for commencement, which is Tuesday, and my mother would complain incessantly in this heat. Then the next day I'll be heading back with them for one final summer at home. Graduating will be a relief, but spending this past year abroad, I don't feel as connected to my imminent alma mater as I imagined I would when I matriculated five years ago. Walking around campus, even sitting here outside the dorm where I lived and ate for two years, just doesn't evoke many feelings. It's so empty—campus, that is—finals are long over, most underclass students are gone and seniors are just sitting. Sweating and waiting. It actually feels more foreign to me here than anywhere in Europe did. Maybe nostalgia can only be felt as the absence of something, and as I am here, that void is not yet vacant—no matter how insubstantial the filling.

Speaking of insubstantial filling, what a jejune letter this is so far—the weather and graduation logistics? I wonder if you're still reading. But no, I know you are, waiting to see some spark of life from me. I didn't know whether I should write you to be honest, but since you asked me to, I decided I would. It's more difficult than I thought, finding the right words. In general it's hard for me to stop thinking about the past nine months abroad, and even though you were only in my life for one of those days—but two nights!—they were pretty memorable, Miles. I remember our adventures in Paris with fondness. It was so hard leaving that morning. I'm sorry I snuck out, but it was already past the time and I just kept looking around and thinking of Albertine as she left. "*Pauvre petit chambre.*" It's the saddest sentence in Proust. Knowing they will never see each other again and knowing we were in the same situation. I wanted to die. I couldn't have left if you were there looking at me. This will sound disingenuous, but given all you have been through in life and the fact that you are seven years older, I think maybe that day meant even more to me than it did to you. Just in a different way.

No one here—no one—can relate to what I've experienced. I know Italia is hardly central Africa, but it was still a different culture. Felix doesn't exactly mock me about my culture shock, but he sure isn't sympathetic. We just don't talk about it, which has made for a lot of uncomfortable silences. But I'm sure you don't want to hear about him.

How are you? Where are you? I assume you're back in Salerno if you are reading this, so I guess I mean when did you get back? Did you find your father? I don't know whether I hope you did or not. I want to thank you for the dictionary. When did you sneak it into my bag? It doesn't seem like we were ever apart long enough for me not to have noticed. I didn't actually discover it was there until I started to pack for the train back to Firenze. I wondered if you put it there so that I would bring it back to you, but it was too late, I would have missed my train. And selfishly, I wanted to keep it. To remember you. Unfortunately I had written my address in it, under alidade, thinking maybe I could continue to offer you some direction, but you never got to see it. Maybe you will write me now, but if you don't I guess I'll understand. It is so evocative flipping through it. I showed a few friends and tried to explain to them. They don't get it. They can't get past the fact that I am not a chemist. I picked a word for us the other day. Page 223. March 22. The day we spent together. The word was *mélodieux*. Melodious. Musical. I thought that was a pretty apt adjective for our time together. Anyway, thank you, Miles, whether you intended for me to keep it or not.

I stayed in New York with my aunt for two days after I landed and Sunday morning I woke up jet-lagged at about 5 a.m. I went out and got coffee at Zabar's and walked across the park to the Metropolitan Museum and was probably the first person inside when it opened. I walked around a little, but mostly just stood in the sculpture hall and looked at Rodin's works. I thought about you. I know you said you were never there, Miles, but it kind of felt like you were that day. The Orpheus and Eurydice is so breathtaking. They're emerging from a roughly hewn wall of marble. Orpheus covers his eyes with his left hand. He doesn't want to see. Eurydice's right arm is draped, from her wrist to her shoulder, along his right arm and the inside of her left wrist rests on the back of his hip—right where you said I was magically soft! The look on her face is so yearning, so full of longing, but exhausted, bordering on hopelessness. It's almost too sad to look at. But I did. For a long time. I think I always imagined the two of them so happy until the moment when Orpheus turned around, but maybe that's not what happened. Maybe Eurydice was scared all along. Maybe she didn't know where she was going or even who was leading her. Maybe she was crying to be allowed to go back, even though it meant going back to Hell. Maybe Orpheus just wanted to give her hope, to let her know that she was loved, and that was why he turned around. Sometimes it's more important to know that—to know that you are loved—even if you end up losing the person who tells you. Or the person you tell. That was what

I thought as I stood there and I just wanted to write you about it. I wish we could have seen it together.

Well, this page is almost full and I don't have another piece of stationery since my first two attempts at this letter came out even more awkward than this one, so guess I will say good-bye. I don't want to, but *adieu, soldat.*

Con tutto il mio affetto,
Alice R., of the field

• • •

I got that letter in mid-July when I returned to Italy. I wrote back but she never replied. Or maybe she did. Maybe it got lost. That's what I tell myself although I know it isn't true. I think about trying to get in touch again, with the computer or something. But I never knew her last name. Alice R. Maybe I could find it. But she told me what she wanted to tell me. And that moment's past. That movement's through.

5. Satz.
RONDO-FINALE.

Tempo I. (Allegro ordinario. ♩)

Oyez! Oyez! Oyez! Hear Donner rumble through the roof. Poorly sealed window panes rattle in their frames. The storm is here. "*Dunkel ist das Leben, ist der Tod,*" Herr Bethge wrote then Gustav quoted. "Dark is life, is death." Here is night. He called after me. Falling. Minos summons Miles, once Milo, *il est né* Emilio. My chest resonates sympathetically with the rolling thunder, vibrating so primitively I wonder, will I finally crack, a crystal glass, shattered with a soaring high G, spilling loose its contents, my blood from my body. Time for judgment. No more distractions. Mamma, Jerzi, Alice. None can help me. Clotho, Lachesis, Atropos. You wove it, now cover me up on the couch. Alecto, Tisiphone, Megaera. Come pluck out my eyes, leave my sockets hollow and blind, like the hidden ones which stare down on me. Exacting triumvirates surround me on three sides but all that matters is the north. The joke is I didn't even mention the most important thing all day long. All that matters is my Father. We're the three. He. Me, the Son. And someone's ghost. The Roman one, uniting us. And shining brightly o'er my head, the Pentecostal flame, the Holy *esprit. De l'escalier.* The shadow follows me. We are I. O yea. "*O mensch. Gib acht.*" Take heed indeed. But Three's not my symphony. We three not withstanding. Mine lacks vocal warning. Words can be misinterpreted. And Love has nothing more to tell me. Move your sun, spin the stars, I heard it all in just one *jour.* Since then nothing. No more tottering. I teeter on the brink. Now it's just the thunder. I hear you grumble. More so than when I sat down this morning, everything is cluttered in this cavern. Sorrows that for years had slept soundly or at the least had been dampened, buried, tied up in a corner, were awoken, uncorked, uncovered, loosed. Can't repack Pandora's opened anything. Now they all sing, ring in the wings, clangor, clang, clang, jangling my edgy nerves.

I put down my pen, possibly for good I believed, when moments ago a silhouette appeared beneath the transom. It looked like Jerzi, emerging from my French *souvenir*, but then I decided it must just be the waiter coming to check on me. I gave him all I had in my pants pockets, all the coins, all the bills, from all the places I've been carrying around. One less burden. No more money. No bail. Just sink. Hit the ice. Cocytus is frozen finally. Maybe if I had sentenced myself, took today seriously instead of musing on my past, the storm would have just blown away. If I had attempted to understand how I did what I did. Not ignore what I did do. Did did, did do. Still can't write it. My wits are gone again after recovering during that brief respite and I must go out, Lear-like, into the storm. Yes, T. S., I must heed what the thunder says and, in the night, seek Shantih shantih shantih.

• • •

Outside, the fresh air, saturated as it is, has done some good. I have stopped to rest near the university, between the columns of a church whose denomination I cannot determine through the rain. No, the storm is not to blame for my ignorance. Wicked weather aside, it comes down to the fact that I don't know the language, God's or Croatian, and therefore cannot translate what the letters spell. "*Mein Herz ist müde*," but tired heart or not, I won't collapse like Kundry. I'm not the Lonely One in Autumn only. I'm always that way. I'm accustomed. More blows will come and I will bear them, Boreas. After trudging along *Vukovarska* in your bluster, past its end when it changes to *Bihaćka*, I quickly turned down *Kliška*, and not more than five hundred feet later a smell so familiar—yet so forgotten—grabbed me through the wet night. This will sound simplistic, almost childish, but it was the smell of sugar. Specifically, the almost sickeningly sweet smell of confectioners' sugar, so intense it seemed as if my teeth would decay if I inhaled too deeply. That was the smell of my youth, the smell of *Due G's*, the smell of my first, conscious, morning sniff. And it was the smell of Mamma, who could not sneak up on me because my nose would hear her first, before her footsteps reached my ears, and I would duck down behind a chair and wait for her to enter the room and then leap out and scream BOO! Mamma always laughed and chased me down and when she caught me, she tickled me, singing *O mio bambino caro*. She loved that aria. I had forgotten that fact. I don't think she knew it was actually *babbino*. I wonder what other words she transformed. B to M. Alice changed B to A when she blew. I changed Emilio to Milo to Miles. Lost one I. Cyclops. Lost one O. Oh no. Swapped them for an S. I hear E-O-S. Eos. The dawn. Oh yes. Aurora. The aura of sugar she unwittingly stole from the bakery enveloped her, a pleasant harbinger, a hint of the warmth with which she protected me from those cold winter breezes, a hint of warmth that said spring, rebirth, was approaching. When Mamma was lost to me that sweetness was gone. But before then, back beneath her cloak during our morning walks, I would inhale so much saccharine vapor that my dreams upon resleeping on the couch were littered with candied landscapes. Oh Mamma I miss you. More Mahlerian tongues, they continue to alight, light, enlighten then frighten me. Mamma, maybe you were right. "*Die Englein, die backen das Brot.*" You are an angel and bake bread for your God. Maybe that's your fate. Maybe it's your present state. But it's not mine, the Fourth. I must move.

• • •

Didn't make it very far in that interval. I reached *Kačićeva* and, at the bus stop, turned left onto *Porinova*. Again left, always sinistral with me. Only Alice was on the right. I blame my ankle. I stumbled into the intermission audience sheltered beneath the portico in front of the *Hrvatsko narodno kazaliste u Splitu*. Those words I speak. Croatian National Theater in Split. Arts not religion. I am mingling. Well, not really. I have avoided looking at them, well-dressed, drinking, chatting. "*Schön gekleidet, trinken, plaudern.*" Nor have I read the posters announcing the evening's program, now partially completed. I never want to know what I have missed. Whatever it was, they seem to have enjoyed it. The crowd hums with an electricity that I had forgotten existed. In the past decade I have not attended a single performance, preferring to remain in relative isolation. I wonder what they're seeing. Contradiction! In this weather, in this bluster, "*In diesem Wetter, in diesem Braus,*" they're not playing outside the house. Keep the children safe. No dead ones here. That was further east. I only made it to Zagreb. I came out of the hills above Salerno, where I had hunkered down clinging to a ridiculous belief that Carlo would return before his death to be buried beside Lucia. I located her grave in my obsessive trampings through those hills. Ambler in Tramonti. Mahler in the mountains. I spent many days sitting next to it, the grave that is, hoping for visitors. Now he'll never come. At least I know that. Anonymous he'll be thrown into a furnace and with a sublime finality burn up. Blow away. Maybe it has already happened. Maybe he's in the *bora* that I'm facing. Maybe I have breathed him deep into my lungs as my ears inhaled his final screams. Maybe he is in me. We three. The Father. The Son. The other one. Create in me a clean heart, O Carlo, and renew a right spirit within me. "*Nein, nein, das ich mein', mir nimmer blühen kann.*" No, no, never, never bloom again. I'm a wayfarer ever, without words, and One's not mine. *Nicht meine.* Round and round, my mind goes round, my round reasoning, my brother, *meine* mind, Jacques, goes round my round round reasoning.

• • •

I am wheezing at an overlook after climbing a seemingly unending stair. I tried to count the treads but raindrops knocked the numbers from my mind. And other things. From my hands. I cannot see how long I climbed because my map is gone. I released my grip on it after slipping on the stairs and it blew away in a trice. Wet marble. Mary cries. In our final interaction, my map said that I had been wandering in that section of the city called *Varoš*. It led me to the stairway at the end of *Senjska* where I climbed out. My *Trauermarsch* has begun, and as with any funeral march I don't expect to return, but that doesn't make the loss any less acute. Good-bye, my map! May you blow back to the boardinghouse and rejoin your companions, which the widow will eventually throw out with my other unclaimed possessions. I don't know where I am. Below are turbulent seas, darkened islands, and smeared electric lights from Split. It's ugly. There's nothing "*Von der Schönheit*" here.

• • •

I am outside a darkened science museum. No reason. I can't get inside. There is also a gated zoo. I hear frightened animals screaming. Trapped inside their cages. Maybe the scientists use them for experiments. Of course they do. We are all screaming, all trapped, all used. Life is the experiment, Alice. Love and Strife the variables driving the subject in one direction or another, inversely proportional. Teeter-totter. Make Love an A for her, and Strife represented by C, obviously. Death, the end result, the exit, exists in many permutations, Dead, Dying, Done, but a bullet here, a misplaced step, a slip, a push, a genetic betrayal, two chromosomes, an X or why in my case, can affect the outcome in an untimely fashion. The control, that's what my theory is lacking. What's the difference being studied by the scientists? The gods? Faith. No symbolism, just small f. Some grasp it solely through simplistic trust—M for Mamma. Others are blessed. I don't know if I know any of them, so I will just let it be a B.

Death = A/C*[f(BM)+XY]

Solving for faith, that which I lack or have distorted, we get: f is Dead Carlo on top of Alice minus a boy above Blessed Mamma. I was never good at math.

I needed to leave that bar. Bars keep you caged. Now I am trapped in this storm, exposed outside like an animal. Maybe it wasn't the correct decision. I can't escape either. I know because I am sentient. My shoes squish when I step. For an unconscious animal, exposure would be preferable. You can see what's coming. Although the noise, the crack of lightning, the thunder would be more than enough to incite panic. Cages do not matter. Does fear only come from consciousness? From faith. I know not because I am. Nothing. More stairs led me here. I only follow pathways now, mapless as I am. Just climb blind. Blind climbing. Blinding. I'm in Minos's labyrinth. Ariadne! Help me! It's liberating I suppose, losing the thread, no longer relying on some cartographer's version of reality. Lead me out! Wonder and discovery have disappeared from my wandering leaving _an_ering. An erring actually. But I don't know where the extra r is. Alice R. is what I had wished for, her and what I finally found in Zagreb, but who could have dreamed it? "*Wenn nur ein Traum das Leben ist, warum denn Müh' und Plag'?*" If life is but a dream, why is there toil and misery? The nervousness accompanying my feeling of lost—lost, not loss—is making me sick. Panic. I don't stray.

Need no grapnels. My birthday Sunday began with lies. I am safe. Ten years, sitting at her graveside. Everyday. I can see the cemetery out my window. With binoculars. Running into the rain every time an old man whose face is covered by an umbrella approaches her plot. I put fresh flowers on her gravestone every couple of days so that he would inquire of the caretaker, who has shown such interest in my dead wife? Lies. Lies. My old friends. Four? Yes. Three? Yes. Five? Yes, the funeral photo. One? Check. Two? Not yet. Can't get to Six without Two. All these Mahler symphonies flitting through my failing mind. But, no Six, no boom. Then Seven's held off, too. Why did I do it? When did I snap? What did he say to set it off? Why did he flap? Push. *Lebe wohl.* Well, you can't live well. Poor vole. Watch out for the owl. A owl. AWOL? A WOL. A wohl. Ah well. Flap on, owl. Hoot. Hoot. Howl. Flap on.

• • •

"*Ich suche Ruhe für mein einsam' Herz.*" I am seeking rest for my lonely heart. I have finally found it. Arrived at my *Abschied.* Farewell. My earthly song is ended. I am alone in blackness. Back at the beginning. Trapped at the end. Whichever, it's all circular. There flows Lethe past me again. And again. I'm unsure of what my blind pen is putting on these pages in the dark. I am in a small, stone church. Fittingly it's still Sunday. I had to force the door, God forgive me. It gave easily enough, rotten wood splintering alongside the lock. If this building had been in my runaway neighborhood it would be filled with junkies, whores, corpses. I could not take anymore of the storm. *Ich bin der Welt abhanden gekkomen*, but even though the world has abandoned me, I don't care. What is the world worth, Mahler asked, *was kost' die Welt*? For some time I have not been on the path. I wandered in *una selva oscura.* No Virgil, no Orpheus, to lead me. Nor Alice anymore. The letter is gone. This building appeared before me. I saw it in the lightning. Which incidentally is spectacular. Some trees probably disagree with me since they are burning. Burning in the rain. There had been a drought. Not now. They're all here. Fire. Water. Earth. Air. Chaos coming. Seesaw. When a bolt of lightning flashes, I see through a circular window above the door where I entered. I'm inside a camera, *obscura*. C saw. He saw. Finally. I am Stellio getting fed in his Speed Graphic twomb. Twin tomb/womb. Locked in my box until I find what I need to get out, to survive outside. I am starving. I am at the final stage, frightened eyes staring out of the darkness into God's repeated photos. Thirty-three. XXXIII. Those same eyes that I recognized in the park in Zagreb as he shuffled past me. In a fulgurous flurry I look up, around. In front of me my shadow falls. Hello Emilio. Father. Son. And the shadow of the dead me. We three. Across the floor and up on the wall is a cross the floor and up on the wall is a cross the floor. Ha. The record skipped. Not really. It's a faded painting. It really is. A *Röschen rot*. There it is! Two. The countdown is complete. Maybe a symbol of Mary. Maybe Mamma here to mourn for me. I'm ready. Ready to blow. Again. Accept my punishment. Say good-bye. Although if I came from that original Seventh, but did not actually appear until the Rainier shot, then my half life is forty-nine. I would still have two more years. But then I would be split, half of me would be gone. That is nonsense. The park alongside *Ribnjak*. O! false security which I used to take from being able to locate myself. You are here. *Voici*, Alice. No. The sun shone, brightly I believe. It didn't mean 'of the field.' She knew that. Most days when wandering in a park I thought of her and our brief time together. *Ein Engelein. Nicht mein*. Not mine. I no. Flowers make me think of her. Butterflies. Red. Light. Laughter. Life. Love. *Leben. Liebe*. L. Letters. More letters. Loss. The letter is lost. The fingertips of a saleswoman once placed change in my hand. When she dropped it in, I raised my palm to accept the coins, intentionally initiating contact just to feel something. Alice's fingers were finer. Supple like a pianist's. Smooth and thin like young birch branches. Soft as osier. Her peplum coat brushed the back of my hand. I wonder where you are today. You haunted my hotel room for the rest of my stay. When I would enter in at night after a day of imagining what it would be like if the scientists studying me beneath the Rainier Mesa had built a glass pyramid so I could look up and see the sky instead of a starless rocky ceiling, you would be sitting on the bed. Is that a star I see? *À la belle étoile*. Always sitting, never reclining. No, I'm in a cage. Always clothed, never naked, like on the night when you said I want to see you. As soon as I walk in the door you rise, O little red rose, and say, "The final word is *Adieu*. Page Two. One for each of us." To God. Alice. Not really of the field, but too kind to tell me. Then you would be gone, falling through the floor or blowing away before my eyes. Are you a mother? Maybe you named one of them Miles, and when Felix asked you where the name came from, you answered that you pointed to a random page in a Latin dictionary. *O miles belli!* Be a loving mother, Alice. Why can't I win? I am not even fighting. Mount a defense. Dear Lord, that day I was just sitting, watching the flowers wilt in the autumn sun. Their lives were almost over, too. I heard him first. As I did with Jerzi. But no steam. No machines. As I did in a different sense with Mamma. Heard with a nose. As I even did with Alice when she first appeared in the *Salle Pleyel. Pardonnez-moi monsieur*. No. A lie. I felt her first. The touch. The peplum. We just covered that. Anyway, he shuffled. 12 September. One week ago. Unable or unwilling to completely pick his feet up from the gravel path before dragging them forward. That is, incidentally, when the Eighth premiered. 12 September 1910. Three years after. Objection! Relevancy? I have none. I looked up slowly from the feet and their worn but still respectable-looking shoes, to the wrinkled trousers with their loose knees, serge blazer with a rip at the left pocket where a hand was buried. Was he reaching for my books? Alice has the dictionary, from me, from my pocket. The right hand held a walking stick that was more neglected than relied upon, like Mamma and me. A v-neck sweater. His chin was shaved. The upper lip. The nose. I don't know. A nose. Alice knows? But then the eyes. Blue. Yes, I'm sure. Mine are that eroded beige. *O Augen blau*. Azure almost. They seemed backlit, eerily fixed on me. *Veni*, my creator said. Not really, he was silent. Regardless of never having seen his in color, my mouth probably fell open. I knew them. Him. He nodded, but in an ignorant, friendly greeting. I don't know what I did in response. He went shuffling on his way.

Let's take a short break. On 4 September a picture of School Number 1 in Beslan, Russia, ran in the *Herald Tribune*. The fifty-two-hour hostage taking was over. Hundreds killed. Hundreds more injured. There were two explosions. Six and Seven. Not those. These blew children up. Exploded them, not inflated them. Sent them in the sky. Not to heaven. Or maybe. *Kindertoten*. Unstuck me from the cemetery. If I could add, the look in those blue eyes was similar to the lack of comprehension that Jerzi showed after I smashed him in the face. Jerzi, whose eyes were always so expressive, so full of musical emotion. Anyway, the photo showed a small child, age eight or seven—let's say seven for fun—no shirt, in front of what used to be his school. He had no pants either. Or shoes. Just a sash really. Not like at a beauty pageant. More like Adam hastily hiding his shame with whatever could be found. His parents had not been found. The child's. We know Adam's, don't we, Father? They were probably dead inside since many parents had also been taken hostage when the militants arrived. It was the first day of school. Children had brought balloons. How cute. One woman watching from outside talked about a sudden "cloud of balloons" above the school. She theorized it was the moment all the children panicked *en masse*.

Let go what was in their hands to cover their eyes, or scream, or reach for someone. Mamma let me go, too. But I didn't die. Yet. Alice held tightly, the whole time. Saved me. Behind the child, bodies and chaos. BC. Before Christ. Dead eyes. Where is the A? Anyway. The child's eyes. Jerzi's eyes were empty also after I hit him. Irrelevant. You said that. His legs and arms were soiled. Blood. From his dead classmates. On his cheeks and chest, too. Blown up children on his bare skin. Maybe some from his dead older sister. The article said he had one. She wasn't found either. He stared straight at Carlo's camera. The article is somewhere here. No, I guess it isn't, your Honor. I can't feel it. I seem to have left some things behind, either in the bar or when I fell or lost my mind. My right pocket is completely empty, except for a small puddle of water somehow cradled by the fabric. I'd like to enter the water as a promise of my flood to God that never again will I give him a rainbow. That is normally where the map would be, too. Gone, we know. My articles? Gone back at the room. Music names them for us? Gone sometime today. Alice's letter? Gone. Gone. Gone! Best not discussed. It was safely folded and stowed at the back of *Metamorphoses*, which lives in the left pocket. And it isn't here. I don't think I've mentioned it, but it is in those volumes that I am writing these recollections today. I am trying not to disturb Carlo's changes and so I write anywhere that is still blank. Well, I was. Now I can no longer see, so I might just be putting my own words on top of his. Doesn't matter. I'm almost to the end. I write small and very neatly in a sort of block script of my own invention. My pen doesn't write well on the dried blood, so even if it's just a smear I jump over it. Now I can tell the bloody spots by feel. He was seventy-eight years old. Carlo. My father. Dad. Pop. Daddy. Ha. Daddy. That guy who just shuffled past me. Him? What a blinding flash of lightning. The thunder answered immediately. Maybe this will be my tomb. They are communicating quickly. Wait. I spied a candle below the faded rose. Victory. At least I won't spend my last moments in the dark. Although the candle is really superfluous because the lightning is flickering on and off so consistently now it is like a strobe. I almost appear stopped. It's kind of cozy in here with the candlelight. I am sitting on some sort of marble altar apparently. There are two rows of wooden pews. The farthest one, closest to the door, I knocked over on my way in and jammed the door closed with it. I wonder if there was a service here today or if I am the only congregant to visit. The most this place could hold is probably twelve. It's really small. *Pauvre petit église*. Probably been here for centuries. No crucifix on the wall. Probably stolen. Just that painting of the rose with some stuff around it. Maybe Jerzi never played the violin again. It wouldn't have been easy for him to acquire a new instrument. I actually feel terrible for taking something that was so meaningful to him. A piece of his soul really. Almost like taking his life. His faith. His hope. His path to God. He probably felt dead. I would apologize to him if I could. I'll try. I'm sorry, Jerzi. You didn't keep Carlo's existence from me. You tried to help, tried to parent me. You were just a drunk and a liar. I forgive you. Maybe that will help my cause. I must be on top of Marjan Hill. Although it wouldn't change anything, I wish I knew for sure. Anything. This morning I thought Marjan would protect Split, act as a wind break, keep me and the city safe. Keep us together. I guess being on top of it negates its purpose. Aha! Dead Carlo on top of Alice negates her purpose. I feel certain the church won't be destroyed by this storm. It's not even leaking. It can handle a little bit of doubt. I'm the one who'll lose. It was when I put the paper down and went to the train station and then to Rome and then to Ciopino and flew to Zagreb. I wanted to go all the way to Beslan, but there is a war going on in that area I was told, and that's not going to happen. Not going to happen, son. Have to keep it guarded. Have to keep it, guard Ed. Maybe that's your name? No one in.

I hadn't left in a long time. I wasn't scared of travel or anything like so many people were with all the terrorist attacks. I simply sat in a cemetery. Who hasn't done that? After Alice, I chased Carlo for another six years or so and then I'd had enough. I found the grave. If it wasn't mine, that was fine. I just needed to stop. I justified my inertia with the belief that he would come to me. He would come to her. I certainly had no idea he would be in Zagreb, let's be clear. It could not have been premeditated. I don't even know if he took that photo. I didn't ask him. About either. The one of Moro or the kid with the dead sister on his face. Even the one of him in the dark. He could have been a hostage at the time. Maybe he got taken by the *Brigate Rosso*. How do I explain such an astronomically unlikely encounter? I mean, really. It is one of the truly aggravating aspects of the Zagreb experience, that God, excuse me, you, Father, or father, whoever, decided to intervene in my life at that point. Let me sit. I did meet Alice, too. Maybe the intervention the second time was in Carlo's life. Maybe it was payback for killing the kid who killed the lizard who lived in the camera who ate the bugs who swallowed the fly. I don't know why. It can only be fate. Sorry Alice. There is no other way to explain it. It was meant to happen. Try as Carlo did to avoid me, I found him. But I did then let him walk away. Well, I didn't let him so much as when I awoke from my stupor he was already at the upper end of the park. I got up and started to run after him but stopped. I didn't want to confront him yet, so I followed cautiously. I doubt he would have even noticed me if I had trailed directly behind him. I caught up at the base of *Gornji Grad. Gornji Grad.* GG. *Due G's*. Fitting really.

My ankle hurts. I think I broke it for good getting into this church. And I have a giant splinter in my hand. A big, sharp splinter stabbed right into the fleshy part of my right hand when I first tried to shove the door shut against the storm. All I need is a kidney failure or an appendicitis and I've got the stigmata.

Bless me. All those days in Corona when I limped home. Kicked so many times. Who would think to kick a kid? Who would think to take a kid hostage? Who would think to abandon a kid before he was born? It is true I followed Carlo to wherever he was staying, but it was somewhere that I can't really recall now because I don't seem to have any maps. Can that be remedied? A map for me, please. Hello? We went up the funicular, that much I remember. I stood outside his hotel to see if he would emerge for dinner. He didn't. I was going to rob him. For fun. I wasn't armed. I had seen it happen enough times in New York that I had a good idea of what to do. I was just going to yell things at him, like a lunatic. Maybe that line from Lucia. *L'universo intero è un deserto per me senza Lucia*. His reaction would have been interesting. Maybe hit him with his cane. Just lightly. If I still had the Speed Graphic, well, that could have been bad. Smash his fucking face in. Oh, dear. Excuse me. But if I still had the Speed Graphic, I wouldn't have been standing outside his hotel because I wouldn't have stolen the score. And read how grieving fathers really react to lost children. Anyway, he didn't come out. The next day I wasn't quite so angry. At first. I went early in the morning, very early, and waited. What if he had left? I should have broken in during the night and attacked him. I object to my own implication. Strike that. I wouldn't strike him. Speed Graphic. Check. It was frustration. I knew he wouldn't leave. God would not let that happen if he had put us in the same park in the same city on the same day almost forty-seven years after Carlo had tried so hard to get away from me in a different city in a different country before I could even use eyes to recognize him. I couldn't see color back then. No red. No nothing. No cones. I was merely some cells in a uterine wall. He was there. Not in the uterus. In his hotel. And it wasn't even the photograph that made me leave Italy. Well, I mean, it was the photograph, but it wasn't solely the fact that I believed it was taken by Carlo. I had seen a couple of others in the intervening years, and I just didn't bite. Even if he took it, he would still come to the cemetery. I was tired. And what if I missed him when I was off chasing a phantom. No, it was the dead children. Does that help my case? That's what made me go. Dead children. I followed Carlo to a café. I was so nervous. Before the exhibit in New York, I had covered so many scenarios whereby I would confront Carlo—remember I provided some sample answers several pages back—and yet I had no idea what I wanted to say now that the day had arrived. I thought about saying the same thing that Alice had said to me. Well now we're alone so no one can separate us. We finally get to meet. I'm Alice. But I'm not. So I didn't. No one can separate us anyway. Not anymore. I feel you in my lungs. Scratchy like Mamma's old scarf. He wouldn't get it, though, since he never met her. In the end I believe I actually said what I first said to Jerzi. My name is Milo. What's yours? Is that what I really said? It didn't work the first time. I'm having trouble remembering.

Something is moving in the corner. I am not getting off this altar to investigate, but in the latest lightning flash, something moved. I swear. I don't swear, but I promise. I feel like God is taking pictures of me in here. Did I mention that? Am I inside or outside the camera? The courtroom? Are cameras allowed in the courtroom? Can I say aloud my question? Am I the film or the subject? The recorder or model? Am I trespassing since I don't believe? And let me make that clear. I still don't, even after Zagreb. I am not going to be one of those deathbed converts who throws away a lifetime of disbelief in one panicky moment. It does seem as if I am addressing God occasionally, but that is just to plead my case for his nonexistence. He's not answering. I'm confused. Next question. Maybe I am squatting again. I will not acknowledge the landlord, the owner of the land, Lord. I will pay no rent. Not acknowledge the lord. No pay rent. No parent. Take my soul. It is worthless at this point. I just want out. End the storm. Let me go. When Alice laid down next to me and traced her fingers along my cheek and down my neck and chest and stomach, it was like a hummingbird was trapped beneath my skin. I couldn't regulate my breathing. That feeling was positively tranquil compared with my state after first speaking to Carlo. I never felt it again after her. I honestly don't know how I got the words out. I sat down at the small table next to his and said them. He said. An American. Hello Milo. I am Carlo. Don't not contract like Jerzi. Say I'm. It felt so strange and somehow fitting that he didn't call me by my real name. That was why I lied. I didn't want him to know me. He sounded kinda like an old man. A kind old man. It was an act, I'm sure. It's a lizard. In the corner. A lizard is crawling on some piece of church furniture that looks like a sideboard in the corner. I hate lizards. The dead one in the book is fine. But alive? No. If I see it again, I'm throwing Stellio's corpse at it. As a warning. Maybe it's after the wine or wafers. I wonder if there's anyone buried in the floor. It seems like there usually are in churches. Maybe I'll end up down there. Hammered in by a falling crossbeam. The day was the premiere of the Eighth. I mentioned that already. In Munich, in Munich in 1910, which I had not said yet. Overwhelming success. Just like in Beslan. The Eighth has a bunch of dead boys taken too soon, just like in Beslan. Though they can still sing. *Wir wurden früh entfernt von Lebenchören*. We were early snatched, from the choir of the living. Nicely put Goethe. Or Gustav. Either. Both G's. And roses are important, too. I wish Alice would come for me. Me and Carlo. After all that time spent thinking about our meeting. All the days we spent together staring at Lucia's mom through the lens of the Speed Graphic. Lucia's mom crying over her dead daughter. While I waited for my turn I wondered what I would say. I wasn't listening. I could have started with I'm your son. But he could have denied having a son. Left me hanging there just to absolve everyone else. Hanging there so disbelieving boys could masturbate to me. He could have said his name was Jeremy. It really is a lizard. There is a lizard in the corner, and it has noticed me. It seems to be smelling the air in this direction. Is that what they do with their tongues? Do their eyes hear and their noses taste? That actually explains my experience with Alice. All senses intermingled. There are two. There are three. There are four, four lizards in the corner.

Okay, maybe I panicked. I have thrown Stellio. Forgive me father. You kept him for so long. It had absolutely no effect. The lizards have disappeared but not in fear of a corpse, I fear. They are regrouping. I have grabbed a smooth black rock from the altar and I hold it in my left hand. I spied it in yet another photomnicient moment. Why is it here? It is remarkably smooth. Obsidian? Oblivion? I'll throw it next. Despite the vibrato in my voice, I managed to learn that Carlo was a sometime photographer on his way back from a trip. I never asked from where. Or where he lived. Part of me didn't want to know. Didn't want to confirm or deny any beliefs I held. Didn't want my faith crushed. Ignorance is bliss. Cliché! Strike that from the record, steno. I told him I lived near Salerno. He said he loved Italy. I said I was married. He said he once was. My wife was pregnant with our first child. He said congratulations and then sorry but he had an appointment with a publisher. He tried to shake my hand but I intentionally knocked over my coffee when reaching up, spilling it on my pants and slightly scalding myself, so that I didn't have to touch him like that. It was worth it. The pain. I quickly said maybe I'll see you tomorrow and pushed past him to the bathroom. I splashed water on my face. He didn't go to any meeting. I have pocketed the black rock as the lizards have already reached the altar. When they disappeared they must have taken to the floor. Decided to bring the fight to me. I used my shoes. I took one off and smashed two lizards that had climbed up next to me. *Mors factus sum*. I was so disgusted with my actions that I dropped the shoe. I thought better of it and removed the other one just in case. So now I am barefooted like all the children in Italy during the war. He went back to his room, so maybe the meeting was on the phone. Maybe it wasn't a lie. I waited for him the rest of the day, but he didn't emerge again. I began to believe there was another exit from the hotel. When I finally stopped watching the door at ten in the evening, I went for a walk around the block only to confirm that I was correct. The lobby ran the width of the building. I had just been lucky in the morning when he had decided to exit on my side. I am *felix*. That realization caused me some anger. There was another lizard on the altar but I saw him crawl up, right in front of me, and quickly killed him. I thought I heard this one hiss, but of course that's my imagination. Lizards don't hiss. Do they? At his size? He seemed a bit bigger than Stellio's corpse, but the latter is desiccated, so they were probably the same size in life. I can't compare because now they're both gone. Now I have none. No pay rent. Now I'm distracted. There are more over where the first one came from. I'm under attack. The next morning I was torn. I didn't know which exit to watch. I wished I could split myself in two and guard both doors. Put the guard at the wrong one. I chose the one from the night before and entered the hotel. I found no lobby in which to sit. In New York I slept an entire night in a lobby once because Vanessa was going to be out using her hands and come in tired and stinking of come in tired and stinking of come in tired. Another skip. Damnit. And another lizard. There. Come in come. Come, she used to cry. Tired. I couldn't be alone. Just people around. It was two nights after the photography exhibit. I think the night right after I scared her. She didn't want to be needed. She did the needing. Needed companionship, but it didn't have to come from me, and the me didn't need to be needy. That night ruined it. I asked the clerk for a business card and kept walking through to the other side and out. I grew anxious. I grew angry. I walked back in the door and looked up to see if there was a camera. No. No security. I stood there, immediately inside. I could see to the other end of the building, but the desk, which was set back, was out of sight. Where the hell was he? Every so often I had to move aside because someone opened the door behind me. That was annoying, it's true. Or a guest came walking down the hallway toward me and I would simply smile and open the door for them. Most of them did not smile in return. I became slowly invisible like the runaway me. Finally I saw he. Him. I have just done something very unfortunate. After noticing several more lizards atop the altar, I went to sweep them off in haste and in doing so I have knocked the candle onto the floor. I reached for it as it fell but missed. It burns still, but that can't continue for long. The flame will die. Carlo was walking away from me. Something just fell on my head and slipped down my back beneath my shirt. In haste I removed it and rolled on my back. I only succeeded in scraping myself. It did not feel good, not like what Alice did. Or Mamma's caresses. Well, that's it for the candle. And the lightning seems to have slowed almost to a stop. Blackout again, Glenn. There's a glow outside the window, though, as if dawn were approaching. Eos, it isn't, although someone may be crying soon. Missing me. It must just be the burning trees. I followed him through the lobby. The clerk didn't acknowledge me. It had worked. I couldn't be seen. Something has fallen again, on my left shoulder this time, and when I went to smash it, I stabbed myself with the pen. It is incredibly painful. I must be writing with blood. How strange. They glow. I looked up and there they glow. The lizards are glowing in the dark. There are dozens of them. They cover the ceiling and are crawling down the walls. They really do look like stars. I wonder if they sounded an alarm. I threw the rock to frighten them but that was silly. I winced when I released it and the rock went through the window. I have broken the camera.

Smashed the glass. We headed toward the funicular again. Before we reached it, I approached him. For whatever reason I decided to attack. The lizards. Can't catch me that easily. I stood up and swung wildly at the ceiling. It was a ridiculous attempt to dislodge them. The ceiling is much too high. I didn't even come close. Do you remember me? Why yes. How are you today? I ignored the question. Objection. Rejected. I will carry on. Silence. Where are you going? I must have sounded threatening. He felt frail. To the market. Why are you following me? Why did you leave me? I told you I had a meeting. I smell smoke. But the candle is out. Maybe it's coming in through the broken window, piling up on the church ceiling. Yes, the stars are fading. My hand is really bleeding. Or my shoulder. Blood. Fire. Some vapor. This could be that Pentecostal meeting. The Apostles and the ghost. The painting in Notre-Dame. Pose Alice. Say cheese. The birth of the church on my birthday. Are there not many ways down from *Gornji Grad*? It's a kind of promontory rising above Zagreb. The old town is up there. And a castle. I don't really remember. And as I have covered there is no possibility of consulting with a map. Could I please have something to help me navigate my way out of this? An alidade, maybe. Or an Alice if there is not an alidade available. There's the funicular. Did I say that? Some winding roads. Stairways? I just climbed some so I'll say yes. Yes, there are stairways. Those pews would just fit Jerzi and Alice and Nonna and Nonno and Vanessa and the dead violinist who was thrown down the air shaft and the librarian and the security guard and Mahler and *Putzi*. There are two seats left in the jury. Leave Lucia. Sit down Carlo, Mamma will arrive momentarily. Bringing her bread and her scales. I found your camera. The one I lost yesterday? No, you old fool. I miss it dearly. I don't care. And your books. Did you leave them for me? I don't understand what you are saying. I know about the boy. What? I didn't think I was speaking clearly. Maybe my words were coming out differently than they sounded to my ears. I tried again. I saw your picture. Do you still weep? I think something in his eyes finally understood. It must have been very confusing. Stellio? The lizards are crawling all over the altar now. I think they too are fleeing the fire. Or the smoke. Lucia? But she died. I was just hitting him with words. One at a time. He actually seemed very nice. Just scared. It was really shocking, I'm sure. Francesca? Who are you? Did you ever love her? How could you leave her, let her fall? Who are you? He started to back away from me and I reached out to grab him. Did you? Did you ever love Mamma? I need to hurry up and get out of here, but the lizards won't let me so I'll continue to write. And the spirits on the pews haven't reached their verdict yet. We have. Oh well. As if I don't know it. They are on my arms now, the lizards are. I can't shake them off. I yelled. Francesca! My mamma! I lost her. I didn't really care about Lucia but I just sat there. Every day. His eyes were frightened. He didn't weigh very much. Tissue-thin. Staple him to the ceiling. Another *somnia vana*. I hear bells. Lots of bells. The haze is growing lower. Or was that in Zagreb. Maybe it's my ears ringing. The lizards' sharp tongues seem to be searching for something on my skin. Smelling me. Don't they sniff the smoke? All around me bells were tolling. It was like that with Mamma and I just couldn't hear. The last time I saw her. I only wanted them to understand. I was hurt. Maybe it's an alarm. Fire! I'm your son. He didn't understand. I shook him. I am your son. She didn't care. Shook again. Mamma, I tried. Your son. Why did you marry her? He closed his eyes. I think he was praying. Look at me. Mourn me, Mamma. I don't think I pushed exactly. Look at me. Something just slipped. Look at me! I reached up to open his eyes with my fingertips. It was an accident. I poked too much. It was bloody. They are everywhere. It actually feels so good. I seem to be coughing quite a lot. I was not gentle. I'm going to have to make a run for it. Risk the lizards. The judgment of my peers. Mahler will let me out of here. Backward down the stairs. If he had been looking in the right direction, maybe he could have caught himself. His eyes opened though. So I got what I wanted. I reached for him but couldn't catch anything. Just the air. He fell too quickly. I kept looking at him. So I could remember it. Capture it. I wished I had his camera still. It was all there. The fear. The regret. The recognition. The sadness. Everything I wanted. I framed it perfectly. All the way down I watched. And when he finally stopped falling, I turned, and I ran.

Firenze—New York City—Leland, 2009–2014

CPSIA information can be obtained at www.ICGtesting.com
Printed in the USA
LVOW10s0946120815

449790LV00006BB/263/P